# A TALE OF BEAUTY AND BEAST

# A TALE OF BEAUTY AND BEAST

## A RETELLING OF BEAUTY AND THE BEAST

## MELANIE CELLIER

LUMINANT PUBLICATIONS

A TALE OF BEAUTY AND BEAST – A RETELLING OF BEAUTY AND THE
BEAST

ISBN 978-0-6480801-4-5

Luminant Publications
PO Box 305
Greenacres, South Australia 5086

melanie@melaniecellier.com
http://www.melaniecellier.com

Cover Design by Karri Klawiter
Editing by Mary Novak

*For Elodie Amelia*
*because a best friend can be almost like a twin*

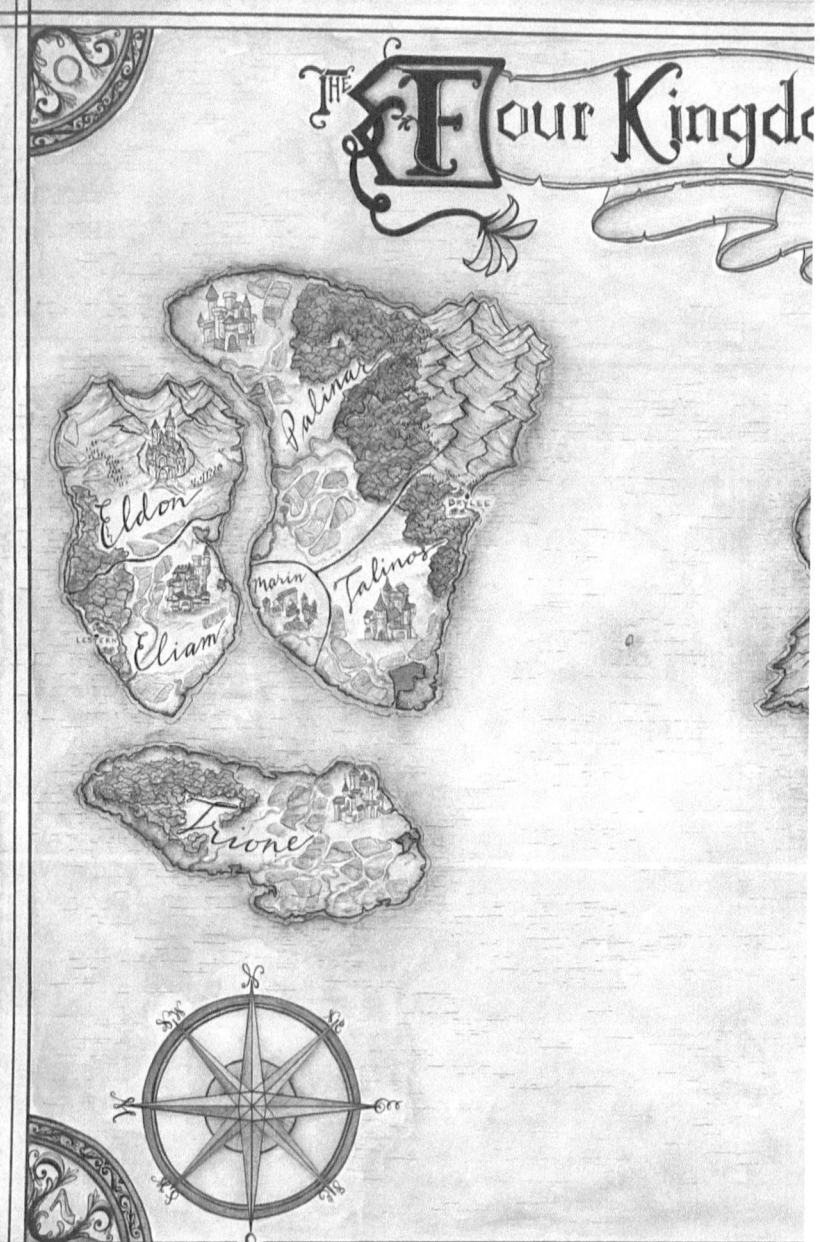

OMS
and Beyond
RANGMEROS
Northhelm
NORTHGATE
Rangmere
BORDER CROSSING
Arcadia
WINTER CASTLE
ARCADIE
The Great Desert
LANARE
Lanover
CATALIE
INVERNE
LARGO
BANISHMENT ISLAND

# PART I
# THE CASTLE

# CHAPTER 1

*I* had been riding all day, and the sun was now starting to set in spectacular streaks of red and orange across the plains. But still I pressed on, too afraid to stop. A howl rose above the sound of the wind, and I shivered from more than just the cold. Did that call sound closer than the last?

A second and then a third wolf took up the chorus, and I decided they were definitely closer. What would happen when night fell? Maybe I should stop and try to light a fire now. Would the flames be enough to keep them away from me and my mount? I looked at the emptiness surrounding me. Where would I find fuel for a fire in this desolation?

*Sophie? Where are you now? It's starting to get dark.* My twin's projection sounded in my mind and broke me from my panicked thoughts.

I took a calming breath before answering. *I'm riding, there's still plenty of light left here.* The fear had been mounting all day, but I had tried to keep it out of my projections to Lily. She was worried enough about me as it was. But it was hard to keep the emotion away from my words, especially when I was sending my thoughts directly into her mind. She almost certainly suspected the truth, but she also knew I wasn't going to change my mind and turn back.

He promised I would be safe, I reminded myself. My new betrothed. He promised. The exact words of his missive had been, 'I cannot stop you sending an escort, of course, but only my betrothed is guaranteed safe passage'. Not exactly an encouraging message, but it had explicitly guaranteed my safety. And, since he had demanded I come alone and immediately, he could hardly fault me for stepping outside of his directions. Which meant my current predicament was entirely his fault.

My twin's earlier warnings repeated in my mind. *He's a monster! A beast! You can't trust him.*

She was right, of course. At least as far as we knew. And I didn't trust him, not at all. But I did trust in the power of the ancient laws. The ones that created a formal, binding betrothal between the ruler or heir who called a Princess Tourney and the princess who won the secretive competition. The laws that bound every person in these lands and decreed that not even the one who had called the Tourney could disrupt the subsequent betrothal. Which surely included not letting the bride-to-be get eaten by wolves.

I had seen the power of this ancient magic all too clearly during the long weeks of the Tourney—the competition Lily and I had been forced into when we arrived in these lands. Our diplomatic delegation from our own kingdom of Arcadia in the Four Kingdoms had arrived at just the wrong moment. And since the High King himself had set up the Tourney many generations ago, we had been unable to escape it. I had seen the ancient magic create realms and bring them crashing down. I had even seen it hold back death. It was this same magic that had apparently cursed the Beast's kingdom of Palinar. Surely it could also keep me safe.

And so, here I was, riding my horse all alone through an empty wilderness while wolves howled around me. Not exactly a promising beginning to a betrothal. But the ominous words of my new fiancé's message had been clear. Only I was safe. Only I was protected by the Tourney.

And it wouldn't have been only guards accompanying me if I had waited. My twin Lily and her new betrothed, Crown Prince Jonathan of Marin, would have insisted on coming as well. Who knew how many lives might have been lost in their efforts to protect me?

*Where are you going to spend the night?* Lily's worried projection reminded me that she was still adjusting to the whole idea of me going off on my own. I hadn't exactly discussed it with her when I had snuck out of the palace on a stolen horse. I stroked the neck of my mare, Chestnut. I had befriended her weeks ago, and she had happily accompanied me today. The poor thing hadn't known what she was getting herself into, of course.

*I'll let you know when I work that out,* I responded, injecting some humor into my projection. It gave me comfort to carry my twin's presence with me in my mind, even if she could offer no practical assistance. We had never been apart before, and I liked the reminder that we were still connected. That we had a link no one could break, a Christening gift from our godmother. *A greater bond than ever twins have shared before.*

And with our old nanny having passed away, only Jon knew of the secret connection between Lily and me that had resulted from our gift. Which meant this Beast was wrong if he thought he could isolate me from the rest of the kingdoms by asking me to come alone. My betrothed had secrets aplenty, but I brought some of my own with me.

The sun had almost disappeared below the horizon now, and I could still see neither shelter nor fuel for a fire. A flash of movement made me whip my head around, but the plains appeared empty. The mare faltered and then picked up her pace without being asked. I crouched low over her neck, encouraging her speed, and peeked under my arm.

Another flash of movement, and this time I caught a glimpse of gray. A wolf! My breath quickened, and the horse must have picked up my tension since she increased her speed even more. I looked again but could now see nothing. How did they hide themselves in this vast emptiness? More of the magic of the curse, I supposed.

My heart beat wildly, and I tried to calculate how much strength remained in my mare. She had alternated between a walk and a trot all day, so she couldn't have much stamina left. I guessed she was running on instinct and fear right now and not much else.

I scanned the horizon again, searching for something, anything. The final rays of the setting sun blinded me and made the landscape strange and unfamiliar. I squinted through it, not sure what I was even hoping to see.

A black dot wavered against the light and seemed to grow bigger. Its shape looked unnatural, too square to be an animal and far too large to be a wolf, so I nudged the mare, angling her toward it. As it grew even bigger, I glanced back again and this time got a clear glimpse of two gray shapes racing after us.

My horse ran at a full gallop now, and my hair and dress streamed behind me. Even so, we neared the approaching object at a surprising pace. It was clearly moving toward us as fast as we rushed toward it.

I began to pull up on the reins just as the last of the sun slipped below the horizon and the blinding light disappeared. The mare responded reluctantly as I blinked in the twilight haze and tried to understand what I was seeing.

The object, a large traveling carriage, had also slowed, so that we both came to a stop at the point of meeting. I twisted in the saddle, but the only sign I could see of my pursuers was a whisk of gray tail before they disappeared off into the fast encroaching darkness. I turned back to the carriage.

The coach itself looked perfectly ordinary, and yet I couldn't stop staring at it. No horses pulled it, and no coachman directed it. It stood still in the middle of this strange wilderness, as if it had arrived at a prearranged stop.

"Good evening," I called, tentatively. No one responded. I looked around again, but the wolves had not returned. Whatever this strange apparition, it seemed to offer us some protection from them.

I swung down from Chestnut, keeping a tight hold on the reins, and approached the window. I couldn't see the inside in the evening gloom, so I took a deep breath and opened the door. I reached out toward Lily in my mind as I did so, anticipating the need for extra courage, but nothing greeted me except the empty inside of a carriage.

*What? What is it?* She responded instantly, clearly on edge.

*I...I don't know.*

*What do you mean?*

I chewed on a loose strand of hair as I peered inside, wondering if I'd missed something. *I've found a carriage. But it's empty.*

*In the middle of that wasteland everyone is always talking about? Maybe someone abandoned it when their party got attacked by bears or something.* She didn't sound happy.

*Maybe...Except it drove up to me.*

*It drove up to you? Well ask the coachman then.* Lily sounded a little exasperated now.

*There isn't a coachman. Or horses. The carriage just arrived on its own.*

*What?! That's it. I'm coming after you.* She didn't say anything else, but she hadn't completely cut off the projection toward me, either. And I knew her well enough to read the emotions she was sending. I could easily imagine the scene: Lily jumping up, ready to storm off into the night, and poor Jon being left to guess at the content of our silent conversation. After a moment, her emotions calmed and then changed. I cut the connection on my end, too tense to cope with her new feelings of tenderness and love. Obviously, Jon had managed to talk her down.

I spotted a piece of parchment resting on the floor of the carriage and leaned awkwardly in to pick it up. Every minute the light faded more, so I rushed to read it.

---

To my betrothed,

This carriage will provide you, and only you, safe passage to my castle. It is the official carriage of the royal family of Palinar and nothing in this land will harm you while you are inside. Tie your horse behind, and it will remain safe also. Sleep inside the carriage, and do not attempt to alight at night.

Prince Dominic

---

I frowned and went back to the beginning, but I could barely make out the words in the increasing darkness. And I didn't want to waste the remaining moments of dim light. Hurrying, I unsaddled Chestnut, thrusting the saddle and saddlebags into the carriage. I rubbed her down and secured her to the back.

The whole thing was madness. Utter madness. But I had no choice. The plains had offered no other option, and the wolves *had* run away at the arrival of this magical vehicle. I stepped inside just as blackness overtook my surroundings.

I waited a moment, but no magical light appeared to break the dark. Too bad. I groped blindly through my saddlebags and managed to cobble together an evening meal by feel. I didn't bother attempting to wash or tidy myself in any way, what would be the point? I explained the situation to Lily as I ate, glad to be able to project and chew at the same time.

She seemed incredulous but accepting. *Perhaps you're right,* she projected with a sigh. *Perhaps this betrothed of yours will protect you.*

*Don't sound so unhappy about it!*

She laughed at that, before sighing again. *I just wish you hadn't gone off on your own.*

I didn't bother to reply. We'd already spent over an hour discussing it earlier in the day, and my muscles ached after a full day in the saddle. It had been too long since I'd had the opportunity to go for a long ride, and my body was out of practice. I arranged myself as comfortably as possible on one of the seats of the carriage.

*Goodnight Lily.*

*Goodnight Sophie.* Her warmth settled around me like a long hug, and I sent the same comfort back to her. She had no idea how much I wished she could have been here in person. Despite her presence in my mind, I had never felt so alone. I had never been so alone.

Perhaps it was that loneliness that shaped my dreams. Because as I drifted off to sleep, I could have sworn I heard the familiar chatter of servants. Only these ones seemed to be discussing me. Apparently, they found me beautiful enough, although for what they didn't say. It was my strength they doubted. I wanted to be outraged—I had fought my way through a grueling Tourney and then braved the wastelands alone to get here—but I was already sinking deeper into dreamless sleep. And maybe the dream voices were right. They came from my own subconscious after all, and who knew me better than myself?

# CHAPTER 2

*A* jolt made me roll off the seat of the carriage and crash to the floor. We had started moving. I groaned and pushed myself to my feet, rubbing my hip bone. The wheels hit a bump, and I staggered before hurriedly sitting down. Rubbing my eyes and yawning, I grumbled to myself at the rude awakening.

After checking that Chestnut trotted behind us, I munched on a cold and unappetizing breakfast. I wondered how long before Lily woke up...then if I could possibly fall back asleep while the carriage was moving...and then I surveyed the chaos again and sighed. I supposed I had better tidy up. The Palinaran royal family had several castles and palaces, and I wasn't completely sure where I was going. Which meant we could arrive at any time.

I tidied all of my belongings neatly back into the saddlebags and used a small mirror to tidy up my hair and dress. When I felt as satisfied with my appearance as was possible in the circumstances, I settled back to watch out the window and await developments.

When the light began to fade, I gloomily surveyed the chaos of my belongings that had once again spread throughout the carriage. The hope with which I had packed them in the morning now seemed foolish and naive.

I sighed. Lily had done her best to keep me entertained, but there was only so much she could do from afar. She had even read me one of my favorite fairy tales for a couple of hours, but then she had been called away by other duties. She was betrothed to Marin's crown prince, after all, and Marin was currently full of foreign delegations. Treaty negotiations were still underway between our own kingdom, far away in the Four Kingdoms, and all of these lands except Palinar. She could hardly come up with an excuse for spending the whole day locked in the library reading.

I had thoroughly examined the inside of the carriage by this point, of course, and had been unimpressed to find my betrothed had failed to include any supplies. Thank goodness I had packed myself a generous supply of food and water before fleeing Marin.

As I munched on another cold meal—each one was becoming more unappetizing than the last—my thoughts dwelt on my betrothed. The Beast. Just the thought of him made me shudder —with revulsion or fear, I wasn't entirely sure.

I shouldn't be surprised at the lack of provisions. Why would a cold-hearted monster consider my comfort at all? Millie, Jon's cousin and a new friend, had told us all about how each Princess Tourney was shaped by the ruler or heir who called it. It made sense since its purpose was to find his perfect match and true love. And our Tourney had been frightening and dangerous—a terrifying glimpse into the dark nature of the crown prince of Palinar. So powerful was his curse, that it had reached out through him to corrupt the Tourney itself. What awful acts had he committed to bring such a curse upon himself?

I knew I couldn't possibly be the true love for such a man—if man he still was. The truth was not that the Tourney had chosen me, but that I had cheated, using the secret connection between Lily and me to circumvent the rules and gain an advantage. She had planned to sacrifice herself to save me, but it was a sacrifice I wasn't willing to let her make. I had never tried to work against her before, and my victory had been hard won. A hollow victory if not for the look on Lily's and Jon's faces at our joint betrothal ceremony. I would sacrifice myself again for my twin's happiness.

Except I was determined to make it a short-term sacrifice. As I had knelt beside the Beast's proxy at our Betrothal Ceremony, I had promised myself that I would travel to Palinar and find a way to break our betrothal. A way that didn't violate the ancient laws. Then I would find out what the Beast had done to curse his people, I would defeat him, and I would free them. I would make sure that he could never hurt me again. And then I would return to Marin.

It was an excellent plan, except that I had no idea whatsoever how to do it, and two full days of travel hadn't brought any enlightenment. When I fell asleep for the second night, I didn't let my mind listen for any voices—I didn't want to know what my subconscious thought.

*Sophie.* Lily's grim-sounding projection woke me even before the carriage began to move the next morning.

*What is it?* I came awake quickly having only been half-dozing.

*We've just received word from Marin's prison. Cole has disappeared.*

*What!?* I gasped. *What about Sir Oswald and Corinna?* I asked, referring to Cole's father and sister.

*They're still there and claim to know nothing about his escape.* Lily sounded tired. The sky had barely begun to lighten—how early had she been awoken with the news? *The duke has turned out all the guard, and they're searching the city. He seems confident we'll find him.*

Lily didn't sound like she shared her future father-in-law's optimism, and I understood her concern. The duchy of Marin was a city-state—by far the largest city either of us had ever seen. It must have a great many hiding places. And that was assuming he hadn't made it across the border into southern Talinos, or across the straits to one of the other kingdoms.

I groaned. The duke was never going to find him. And who knew what danger Cole would stir up? Every indication suggested he had been deep in his father's plot to steal Jon's father's throne—a plot we had only just managed to foil. And his treachery against the duke was actually the smaller concern.

The darkness we had defeated in Marin, had started in Palinar. The locals assured us that a curse so large and so devastating could only be the result of a kingdom turning their backs on the godmothers and breaching the ancient laws.

Except no one knew what laws had been violated. Or even the exact nature of the curse. They had simply noticed one day that no one had been seen leaving Palinar in weeks. Weeks that became months. Travelers and merchants who attempted to enter turned back with tales of desolate wastelands roamed by wild animals. A new feature in the once prosperous kingdom.

The last group had turned back after rescuing a man who had been mauled by a bear. I had sought out the man after winning the Tourney, but the rumors had been true. While his physical injuries had been healed, his confusion of the mind remained. He raved about a curse and a beastly prince, but his words made little sense. Of the other royals, Prince Dominic's parents and younger sister, he would say only that they were gone.

Palinar was cursed along with my betrothed. Emptied of people and full of wild beasts. Shrouded with darkness which had begun to infect the other kingdoms. Its power had even reached out through Prince Dominic and twisted the Tourney he had called, nearly destroying Marin.

And Cole and his family had originally come from Palinar,

moving to Marin long before the curse had cut Palinar off from the other kingdoms. But Jon, Lily, and I believed they had not escaped the reaches of the curse. The pride and greed in their hearts had provided fertile ground for the darkness that had already spread so far out of Palinar.

So, if Cole had escaped, that meant the curse had another agent roaming free, spreading the seeds of destruction further afield.

*Let me know how the search goes,* I projected, desperately wishing I could be there with Lily and Jon instead of riding alone in a strange and magical carriage toward a strange and terrifying fate.

She agreed, but she sounded distracted, and I knew I wouldn't be hearing any more of the story today. I wished I had been able to pack one or two books, but my saddlebags had been full to overflowing with basic necessities. There had been no room for such luxuries, and I hadn't expected to have the opportunity to read. I didn't know if a book would be enough to distract me right now, with yet another worry chasing around in my mind, but even the feel of one in my hand would have been comforting, like a little taste of home.

My sister-in-law, Alyssa, had been largely responsible for the education of Lily and me, and she had a never-ending love of books. Lily had never stopped grumbling about it—although I noted she spent a lot of time in the library studying between Tourney events—but I had come to share Alyssa's love. Or at least her love of fairy tales. Stories were exciting, since you never knew what you might find, what answers they might hold. But, at the same time, books were also solid and dependable; once you found a favorite, it never changed.

Would my new home have books? It was hard to imagine the infamous Beast sitting down to an afternoon read. I just hoped whichever castle he had chosen for his lair had a garden. If I couldn't have fairy tales, I hoped I could have roses. Since summer had only just started, the ones in Marin had still been in bloom, and I had been sorry to leave them. Books reminded me of the comfort of home, but roses filled me with an alluring sense of hope. For surely any wonder was possible in a world that could produce such beauty?

Which made it just as hard to picture the Beast surrounded by roses as books. Nothing but disappointment could be gained by hoping for the familiar comforts of home in the trial ahead of me. Better, by far, to prepare myself for the worst—almost a certainty given the situation. Especially since I had now spent two full days traveling through Palinar, and I couldn't remember having seen a single flower.

Lily kept me updated but, unfortunately, she had no real news. The search continued, but they had found no sign of Cole. The hours dragged on, and I ate the last of my food for a midday meal. My water was running low, too, since I hadn't dared to fill it at any of the streams we had encountered during our rest breaks. Chestnut apparently had no qualms slaking her thirst at the waterways, but I didn't trust anything in this cursed place. I could only hope we arrived at our destination—wherever that was—soon.

The carriage jolted and bumped, as the wheels hit a new surface. Peering out the window, I could see nothing but the endless plain, so I climbed onto the other seat to look out the front window. The road stretched ahead of us, its surface rougher than the smooth path through the flat wastelands.

We seemed to be slowly climbing uphill and, in the distance, I could see a line of trees. They disappeared into darkness, so I could only assume it was the start of a forest. I sighed. On the one hand, a change of scenery would be nice, providing a sense of progress that had eluded me in the constant plains. But on the other hand…I didn't like the idea of trees pressing in close to the side of the road. I would have no line of sight, and the memory of the wolves still lingered in my mind.

Given how far away the trees looked, we seemed to approach them impossibly fast. Soon the path was indeed cutting its way through a forest, thick and dark. To make it worse, the temperature had started to drop, despite the season, and I heard the distant howl of wolves.

The carriage raced through the trees, and I shivered as the air continued to grow colder. Rummaging through my bags, I put on a cloak. I had no sooner fastened the garment, than I saw a snowflake drift past the window. Soon it was joined by another, and then another, and then a larger flurry.

Within minutes it was snowing constantly, patches of white building between the trees. Yet another sign of the disease infecting this kingdom. Marin had been bright and sunny and full of flowers when I left, as summer should be. But apparently in this forest it was perpetually winter. My last hope of any flowers dissipated.

Before long I started to worry that the carriage would become bogged in the snow. And the howls of the wolves sounded closer, unless that was just my anxiety fooling my mind. Our pace slowed, although the snowfall did not, and I peered out the back at Chestnut. She looked uneasy for the first time since I had tied her to the vehicle. Was it the wolves or the increasing snow? Possibly both.

I reached out to Lily, wanting to update her on my situation but also looking for comfort. She was asleep, however. Napping, presumably, after her disrupted night. I didn't try again, not wanting to disturb her rest.

The snow built up on the road until I felt sure we would be forced to stop. But just before the drifts became too deep for passage, the carriage swerved. I nearly lost my balance, sliding across the seat, and had to scramble back into position. I wanted to see our new path.

I hadn't noticed a branch in the road, but then I had been considerably distracted. The new path appeared better tended than the main one, and the snow seemed to be lightening. Mounds of white heaped beside the path, but none had settled on the road itself, yet another marvel in this unpleasant place.

It occurred to me that I might be finally nearing my destination. In a flurry of movement, I collected all my escaped belongings and squeezed them into the saddlebags, not worrying about what I was crushing in the process. For a moment, I considered trying to change into a fresh dress, but I quickly abandoned the idea. The rattling carriage would make a poor dressing room, and I didn't like the idea of being caught half way through the process. I regretted the lost opportunity, though. I would have liked to impress my new fiancé and demonstrate that a princess of Arcadia was a person of significance.

I was coming alone into his home, but I didn't want him to think me weak and defenseless. I hoped his letters—calling the Tourney and then summoning me to him—were proof that whatever beast-like qualities he possessed, he retained his mental faculties. Surely, he wouldn't risk bringing further harm to himself by violating the covenant of the Princess Tourney, not to mention antagonizing a new kingdom of whose strength he knew nothing?

The carriage turned again, and I gasped. The rest of the forest dropped away as we rolled through an aisle of orange trees. Despite the snow heaped on the ground, the branches of the trees bore both fruit and blossoms—an even more impossible feat than snow in summer.

A shiver ran through me at the beautiful and chilling sight. Welcome to my new home.

# CHAPTER 3

*A*s we approached the end of the aisle of trees, I glimpsed
visions of a garden spread to either side. Greenery blossomed from the snow with bright colors splashing against the
white. My earlier desire for flowers passed through my mind,
and I shuddered. How could I ever enjoy such eerie, enchanted
blooms?

The carriage drove out from the trees and came to a stop in
front of a large castle. A wide, shallow staircase of gray stone led
up to vast wooden doors. The building branched off in both
directions, huge, imposing, and dark, full of twisted stone and
dim shadows.

I could see no sign of anyone. The snow had ceased to fall, but
the chill in the air remained, and I had no desire to remain in the
carriage after my long voyage. And yet still I lingered, trying to
convince my legs to move and carry me into this strange
unknown.

The door of the carriage swung open of its own accord, the
message loud and clear. I reminded myself I hadn't come this far
to lose courage now and hauled my saddlebags out into the snow,

unwilling to leave them in an enchanted vehicle that might disappear at any moment.

Once I stood beside them, I hesitated, however. My rumpled dress and travel stained face presented enough of an undignified appearance without tottering under the weight of heavy bags. Finally, I decided to leave them in the snow, next to Chestnut, who I untied from the carriage and secured to one of the stone balustrades. Surely I would find some servants inside the castle and could request them to care for my mount and possessions.

Taking a deep breath, I climbed the stairs, my stiff legs protesting the sudden exertion. As I approached the doors, I wondered if I would have the strength to push them open. I needn't have worried, however. When I reached them, they swung open of their own accord, just as the carriage door had done.

I peered into the cavernous entryway revealed by the open doors. Would my betrothed now appear? Had he been the one to grant me access to his castle?

But, once again, I could see no one. I walked inside, trying not to let my trembling legs disrupt my steps. I had never encountered a royal residence that felt so...empty. Where were all the people of Palinar?

The doors closed behind me with a thunderous crash, and I jumped. Whirling around I tried to control my dread. For now, my future lay within this castle, it mattered not if the door were open or closed—I was effectively trapped here either way. Still, I felt an unreasonable relief when I discovered a small, normal-sized door within one of the larger ones and found it unlocked. If I couldn't find any servants, I would need to tend to Chestnut myself—which was, of course, the sole source of my relief.

With the doors now closed, the air temperature inside the castle felt significantly warmer than outside. Without conscious thought, my feet led me to a fire burning in a large fireplace against one wall. Would Lily be awake by now? I decided I didn't care. The situation was simply too strange not to share with her.

*Lily? You won't believe where I've ended up.*

The emptiness around me reverberated in my mind. I froze and called out again. *Lily? Lily!*

Still nothing. My heart, which had already been beating fast, sped up. For a moment panic overwhelmed me, and I screamed her name over and over again in my mind. *Lily! Lily! Lily!*

Horrible possibilities streamed through my mind. She had fallen from her horse and been killed. Cole had found and murdered her in an act of revenge.

I tried to stem the panic. My twin could not have died without my sensing it. We were too connected for that, I felt sure of it. You couldn't lose half of yourself without knowing about it.

Perhaps she was simply busy, and unable to respond. But that thought brought no comfort. If Lily were distracted or asleep, she might not answer, but I would still sense her presence at the end of my projection, as I had done earlier. I could even wake her, if I needed, as she had done to me in the carriage. I tried to remember the last time I had spoken to her and couldn't pinpoint it.

We had never found a physical limitation to our communication, but we had never been so far apart before. Perhaps the distance was simply too vast. I tried again, more calmly this time, paying attention to my projection. My silent words flew out, projecting away from me in a way my ordinary thoughts did not.

I expected them to fade out, overwhelmed by distance, but the sensation more closely resembled slamming into a wall. I had been too shocked and panicked to notice it earlier, but it felt unmistakable now. My knees gave out, and I sank into a soft armchair pulled up to the fire.

I was on my own. Truly on my own. Uncontrollable shivers shook me. Lily and I had been connected since before I could remember. I had never really been alone before. Fear rushed over me, roiling in my belly and clouding my mind.

My connection to the outside world was gone, along with my main source of companionship. What if something did happen to Lily? Would I sense it behind this strange mental wall? I had found courage to face the Beast because I knew I would carry my sister with me. But he had stripped even that away from me.

Anger and hatred welled inside me, burning back some of the fear. Was there anything I was not expected to sacrifice?

A soft sound from the other side of the entryway made me leap to my feet. The light of the fire beside me faded into dimness on the other side of the room, but enough light remained for me to glimpse movement.

I drew back, the fear returning to the fore. Then I stiffened my spine and fed the anger, driving back the terror. "Who's there?" I called loudly. "Show yourself."

The dark figure hesitated and then stepped forward toward me.

I gasped and moved to place the armchair between us. Prince Dominic, for surely it must be he, towered above me. He wore no circlet or crown, but he carried himself like someone used to wielding power and authority.

His broad shoulders barely fit into his jacket, the material bunching strangely around their unnatural shape. His light brown hair reached to his shoulders, matted and wild, and the backs of his hands, the only bit of skin I could see other than his face, looked abnormally hairy.

His mouth and jaw seemed to sit oddly, but otherwise his face looked surprisingly human, more so than I had expected and feared. The relief soothed some of my initial shock. Perhaps I had been unnecessarily apprehensive, the strangeness of the castle and his furtive arrival exacerbating my nerves.

I tried to focus on his eyes, which were a strangely piercing blue, and were the most normal looking part of him. In fact, I thought I detected hesitation and uncertainty in them. And if he felt nervous, even a little, it meant I had some power in this situation, too.

I forced myself to step around the armchair again and drop into a curtsey. I waited for him to speak, but he said nothing, simply measuring me with those bright eyes. Anger, fear, frustration, and resentment swirled through me in such a confused mess that I began to feel numb to all of them. He had brought me all this way alone; did he truly have nothing to say?

I broke the silence. "Greetings. I am Princess Sophia of Arcadia. I assume you are Prince Dominic, my betrothed."

He inclined his upper body slightly in acknowledgment but still said nothing, too haughty or sullen to speak. I reached out to Lily in my mind, knowing she would share my outrage. The emptiness in my mind hit me again, and I nearly collapsed. A single tear managed to escape my eye.

I glanced back at my betrothed, and saw that his gaze had fixed on my face where the drop of moisture still rolled down my cheek. How dare he stand there and judge me. I snapped.

"They call you the Beast, but I had hoped some part of the royal prince remained," I spat at him. "I see now that I was wrong. They told me your kingdom was once the largest and most magnificent in these lands. How far noble Palinar has fallen."

An expression that I couldn't read passed across his face. And then he opened his mouth, and I saw why his jaw looked misshapen. Inside he had a row of fangs instead of normal teeth. They glistened in the firelight as a low menacing growl rippled through the room.

I stumbled backwards and hit the chair, my own mouth dropping open in horror. He stepped toward me, and I rushed to put the piece of furniture between us again. I couldn't imagine the chair would prove much of an impediment to him, but something about my action angered him. He threw back his head and roared.

The deafening sound filled the entryway, and the last of my courage disappeared. I turned and fled, pushing through the first door I found. I ran through stone passageways, noticing nothing of my surroundings, all my attention focused on listening for sounds of pursuit.

Candle sconces sprang into flame ahead of me, lighting a passage through the castle. I considered fleetingly that the lights might be leading me into a trap, but I couldn't face any of the dark, unlit corridors. My legs protested the exertion after so long immobile in the carriage, but my terror kept me moving forward.

Ahead of me the lights stopped, but I had time for only a single pang of apprehension before a wooden door in the corridor wall swung open. The warm glow of a fire poured out to fill the darkness. I pivoted and threw myself into the room, slamming the door closed behind me.

I leaned against it, my heart pounding and my breath rasping through my throat, while I surveyed the room. The large bedchamber was lavishly appointed in green and gold, the furniture solid and elegant. The four-poster bed looked soft and a small fire burned cheerfully. Best of all, the room looked completely empty.

I checked the door for a key, but found none. A small chest of drawers stood against the wall next to the door, so I pushed it, heaving until it slid across the doorway. An image of the Beast's broad shoulders flashed through my mind, but I ignored it. The room had heavier pieces of furniture, but I would have no hope of moving them. This one would have to be enough.

My stomach rumbled, my body overruling my fear with other needs. For the first time, I noticed a small table tucked next to the fireplace and laden with a tray of food. I looked around the room again, but I was still alone. The bowl looked as if it held some sort of stew, the aroma rising from it enticing enough to make my mouth water. Sinking into a well-placed chair, I devoured the fresh, hot food, calculating the hours since I had anything other than travel fare. Already the long, boring voyage seemed impossibly distant.

When I had finished, I knew it must still be early, but I had no desire to step foot outside my room. Instead I explored the inside, examining the large desk and peering into the wardrobe. As I pulled the ornate walnut doors open, I stumbled back, gasping. A row of dresses hung inside, several of them recognizable as gowns from my saddlebags. Rushing through the room, I pulled open all the drawers I could find as well as the large chest at the foot of the bed. I had soon located the entire contents of my bags, carefully distributed around the room.

Shame filled me. In my fear, I had completely forgotten about my saddlebags and, more importantly, Chestnut. I had left her shivering in the cold while I filled my belly and warmed myself.

I looked around the room again. I had still seen no physical sign of a servant, but someone had clearly retrieved my bags and unpacked them. Surely the same person would have cared for my horse. It seemed a certainty. Surely...

I regarded the drawers in front of the door doubtfully. Should I go and check on Chestnut? I couldn't remember the way through the castle, but perhaps the candles would show me the way again.

I imagined myself stumbling through the dark, stone corridors, straining to hear the soft footfall of the Beast around each corner. When I shook myself from the vision, I found my hands had already stripped off my dress and pulled my nightgown from a drawer. I flung it over my head and dived beneath the covers of the bed, blowing out the candles as I went and leaving only the soft glow of the fire to light the room.

I buried my face in my pillow and wept. I could only hope my mysterious helper had indeed cared for Chestnut, and that the poor animal wouldn't have to pay the price for my cowardice. Because I had come so far but now, at the end, my courage had failed me. Lily would have been braver. The thought of my sister only increased the flow of my tears.

# CHAPTER 4

*I* must have fallen into an exhausted slumber, because when I awoke, the fire had died and daylight shone through the windows. I reached out instinctively to Lily in my mind, and the emptiness hit me like a physical blow. Curling in on myself, I fought back a fresh wave of tears. I had always known coming here wouldn't be easy, but I had thought I would have Lily in my mind to give me strength. How would I survive alone in this strange place?

I let my mind dwell on Marin for a moment. Had they found Cole, or were they still busy turning the city inside out? What was Lily making of our sudden disconnection? I knew she would be sick with worry and hoped Jon had prevented her from rashly rushing after me. I thought of her galloping toward Palinar, and the howls of the wolves sounded loudly in my mind. I shivered.

Forcing myself to breathe deeply, I sat up. No good would come from moping and dreaming and crying, I needed a plan. Lily and I had never truly understood our unusual gift; it had always simply worked. Until now—suddenly—it didn't.

I sighed. If only we had spent more time experimenting and trying to understand our connection. More information might have helped me in this situation. But, even without it, I was determined to discover what was blocking our connection and find a way around it.

I looked around at the lush bedchamber. Since my questing projections continued to run up against an invisible wall, I didn't think I would find any answers in my room. Which meant I needed to get up and explore my surroundings. The roar of my fiancé from the night before echoed through my mind, as ominous as the howling of wolves.

I took another deep breath and realized I'd twisted two strands of hair so tightly around my finger I was threatening the blood flow. I forced myself to relax and slip out of bed. Instead of the expected cold stone, my feet landed on a soft rug, sinking into the thick piles. I wiggled my toes, enjoying the luxury after my previous nights in the carriage. I needed to focus on the positives, or I would lose every last shred of my bravery.

I examined the room again in daylight. The curtains were flung wide since I hadn't stopped to close them before diving into bed. I walked over to the windows to peer out. From the view, I guessed my room to be on the third floor and vaguely remembered fleeing up stairs the night before. The room had an incredible vista looking out over extensive gardens.

They had clearly been carefully sculpted and appeared well cared for, although I could see no sign of any gardeners at work. No footsteps showed up in the glistening carpet of snow, either. My eyes stung from the brightness of the white, so incongruous against the green leaves and vivid petals. I couldn't imagine wandering through such a strange landscape.

A small glimpse of a stone building off to one side looked like stables. My shame from the night before flooded me again, and I immediately decided to make the building my first goal.

My stomach rumbled, reminding me I hadn't eaten yet, but I resolutely ignored it. I had failed in my responsibility to my mount the night before: I wouldn't fail again.

Pushing aside the chest of drawers, I stepped out into the stone corridor and looked up and down, hoping to see something familiar. But both directions looked the same, an expanse of cold gray, broken by regular sconces. The stable-like building had been to my right when I stood at the window, so I turned left, heading in that direction. I would look for stairs to take me down and then any door to the outside I could find.

As I walked, I pretended to myself that I felt calm and confident—the new mistress of the castle, exploring my domain. But my ears strained for the sound of footfalls behind me, and my eyes flickered toward every shadow, looking for a looming shape.

I saw nothing, but soft noises reached my ears. I twitched and looked behind me, but the passageway remained empty. I walked on, descending a set of stairs that took me all the way to ground level. Again, I heard the sound, like a faint rustling or whispering, and spun around. Still nothing.

I picked up my pace, looking for any promising door, anxious to be free from the stifling walls that hedged me in. The sound, like a breeze through leaves, sounded again, and I broke into a run resolutely keeping my eyes ahead.

A door appeared, and I rushed to it, hoping to find it unlocked. A desperate surge of disappointment washed over me as the door resisted me, and then it seemed to fling itself open, almost tumbling me into the snow outside.

I staggered and regained my balance, striding quickly into the garden. The cold air hit me just as the first sensation of damp penetrated my thin slippers. I should have taken the time to dress in boots and a jacket. I glanced back at the door to find it had mysteriously closed behind me.

I wrapped my arms around myself and hurried on, unwilling to backtrack and unsure I could even find my way back to my room. As I got closer, it became obvious that the building I had seen was indeed a stable. The familiar smell of horses overwhelmed the exotic aroma of the unnatural flowers, and I heard a nicker emanating from inside.

My heart surged with hope. If the castle had horses, it must have someone to tend them. And surely whoever was responsible for that task would have cared for Chestnut after I abandoned her. I moved quickly, almost running into the warm aisle between the rows of stalls.

A couple of horses nickered a welcome, while another one snorted loudly, stomping one hoof. My gaze flickered over them, traveling down the row until I found a familiar head hanging over a stall door. I ran over and flung my arms around Chestnut's neck. We had made it this far together, and I still hated how close I had come to failing her.

She huffed a soft greeting and began nosing at my dress, clearly hoping for a treat of some kind. I laughed shakily and stepped back, apologizing for coming empty handed. Her coat had felt smooth and soft. Clearly, she had been groomed since our trek through the wilderness. I would need to offer my thanks to the stable master—if he ever made an appearance.

A soft sound behind me, like the shifting of weight, informed me that I had company. "Greetings," I said as I started to turn, "I had begun to wonder…" My words fell away as my eyes absorbed my company.

Somehow Prince Dominic looked even more terrifying in the otherwise familiar setting of a stable, his unnatural features obvious in the daylight. I quelled a strong desire to flee back out into the gardens. The Beast towered over me: if he wanted to catch me, I couldn't possibly escape him. Running would only make me look foolish.

He looked as frozen as me, obviously surprised to be disturbed. I followed his outstretched arm to where his hairy hand rested on the neck of a large jet-black stallion who eyed me warily. The stance surprised me; my mental image of him hadn't included an affinity with animals. Perhaps it should have, though, since he seemed part animal himself.

The large horse looked aggressive, and I had to admit that I would be nervous to mount him. And yet I didn't doubt that Prince Dominic could easily control him. Something about the quiet moment between them suggested both power and something softer. For an unthinking moment, I thought that I would like to join him on a ride, to see him galloping across a field on the black horse.

And then my eyes focused on the strange shape of his mouth and the way his shoulders bulged unnaturally under his jacket, his misshapen body a constant reminder of his curse. I remembered who he was and everything I had already suffered at his instigation. My anger flared, but a decent night's sleep and the reassurance of daylight helped me to repress the fear. Like it or not, I was stuck here, at least for now. I needed to find a way to make this work.

I tried to think of something I could say that would balance my true feelings with some attempt at conciliation. "Your stable is well kept and the horses beautiful. Do you come here often?"

He stared at me, the intensity of his blue eyes seeming to communicate a message, if only I knew how to interpret it. He raised his free hand, as if in greeting, and for a moment I thought he was finally going to speak. But instead he gave a long growl, his lower jaw thrusting forward to reveal his sharp fangs.

I recoiled slightly, a burst of energy urging me to be afraid— to run while I still could. But the instinctive response was quickly overwhelmed by an invigorating anger. Since the moment I had stepped foot in these lands, I had been swept up in a series of unpleasant experiences engineered by this prince to force me to come here. And yet he treated me like an unwelcome intruder.

I put my hands on my hips and glared at him. "Do you truly have nothing to say to me? Are we not betrothed, Beast?" I hoped the title would provoke him into speech, but he merely glared back at me.

Our standoff stretched out, as we stared at each other, neither moving. After a long moment, the stallion neighed and tossed his head, disrupting the Beast's hand. The prince shook his shaggy head and transferred his grim gaze to the animal. The stallion ignored him, and the Beast turned and strode from the building.

I sagged a little and took a deep breath. I hadn't made any headway with my new betrothed, but at least I had conquered my own fear. And Chestnut seemed happy and well cared for. Which left me free to begin my explorations.

As I walked back toward the castle, I looked around, sure I would now see tracks in the snow. Sure enough, a set of large indents led from the stable around the main building and disappeared off toward the front entrance. They clearly belonged to the Beast, a name which fit my betrothed much better than Dominic.

No other prints appeared, however—as if the Beast and I were alone in this well-kept place. I frowned. Something was even more wrong with this kingdom than I had imagined. While I tried to find a way around the block preventing me from projecting to Lily, I wouldn't forget my original goal. I needed to find out what had happened here, and how to reverse it. And, hopefully, while doing that, I would find a way to break my engagement. The sooner I could leave the Beast behind forever, the better. I certainly had no intention of ever letting him touch me. I shuddered at the thought of being that close to him.

I followed the footprints, confident the Beast would be long gone to whatever lair he usually frequented. For the second time, I trod the shallow stairs and paused in front of the huge doors. The castle lacked the cultivated feeling of the magical garden. Instead it felt dark and ominous, even in the bright morning light. I felt sure that every crevice in this cavernous place must be full of dust.

The doors didn't swing open for me this time, and I pushed at the small door cut into one of the bigger ones. It swung open reluctantly, and I sighed before entering the entrance hall. The garden still made me nervous, but I found it less repugnant than I had expected. The open air turned out to be preferable to the gloomy castle.

Inside, I faced a broad staircase that rose upwards before splitting into two. I had already decided to follow the stairs as high as they would take me. It seemed too simple to hope that height would allow me to bypass the mysterious wall blocking my projections, but I had to try everything. Just in case.

As I stepped forward my stomach twisted, reminding me that I still hadn't eaten. As if on cue, a door in the far corner of the entrance hall swung wide, allowing me a glimpse of a long, dark dining table. My feet turned toward it, following the instructions of my stomach over my mind.

Sunlight streamed through a row of tall windows that faced onto yet more gardens to the rear of the castle. The oversized room contained the longest table I had ever seen. It looked particularly out of place in this empty land, and the food that had been laid out at one end looked small and lonely.

But when I approached the single seat that had been set for a meal, I realized the size of the table had been deceiving. There was actually enough food for a miniature feast, it was merely dwarfed by the expanse of empty wood. More food than I could possibly eat had been laid out in gleaming bowls and platters. I paused. Was this the Beast's meal? Surely even he could not eat this much.

I peered around the room but could see no one. After a moment of deliberation, I sat. As much as I regretted it, this was my home now, and I had to eat. If the Beast disliked my actions, perhaps he would finally be roused to speak to me.

The food tasted so delicious it was hard to limit myself to only a small portion of each dish, but I wanted to try everything.

I wished I could let Lily know that at the very least I had a warm bed and a full stomach. Loneliness crashed over me. I had never been without a built-in best friend before.

Several tears slid down my cheeks, and for the first time I felt grateful I was completely alone. At least there was no one to witness my grief. As I reached to wipe the moisture away, the rustle I had heard earlier in the corridor swept through the room. It sounded so much like whispering that I twisted, searching the room with my eyes. I was still alone.

I stood up abruptly, and my chair crashed backwards onto the floor. Feeling foolish, I picked it back up before hurrying from the room. I had eaten too much already, and I needed to find a way to communicate with my sister.

# CHAPTER 5

$\mathcal{I}$ wandered through the castle for a long time before I managed to find the tallest tower. The invisible whispers followed me. At first, I got hopelessly lost, wandering through an endless maze of interconnected corridors and rooms. The castle had clearly been expensively and elegantly decorated at some point. But, unlike my room, the majority of it had fallen into dusty disrepair.

The contrast indicated that someone had clearly prepared for my arrival. I remembered the line of lights that had led me to my room. What sort of strange curse was this? Was the castle itself responsible for its own care? I shook my head at the fanciful thought. How could a magic building have fed and groomed my horse?

But the gloomy, shadowy castle, combined with the whispers all around me, fed the mad imaginings. Perhaps it had not been the curse that had warped the Beast's mind; perhaps living here for so long alone had done it.

I shook my head. No. The Beast wasn't mad—he had written coherent letters, after all—he was evil. He must be evil to have brought down such a curse upon himself. And I had seen the evidence myself in the cruelty of the events of the Princess Tourney. The Tourney he had called and that had, therefore, been magically shaped to fit him.

The darkness he had brought to these lands had nearly overtaken Marin—and all the other kingdoms still stood in danger. And yet here he sat, holed up in his strange castle, carelessly destroying the lives of innocent girls he had never even met.

If the castle was dark and terrifying, it had been he who had made it that way, and not the other way around.

*What did the Beast do to curse himself and his kingdom?* I wondered for the thousandth time. I shook off the thought. Filling my head with horrifying theories wouldn't help me fix my projections or find the truth. I needed proof, and I had a whole castle in which to search for it.

After a while of aimless wandering, I remembered again that the lights had led me to my room. Perhaps a friendlier power dwelt here alongside the Beast. He had certainly shown no effort to see to my comfort.

"I'm looking for the tallest tower. Could you show me the way?" It felt foolish to speak the words aloud to the empty air, but it could hardly hurt.

I had no immediate response, and no candles sprang to life to lead me. But I soon noticed a strange phenomenon. When I moved toward the whispers rather than away from them, I seemed to find more open doors and staircases. I began to listen for them, and soon I found myself in an enclosed staircase that spiraled upwards.

As I climbed stair after stair, I caught glimpses through a series of small windows of what appeared to be a second staircase, somehow twisted around mine. And every time I passed the openings, I heard the whispers.

I tried to calm my breathing which kept speeding up despite my best efforts. The whispers appeared to be friendly, but the sound created the inescapable impression that I was ascending upwards in tandem with an unseen group of people. I shivered. I needed this to work. The familiar sound of Lily in my mind would drive away the eeriness of this empty castle.

But it took only a moment to discover that height made no difference to the wall that blocked my thoughts. I threw them out anyway, again and again. At first, I did it out of frustration, but then I began trying to pinpoint the exact feeling of the obstruction. I had never experimented like this before, and it was unexpectedly interesting.

I had always assumed that we had a direct connection and placed our thoughts straight into each other's minds. But it now seemed more complicated than that. Clearly our thoughts traveled to each other. I focused on the sensation of my thoughts flying out from my mind. I felt the way they stayed connected to me, but at the same time I couldn't shake an underlying unease.

I sat on the floor of the top tower room, put my chin in my hands and chewed on a strand of hair. After extended thought, I decided the discomfort came from the sense of being unanchored. My thoughts had always stayed attached to me, yes, but usually they also attached immediately to someone else. My sister. A tether on the other end. I now felt loose, floating in the world without foundation.

The whispers swirled around me, reaching a crescendo. For a moment, I thought I could make out individual words, but meaning eluded me. I shivered, unnerved, but then reminded myself that the sounds had helped me find my way. They had been friendlier than my betrothed, in fact.

A chuckle escaped me. I hadn't even been gone from Marin a week, and I was already counting disembodied, inaudible whispers as my only friends.

"Not that I'm not grateful," I said aloud. "In fact, I'd greatly appreciate it if you could show me the way back to my room."

A low murmur surrounded me and then moved toward the door. I clambered to my feet and followed the sound. Sure enough, it led me down several flights of stairs and through a series of corridors and delivered me to my room. I smiled as I opened the door—I might not have broken through to Lily, but I had learned a small something of the secrets of the castle. And a particularly helpful something, too, given the size of the building, and its confusing layout.

As soon as my eyes fell on my bed, the smile dropped from my lips. The bed had been made and my possessions tidied, but it was the piece of parchment resting against my pillow that filled my heart with dread. I walked slowly over and picked it up.

---

You will join me for the evening meal.

---

The note hadn't been signed, but the handwriting was easily recognizable from his earlier missives. The curt command made me tremble with rage. At every turn, the Beast was determined to strip away my freedom. I immediately determined not to go.

Several hours later, as I once again paced up and down my room, I doubted my decision. I wished I could consult Lily. My stomach had started reminding me that I hadn't eaten since the morning. And when I had hopefully asked the room if a meal might be forthcoming, nothing had happened except a brief swirl of whispered noise. The murmuring sounded more distressed than usual, but no assistance appeared.

I lay down on top of the covers and let my head sink into the pillows. My defiance had seemed entirely justified when I first read the note, but perhaps I had been too hasty. I needed to understand the curse and the Beast if I was to find a way around the betrothal. And what better source could there be than my betrothed himself?

As the last ray of sunset pierced my window, I scrambled off the bed and hurried over to the wardrobe. The doors flung themselves open before I could touch them and, for the first time, I smiled at the strange behavior of the castle. I hoped it meant I had been right—a second power existed here, and it wished to help me defeat the Beast.

A breeze rushed through the room and rustled one particular dress. I pulled it out and examined it, frowning. I could tell, even without trying it on, that the soft material would fall flatteringly, clinging to my torso and waist before swishing elegantly around my hips and out into a small train. But I felt no need to dress up for the part-monster who was essentially my captor, and the room's desire for me to do so made me question my earlier assumption as to whose side it was on.

But as I reached to return it to the wardrobe, my hand stilled. The Beast insisted on treating me brusquely, as if I had no position or importance. If I wanted to remind him that I was a princess from a powerful kingdom, then I needed to look the part. Reluctantly I dressed and examined myself in the full-length mirror. Sure enough, knowing that I looked elegant and regal boosted my confidence.

My stomach rumbled, and I hurried from the room in a swirl of satisfied whisperings. As I followed the sounds back to the entrance hall, I told myself that my decision most definitely had nothing whatsoever to do with my hunger, or the delicious food I had been served in the dining hall that morning.

My steps slowed as I reached the open door, the glow of flames pouring out into the entrance hall. I took a deep breath and stepped through, half noting the blazing fire in the huge fireplace as my eyes locked onto the hulking form occupying the seat at the head of the table.

His shaggy head came up at my entrance, and he pushed back

his chair, standing silently. For a brief moment, our eyes met, and his piercing blue gaze froze me in place. How could such a monster possess such eyes?

He seemed caught off guard by my appearance, a response at odds with his command that I attend the meal. Then I stepped forward and the unsettling moment was broken.

I had to remind myself to be glad when I saw that my spot had been set at the Beast's right hand rather than the distant foot of the table. I had told myself I wished for a chance to speak with him, but in truth I had hoped to have the long table between us.

I took my place, and the chair pushed itself in behind me. I noted, distantly, that the moving furniture didn't even surprise me. I was growing accustomed to the oddities of this castle. The scrape of a knife drew my eyes upwards, and I had to suppress a gasp at the sight of the Beast's gleaming fangs, jutting from his human mouth. Apparently, I had yet to grow accustomed to my betrothed.

I quickly looked down again, hoping he hadn't noticed my moment of intimidation. A childish part of me wanted to return his earlier rudeness with silence of my own, but the larger part anticipated our first conversation with reluctant interest. I had spent so much time imagining the motivations and mindset of this man, and yet I had no idea what he would say.

But the Beast did not speak. Instead he ate steadily, his hairy hands curling awkwardly around the cutlery. I followed his lead, glad to fill my stomach and gather my composure before launching into the inevitable conflict.

The first course gave way to the second, and the glances I stole at him increased in frequency. The strange shape of his mouth clearly made eating difficult, but he persisted without comment. Twice when I looked his way, our eyes met. Both times I looked quickly away and then spent the next minutes trying to interpret the strange expression I had glimpsed on his face.

The third time I refused to look down, holding his eyes

instead, my own full of defiance. His eyes, as they met mine, seemed to glow, the warmth in them more unsettling than the harsher emotions I had glimpsed previously. Eventually I looked away, hating the faint flush which I could feel staining my cheeks. He had no business having eyes like that.

I rushed to cover the awkwardness of the moment, sick of waiting for him to speak. "You may call me Sophie, if you like. Everyone does. I only use Sophia for formal occasions." I paused to give him a chance to reply, but he remained silent, so I pressed on.

"I suppose you must have been surprised to see me. My kingdom of Arcadia lies far across the seas—one of the Four Kingdoms. We are large and prosperous, and my family wish to expand our diplomatic and trade ties. My sister Lily and I were part of the delegation sent to Marin to open negotiations. We arrived in time to be caught up in the Princess Tourney which you called."

Surprised was probably an understatement. The Four Kingdoms had been cut off from these lands for generations. For so long, in fact, that our people had forgotten that a flotilla of ships ever left our shores to seek new lands.

Yet, apparently, those ships had sailed away and found these lands, pristine and untouched. And then they beseeched the High King to set a wall of storms between us. Back then it had been the Four Kingdoms that had forgotten the High King's decrees of true love and had turned their backs on the godmothers. Those who fled had sought protection from us.

In the intervening generations, much had changed. And perhaps that was what had caused the storms to disappear, and our lands to find each other once again. Because now the Four Kingdoms flourished. The godmothers had assisted the rulers of each of the lands to find true love and, as decreed from the High King's Palace of Light, the result was peace and prosperity for kingdoms ruled by love.

Except Lily and I had found peace a little boring—a fact I now heartily regretted. When an Emissary had arrived unexpectedly from this unknown land, we had responded to the promise of adventure with enthusiasm. We had joined the return delegation to the duchy of Marin, and had found adventure enough in the danger of the Princess Tourney. The ancient laws of this foreign land had worked against us then, even as they protected me now.

Thoughts of the Tourney sparked a flare of resentment inside me. Lily and I had suffered in many ways during the competition, and it had nearly sabotaged Lily's chance at true love. All because of this silent creature sitting beside me.

A small voice in the back of my mind whispered that it had sabotaged my chance of true love, but I suppressed it. I would find a way free from this forced betrothal, whatever it took.

I glanced back at the Beast again. I hoped he had absorbed my words about my kingdom. I wanted him to know they would not sit idly by if he attempted to harm me. Should I tell him so outright? Or would such plain speaking spur him to anger? I weighed the risks either way.

While I considered, the silence between us lengthened. I had moved past anger into incredulity, at this point. Did he really intend never to speak to me? What purpose could he have in such behavior? He had been the one to summon me, although I could hardly imagine why, based on his actions so far. I had feared on the journey here that he might expect too great an intimacy, but the opposite seemed to be true. He did not even want the most basic of interactions.

But, on the other hand, he had demanded my presence at the meal. The contradictions made little sense, and I was sick of feeling uncertain and confused. I had tried being rude on the night of my arrival, and I had now twice tried being polite. I would ask him directly for an explanation—of the Tourney, of his curse, of his behavior.

I opened my mouth to do so just as he shifted toward me. The huge bulk of his shoulders rippled with strength as his large hand stretched out. I remembered we were alone and how capable he would be of crushing me and closed my mouth again.

A strange energy coursed through the huge, mostly empty room. The flames made the shadows dance and weave around me, and the air overly warm. I began to feel I was in a dream. It took me a moment to notice that the Beast had been holding another small piece of parchment out toward me. By the time I recognized the object, he had dropped it beside my plate.

My hand trembled slightly as I picked it up.

---

Will you marry me in the morning?

---

"What?" I leaped to my feet, my chair clattering to the floor behind me for the second time in as many meals. In all my imaginings, I had not considered that he might press for such a quick wedding. Royal weddings took time to prepare and, surely, he could not expect me to marry him while I was alone here without support. Let alone while he and his kingdom remained cursed.

"No!" I almost shouted the word, unable to meet his eyes. "Absolutely not!" I had started to grow a little comfortable in this castle—I had lost the edge of my fear and anger. But the thought of actually marrying my betrothed brought them flooding back.

I turned to rush from the room, only to be jerked to a stop just before I reached the door. His large hand, the nails more like claws, easily wrapped around my upper arm and spun me around to face him. He held me close, although not quite pressed against him, his face leaning down toward mine.

For a mad moment, I thought he meant to press his lips against mine and I froze, almost incapacitated by revulsion. But he made no move to close the small distance between us, instead pinning me in place with his eyes and his firm grip on my arm.

A strange fascination filled me as his eyes pleaded with me for something I couldn't understand. Only that morning I had resolved never to let him touch me. And yet the surge of energy which ignited me now contained as much intrigue as repulsion.

I remembered his hand, soft against the neck of the black stallion. I felt the way his fingers gripped me now, firm and yet not hard enough to hurt. Something about his restrained strength enthralled me in a way I had not expected. What was going on inside the head of such a strange person?

Fancy gripped me, and I imagined that his eyes were attempting to tell me—to pour everything from his mind into mine. That they were pleading with me to free him.

But then my eyes dropped to his fangs, and I remembered. It was I who needed to be freed. This Beast had plucked me from my family, cut off my contact with them, isolated me completely, and now even attempted to physically restrain me.

I stepped down hard on his foot, wrenching my arms from his grip at the same time. Shock crossed his face, and I didn't wait for him to regain his balance. Picking up my skirts I fled from the room as fast as I could run.

# CHAPTER 6

*I* dived into my bed almost as fast as I had done the night before. The chest of drawers again blocked the door, and I had abandoned the gown in a crumpled mess on the floor. The lights had led my way, this time with the whispers swirling around me as well. They had died out into silence now, but I had taken some small comfort from their earlier presence.

I tried to tell myself I was not alone, but I didn't really believe it. I was more alone than I had ever imagined being. I had tried to be brave, but I had failed. I acknowledged now that it had been hunger, not bravery or strategy, that had driven me to dinner. And without my twin to back me up and support me, I had lost my courage.

She had always led us, and I had always been content to let her. Content because I knew that in truth she needed me as much as I needed her. The thought brought a fresh bout of tears. How was Lily coping back in Marin, as cut off from me as I was from her?

But she had Jon now, and a new place in this foreign land as the future duchess of Marin. I had seen a new strength grow in her throughout the Tourney, I had even used it to fuel my own resolve. But now that she was stripped away from me, I saw that it was not enough. Alone I was weak, when all I wanted was to be strong.

For the second night, my tears soaked my pillow, and I could not will them to stop. Eventually, exhausted from my long day, I slipped into slumber.

Once again, I was woken by the sunlight, my curtains still open from the day before. But unlike the previous morning, I didn't have to fight back tears. Apparently, I had finally cried myself out. Or perhaps I was merely distracted by a thought. A thread that had woven its way through my restless dreams.

I struggled now to capture it, certain of its importance. I had been haunted all night by the growls and roars and deafening silence of my betrothed. But also by his haunting eyes, pleading with me. And I had been sure of something in my sleep—a realization that I could no longer recall.

It took me at least a minute to chase it down, the revelation finally bursting through my mind. My betrothed growled and snarled and roared like an animal, his mouth misshapen to fit beast-like fangs. What if it was not rudeness that drove his silence? What if he was actually unable to speak?

I lay in bed for some minutes considering the idea from all angles. The more I thought about it, the more obvious it seemed, and I began to feel embarrassed for not seeing it before. His notes and his pleading eyes suddenly made sense. I sat up in bed, the new knowledge driving away any lingering melancholy. A new challenge had presented itself, and I felt glad for the distraction.

I slipped out of bed, weighing possible means of communication, but paused. A new note had been slipped under the door while I slept. I rushed over to swoop it up, elated by my new understanding. Surely this was a letter from the prince, explaining his incapacity and apologizing for his behavior since my arrival. Of course, I had already worked it out without his explanation, but he couldn't be expected to know that.

But the glow of satisfaction died as soon as I opened the parchment and read the words inside. It could not, by any stretch of the imagination, be considered a letter. Instead it contained only a repeat of his demand from the day before.

---

You will join me for the evening meal.

---

I stared at it, rereading it three times before crumpling it up and flinging it into the embers of the fire. I had allowed my pleasure at solving the puzzle to blind me for a moment. The rudeness of his curt communications could not be blamed on his inability to speak. It came wholly from him. I should not have let myself forget I was dealing with a beast.

I dressed myself in a mood of righteous indignation. Would it really have been so hard to write me a proper letter? I struggled to imagine his clawed hand holding a pen but pushed the thought aside. However hard it might be for him, it could not compare to the trials I had been through in the Tourney. It had most likely been pride that held him back. He had not wanted to admit his limitations, and I felt sure he was not the sort to ever apologize.

I chewed my way through the food that had been laid out for me with more force than was necessary. I suspected that if I wanted an evening meal, I would have to eat it in his presence. And a part of me even relished the prospect. I would give him a piece of my mind and, if I was right, he would be entirely unable to answer back. I couldn't resist a small grin at the thought. What girl hadn't wished herself in such a position at some point or other?

And in the meantime, I had the whole day before me. Going

higher hadn't allowed me to bypass the wall blocking me from Lily, so I couldn't imagine going underground would help. I glanced out the window and admitted to myself that at least some of this conclusion came from the fact that I had no desire to go searching for the dungeons.

The sun shone, despite the snow, and the open air called to me. Perhaps I needed to leave the boundaries of the castle. It might not be a wall so much as a barrier that blanketed this locality. In my anger and fear, I had assumed it was a specific block against me. But, in reality, that made no sense. No one even knew of our ability, so why would anyone plan against it?

One glance at the snow-filled garden, full of blossoming flowers and glossy fruit, was enough to see that this place existed outside the usual laws of nature. I was becoming increasingly convinced that whatever magic fueled this enchantment blocked my projections by chance. I would take Chestnut and ride far enough beyond the castle to test my theory. But not so far that I might lose my way back. I had not forgotten the conditions in the rest of this kingdom, nor the consequences to myself and my family if I tried to defy the ancient laws that bound my betrothal.

Glad for a purpose that would take me outside and into the company of my horse—currently my only friend—I hummed as I hurried my final preparations. I might be talking to Lily again within the hour.

Chestnut seemed happy to see me and eager for exercise. I easily found her saddle and fitted it quickly, glad my parents had made me learn how to care for my mount myself. I had been relieved to see no sign of the Beast, but confused to still discover no sign of anyone else either. Yet Chestnut's straw was fresh and her coat recently groomed.

I thrust off thought of the mystery, too eager to speak to my sister to lend it my full attention. A mounting block outside the stable helped me onto Chestnut's back, and we were soon walking through the gardens.

I had intended to move quickly toward the aisle of orange trees, but my fascination held me back. I let Chestnut wander through the plants at a walk. The hours spent surrounded by the enchantment of the castle had softened the unease the strange garden had initially produced. I could now see the unusual beauty of it—the colors gorgeous against the pure white of the undisturbed snow.

I spotted an intricate rose garden far to my left and nearly turned Chestnut toward it. But at the same time, I saw the first of the orange trees on my right and remembered my purpose. I directed my mare's nose toward the row of trees and urged her into a trot.

The warmth of the sun beat against my shoulders, and I marveled that it did not melt the snow. As we moved into the aisle, I let Chestnut settle back into a walk. I steered her to one side, brushing close against the trees. Clumps of delicate white flowers alternated with plump-looking orange globes. The intoxicating scent of the flowers surrounded me, and I had to stop myself from picking one of the fruit. It looked juicy and delicious, but I didn't know if it was safe to eat something so clearly enchanted.

I felt more relaxed than I had since leaving Marin. It was hard to feel stressed or afraid when every sense was flooded with so much beauty. I breathed deeply and closed my eyes. For the first time in days, I felt hope—as I always did amid the beauty of a garden.

When I opened my eyes again, I noticed a tall set of iron gates, located at the end of the trees. Both sides were flung open, giving free passage into and out of the aisle. And from the look of the grass growing around the bottom of the metal, the Beast was not in the habit of closing them. I hadn't noticed the gates from inside the carriage, but I could hardly be surprised given my state of distraction at the time.

Unconsciously I pushed Chestnut back into a trot, spurred on by the glimpse of freedom ahead. *Lily, I'm coming!* I projected, although I knew she would not receive it.

Before I reached the gate, however, the sound of pounding hooves drew my attention. Flashing between the trees, I caught glimpses of a huge black horse, thundering along outside the aisle. The Beast rode his stallion as if the two were one, moving more gracefully together than I had imagined two such giants could.

I slowed slightly, unable to tear my eyes from the sight of them. Once again, I found myself captured by the controlled power of the Beast. He appeared to be racing to meet me, and for an unthinking moment I felt glad, pleased to have the opportunity to examine his technique more closely.

But he didn't give any sign of greeting or turn his mount into the aisle to ride beside me. Instead, just as I neared the gate, he swung his stallion's head sharply, turning him perpendicular to the path I rode. As he crossed the open gateway, he pulled his horse to a sharp halt, the stallion rearing up, his hooves flashing through the air.

The Beast's roar rang out through the garden, crashing through the still beauty of our surroundings. I scrambled to pull Chestnut up before we were crushed by the stallion's hooves. The mare neighed loudly as I tugged on the reins, lifting her own front hooves as she attempted to pivot away.

Brown mane streamed in my face. A black coat flashed before me. Sharp hooves and dark riding boots streaked past, rising and then falling. And then, somehow, we had avoided a collision. Branches and leaves filled my vision as Chestnut, having regained her balance, took off running. She shot between two trees and out into more open ground, racing toward the garden that surrounded the far end of the row of trees.

I fought to keep my seat and break through her blind panic. It wasn't the first time a mount of mine had bolted, but it had never happened on such unfamiliar ground. Unaware of potential dangers in the terrain, I struggled to get her quickly back under control.

Just as I felt her begin to calm beneath me, the sound of hooves once again filled my ears. I glanced swiftly back, under my arm, and saw the flash of black as the Beast raced toward us. Chestnut, hearing the approach, picked her pace back up.

I bit back a scream. Was he trying to get me killed?

The longer legs of the stallion quickly brought them alongside us. The Beast leaned toward me, reaching out with one hand. With shock, I realized his intention. He was attempting to stop Chestnut.

In panic, I turned my eyes away from the ground ahead and met his eyes for a fleeting moment. "Stop!" I screamed with all the air in my lungs. "Leave me be! Are you insane?"

He seemed to falter at the determination and anger on my face. His pace slowed slightly, and I took a deep breath of relief, transferring my full attention back to Chestnut as he fell away.

The garden raced toward us, and my heart pounded at her renewed speed. I could feel the unthinking terror filling her and wondered if I should aim her toward the castle. She would swerve before she hit the building, but would she throw me off in the process?

As she leaped over the first of the garden beds, I noticed that the ground rose to one side of the castle. Angling her in that direction, I pointed her uphill and toward the clearest ground I could see. I held my breath as we thundered forward, sitting back in my seat and pulling periodically on the reins.

Gradually I felt her speed shift and slow. As the castle flew past us, she dropped down to a more controlled gallop and then slower still. As we crested the rise, she finally transitioned into a trembling walk. I slumped slightly in the saddle taking deep, gulping breaths.

I closed my eyes for a second, heart still racing from the near disaster. The Beast had prevented me from leaving. It was the only explanation that made sense. I narrowed my eyes. He had purposefully blocked my passage and had done so in the most dangerous way possible, without thought for my safety.

I wheeled Chestnut back around and walked her to the front steps of the castle. The Beast stood there, his stallion's reins in his hand and his eyes on me. It was hard to read the veiled emotion in them, although he was calmer than I had expected.

The same couldn't be said of me. "How dare you!" I drew myself up tall, staying on Chestnut's back to give me extra height over the dismounted Beast. "You could have killed me. Do not ever attempt to touch my mount again."

My chest heaved with my angry breaths while the Beast watched me calmly. After a moment, he bowed his head in apparent acquiescence. I felt an ungracious surge of triumph at his capitulation. "And do not attempt to control where I go. We may be betrothed, but I am not your property to order as you will. If I wish to leave the castle, I will."

He froze, not a muscle moving as his eyes tightened. Then he bared his fangs and growled, the sound starting low, but gaining quickly in volume. My eyes widened, and Chestnut shied, reacting to my tensing legs as much as the noise.

She turned her head toward the stable, and I encouraged her to move faster with a further tightening of my knees. As we fled ignominiously, I felt shame course through me. Once again, my courage had failed me.

# CHAPTER 7

*I* trembled the whole time I groomed Chestnut, as the terrified energy of the ride and the tension of the confrontation with the Beast drained away. When I finally made it back to my room, I had regained my calm. Until I saw a new parchment pushed under the door.

---

You will not leave the castle grounds under any circumstances. It is not safe. The gate will remain closed and locked from now on. Do not try to circumvent it.

---

No details or real explanation. No apology for nearly getting me killed. The new note followed the last one into the fire. There was no way now that I would be attending a meal with him, even if it meant going hungry.

As twilight approached, the sound of inaudible whispers filled the room. The wardrobe door rattled and opened, a breeze ruffling the dresses. I resolutely turned away, despite my rumbling stomach.

The whispers seemed to grow more agitated, the soft sound growing louder and more discordant. The door of my room swung open, and I strode over and slammed it shut again. The whispers went silent for a moment before bursting out louder than ever. I went over and sat in a chair by the window, staring out into the garden below as the last rays of sunset burnished the flowers.

More rattling emanated from the wardrobe, but I resolutely ignored it. Material enveloped me, and I yelped inelegantly, fighting my way free of the many layers. I stood up and glared down at the violet dress which had apparently been dropped on my head.

I turned my glare on the room but, of course, it remained empty. "Leave me alone," I said out loud. "I'm not going."

More rattling and rustling spread through the room, and my door swung open again, but I continued to glare indiscriminately until it slowly subsided. "If he wants me to eat with him, he needs to learn to ask nicely."

A sound more like a sigh than a whisper filled the room, followed by silence and the soft closing of the door. I shook my head. I had been right the night before—the castle seemed committed to my dinners with the Beast.

I flopped down on my bed. My defiant stance unfortunately meant a night of boredom as well as a night of hunger. I sat up abruptly. The food I had so far eaten had tasted real enough and had filled my stomach. If it was only delivered by the enchantment and not created by it, then there might be a kitchen full of food in here somewhere. A kitchen where I could requisition a meal.

Given their recent agitation, I doubted the lights or whispers would be inclined to help me circumvent the Beast's orders in this way. But I had spent my entire life in various palaces and castles, and I was starting to get a feel for this one. I suspected I would be able to find my way there eventually.

Listening at the door for any hint of movement in the passage outside, I pushed the door partially open and slipped out of the room. I felt a little ridiculous creeping along through empty passageways in a castle that contained only one other inhabitant —and one who was presumably in the dining hall. But somehow —possibly due to wishful thinking—I had begun to think of the whispers as companions. Slightly misguided ones, perhaps, but company of a sort. And I wasn't entirely sure what they would do if they saw me.

I chuckled quietly. *If they saw me.* Whispers didn't exactly have eyes, and for all I knew they were part of the magic of the castle, in which case I was trying to hide from the walls themselves. But still I trod as quietly as possible, stopping to listen and then peer around each corner.

It took me well over an hour to find the kitchens, by which time I was beginning to fear that the Beast must be finishing his own solitary meal. And I had no idea where he went when he wasn't riding or eating. The thought made me tread even more carefully, but it also made me more determined. I would not go to sleep with an empty stomach while he satisfied his hunger.

When I finally reached a promising doorway, I stuck my head around cautiously. Sure enough, a large kitchen greeted me with a cheerful fire burning in one of the fireplaces. I thought I had become used to the strange ways of the castle, but my knees gave a slight wobble at the sight of plates, cutlery, and food flying around the room. After a moment, I registered the presence of the whispers.

I stood there motionless until a sort of pattern emerged. The remains of a delicious looking feast were cleaning themselves up, scraps making their way into scrap buckets of their own accord and dishes washing themselves. If I hadn't felt so unnerved, I would have laughed at the comical sight.

*I wish you could see this, Lily,* I projected into the nothingness. *I wish you were here.*

The whispers seemed to rise in volume as I thought of my sister, although still stopping short of any clear meaning. I sat just outside the doorway and let myself fall into the grip of sadness and loneliness. What was the point of new sights and adventures if I had no one to share them with?

A loud crash and a renewed surge of whispers distracted me from my melancholy. Peering into the room once more, I saw that shards from a large dish now lay scattered across the floor. I could almost hear a recriminatory tone to the sound of the whispers, and they sounded so much like words that I listened intently hoping to decipher something. They had become much louder since I had first encountered them, and I didn't understand how I was still unable to hear any words amid the rustling, murmuring sound.

I held my breath, tipping one ear toward the kitchen, but still the sound seemed to slip past my consciousness. I thought again of my twin and all the theories she would have about this odd place, and a sudden thought struck me. I had put plenty of effort into connecting with her, throwing my projections out in her direction, but I hadn't put the same experimentation into listening. Perhaps if I could not reach her, she could still reach me.

It was a more difficult prospect, of course, because it required that she be attempting to reach me at the exact moment that I was attempting to listen. But the more I understood and perfected my ability to listen, the more likely I would hear her next time she projected. The thought excited me enough that I didn't want to wait.

I settled myself more comfortably against the wall and closed my eyes. At first, I strained my ears, as I had done moments before, and I had to remind myself that I had never used my mouth or ears to project with Lily. Instead I tried to clear my mind and focus on what it felt like to hear her voice in my mind.

*Hurry up!*

I flinched with shock at the clear words.

*Lily!* I responded instinctively, reaching out for our familiar connection. But instead I hit the mental wall, feeling nothing but a cold emptiness where my usual sense of my sister lay. I took a deep breath, shaking slightly from shock.

I had heard the words. I was sure I hadn't imagined them. I replayed them in my mind and realized the voice had sounded nothing like Lily's. And the words themselves made no sense. I closed my eyes and listened again, this time focusing on the sensation of making my mind receptive, of opening it to whatever path my projections traveled. I made no effort to cast my own thoughts out, and I similarly put away all thought of my sister or the familiar cadence of her thoughts.

*If you weren't so busy gossiping, Tara, you wouldn't have dropped the platter. Now what are we to use to serve the prince's potatoes?*

Yes! I cheered myself silently.

*Oh hush, Gilda, you're always complaining. The castle has a hundred platters.*

*Watch your tongue, girl, or I'll make sure you're sent out to the stables to shovel manure.*

As an outraged gasp sounded inside my mind, I carefully peered back into the kitchen. Most of the food had been cleared away, but a dish hung frozen half inside a large sink of water and several other items hung in various positions around the room.

*You're not head chef, yet, Gilda.* A third voice entered the conversation, deep and slow. *So don't get ahead of yourself.*

*I'm just trying to keep order, Matthew.* The Gilda voice sounded grumpy, but she offered no further comment, and the various frozen objects began to move again.

I swallowed and whipped my head back out of sight. For a long moment I simply sat there, making no effort to move or even to listen. Now that I had stopped trying, the inaudible whispers sounded again.

I closed my eyes and pictured the scene in the kitchens. Apparently, it was spirits who served the Beast and his castle. I shivered. Except the conversation hadn't sounded much like otherworldly spirits. In truth, Gilda sounded very like a head chambermaid from my own palace who had always secretly terrified me a little. And Matthew had sounded so much like a stable master that I could almost picture him. They certainly sounded nothing like spirits.

I considered another interpretation. Invisible servants. I chewed on a fat curl of hair while I rolled the idea over in my mind. So many things began to make sense. The missing people of Palinar. The doors that opened themselves. My guides through the castle. The unmanned coach. Even the words I had heard my first night in the coach when I had been half asleep, my mind relaxed.

A new thought hit me and two tears leaked down my face unheeded. I was not alone here with the Beast, after all. I had a whole castle of potential companions, if I could only find a way to communicate with them. Seeing them would be nice, too, but definitely secondary.

A tiny part of me felt sad to realize that no magical force had been assisting my efforts to defeat the Beast, but I thrust it aside. The inhabitants of the castle had helped when I had asked, which suggested they were friendly. And I preferred a friend to an inhuman magical purpose, even if that magic was helping me.

I reached out with my mind for the voices I had heard, trying to connect with their conversation, but I heard nothing. I frowned and tried again. Still nothing. The sensation of reaching out for Lily and connecting with her mind felt so familiar that I couldn't understand why it wasn't working now. I tried again without success. I couldn't even hear the whispers now.

I stopped trying and relaxed, and the whispers rushed back. I could understand now why I had been unable to hear them more clearly by listening harder. They weren't a physical sound, but a brushing against my mental awareness.

I resisted the urge to attempt to connect to any of them, or to the people behind them, as I usually did with Lily. Instead, I replicated my earlier efforts, opening my mind to an extra awareness and focusing merely on being receptive.

*Aren't you finished yet?*

*Sorry, Gilda.* The voice sounded young, like a child, and guilty.

*You always say that, and yet you're always slow. How sorry can you really be?* I detected a note of affection under Gilda's harsh words.

I expanded my awareness.

*So, then he invited me to go walking with him after the chores are done.*

*He didn't!*

*Really!* Several mental giggles sounded along with the words.

I crawled forward to peer into the kitchen again. It was a different sort of listening from what I was used to with Lily. With my twin, it took no effort at all, a mental connection that bonded me directly to her and required the merest thought from either of us to spring into being. This felt more like opening a new set of mental ears to the general chatter of the world. I could feel no sense of the person behind the words, and I had no channel to receive an impression of their emotions or wellbeing like I usually did with Lily.

But I found, with concentration, I could tell the direction the voices came from. I identified that the voices of the girls giggling over one of the grooms came from several sinks where dishes appeared to wash themselves. And that the voices of Gilda and the boy came from a silver fork that was being polished by an industrious cloth floating in the air.

Matthew, the one who had sounded so much like my old stable master, hadn't spoken again, so I couldn't be sure where he might be positioned. For all I knew he had left the room.

A loud mental gasp rang out, but it ended too quickly for me to tell where it had come from.

I recognized the shocked response as coming from Gilda, however. *It's Princess Sophia!*

I had been caught. I bit my lip and looked around the room at the flying items, not sure where to direct my gaze.

*Where? I want to see her!*

*What's she doing here?*

*What's she doing on the floor?*

A flush crept up my face at my foolish position. I scrambled up off my hands and knees and stepped into the room. "Good evening," I said aloud with as much confidence as I could muster while brushing off my hands. "I don't suppose someone could find me some food?"

*She's speaking to us!*

*Well, not to us exactly. One of the chambermaids told me that she sometimes speaks to the castle. She's very polite, apparently.*

*Except to the prince. I heard she told him off.*

*Told off the prince! I wouldn't dare!*

*Well of course you wouldn't—as is right. You're a scullery maid, not a princess.* Gilda sounded disapproving of the girls but did nothing to silence their conversation, obviously as certain as the rest that I couldn't hear them.

*Oh, and you would, Gilda?* I thought I recognized the defiant Tara. *He was scary even before the curse.*

*As scary as he was handsome,* said one of the gigglers.

*I think she must be very brave,* added Tara, and my heart instantly warmed to her.

*She's as beautiful as we'd hoped,* said a voice I didn't recognize.

*But why was she crawling around on the floor?* The last voice sounded much more doubtful about me than the others.

I cleared my throat. "I apologize for disturbing you, but I would greatly appreciate some food if you could find some. Just some bread and cheese would be sufficient."

*I don't know that His Highness would want us to feed her after she refused his invitation.* Gilda sounded torn.

I suppressed a snort. Invitation. That was one name for his curt command.

*But she's a* princess, *Gilda. Surely we can't disobey her!* I got the distinct impression Tara was merely attempting to distress the more senior woman.

*We can hardly let our royal guest starve,* said the voice I recognized as Matthew. *And she's to be our mistress, is she not? Seems to me she's as much right as any to be giving orders around here.*

*I'm not sure that His Highness would see it quite that way,* said the earlier doubting voice. He seemed to be located near Matthew, and I wondered if he was a footman or a groom.

My stomach grumbled loudly, and I lost my patience. "I don't care how 'His Highness' sees it. I am not the Beast's prisoner, and I will not be constrained by his orders."

Shocked silence filled the room.

# CHAPTER 8

*C*an she...can she hear us?

*Impossible!* But the doubting footman (or groom) didn't sound quite sure.

"Certainly I can hear you," I said calmly, as if such a circumstance was to be expected.

*She must truly be the one!* The scullery maid sounded breathless.

"The one? What one?"

*Never mind their babble, Your Highness,* said Gilda quickly, clearly trying to turn the subject. *Have a seat, and let me get you some food. I'm sure we can find something more suitable than bread and cheese.*

"Truly, I don't want to be a bother." I was grateful for my years of practice with Lily, because it felt strange speaking aloud in response to a mental projection. But I wasn't confident I could project in the general way they did. I felt grateful enough I had worked out how to hear them.

*Bother? No, indeed. You must forgive our foolish words before.* Ah. Gilda's change of tone now made sense. She must be scrambling to remember what they had all said previously.

But I had no desire to alienate the first people I had spoken to in days. Excluding the Beast, of course. "Thank you, and I can't imagine what you mean."

*Please, have a seat.* The kitchen tables were lined with long benches that could be tucked away when not in use, but the head and foot had wide, elaborately carved wooden chairs. One of them scraped backwards, presumably pulled out by one of the invisible servants, and I carefully made my way toward it.

I hadn't collided with anyone in my days at the castle, so I assumed they had all been making some effort to avoid me. But walking among them still made me uncomfortable. I had to resist the urge to stretch my arms out in front of me as I moved.

As I sat, sudden conversation burst out all around me, along with a flurry of sound from various plates and pots and cupboards. Trying to follow their words alongside the cacophony of actual noise hurt my head. I let my concentration drop away, and the words faded back into whispers. I could only hope it became easier with practice, or I would spend each day in a perpetual headache.

When I realized a platter of food had been hovering beside me for some time, I started and reopened my awareness.

*Apologies, Your Highness, is something not to your liking?* The tone sounded a little snide, and I was almost certain it belonged to the doubter from earlier—a footman, then.

"No, indeed, I apologize. It looks delicious." The food started traveling from the platter to my plate on a large silver spoon. I watched it, too fascinated to look away. "May I ask your name?"

*Connor, Your Highness.*

Several other voices started talking at once, and I held up my hand. Silence fell. "I'm afraid it's rather difficult to follow a conversation when you can't see any of the speakers." My connection with Lily was so close that I didn't need her body language to understand her words. Plus, there was only one of her. It was astonishingly difficult to follow an invisible group such as this. "I'll need you to project a bit more slowly, and one at a time."

*Project? What do you mean?* The curious child's voice sounded from the far corner of the room where he had no doubt been banished following my arrival.

*Hush, Gordon! Don't disturb Her Highness.* I could have anticipated Gilda's rushed response.

"No, it's fine. I don't mind." I looked in the direction of the voice. "Gordon, is it?"

After a moment of silence, one of the scullery maids whispered, *She can't see you, idiot!* and Gordon mumbled a quick, *Yes, Your Highness.*

I grinned, sure he must have initially nodded in response. "I don't hear you with my ears, but rather in my mind. Projecting is merely what I call such communication—when you send out your thoughts rather than speaking aloud."

*I don't know anything about thoughts,* Gordon sounded confused. *I'm just speaking like always.*

"Oh." I looked around, wishing I wasn't surveying a room of empty air. "I think someone needs to tell me exactly what is going on here."

Silence reigned, and I imagined them all looking at each other, wondering who was going to speak. I had already pictured faces for them all, I couldn't help myself.

*Well, Your Highness,* said Matthew at last, *it seems we've all been caught up in some sort of...curse.* His voice hesitated strangely over the word, and my brows drew together. *As best we can tell, we've all been sort of...moved sideways. Into some other realm, I suppose.* He sounded uneasy with the talk of other realms. *We can see, hear and interact with each other like normal. And we can interact with objects just fine. But we soon discovered no one outside Palinar can see or hear us at all. We have our animals with us even.* He paused, and I thought of the coach that I had assumed to be horse and driver-less. *Which is why we weren't expecting Your*

*Highness to be so astute, and why we know nothing of this projection you speak of.*

He paused again as if hoping for some sort of explanation, but I remained silent, unwilling to tell him of my gift. When he said nothing more, I prodded him. "But why have you been cursed?"

Another moment of awkward silence and then Gilda rushed in. *Well, as to that, Your Highness, who can say? Certainly not the likes of us.*

I frowned. It was easy to tell they knew more than they were saying. I let it go for now. "But what of the Beast, and his horses? I can see them well enough."

Matthew made a sound like a throat clearing.

*At first the royals were excluded. Alone in a kingdom without man or beast. But then a godmother came and allowed the young prince to see and hear us, here in the bounds of his own castle. She even gave him back his favorite mounts.*

He spoke as if the godmother had been granting the prince a favor, yet his beastly shape suggested otherwise. Or had that been part of the original curse, and she had been unable to lift it for some reason? Clearly there was far more to this story than the servants were willing to reveal. What were they hiding? And who did they seek to protect with their silence?

"And what of King Nicolas and Queen Ruby? Are they at the palace in the capital? Why have they not sought assistance from the other kingdoms?"

*No, young princess,* Matthew's voice sounded heavy and weary. *Their Majesties are no longer with us.*

I frowned at his cryptic choice of words, spooning food into my mouth to give me a chance to think. So the king and queen were dead. And no one wanted to tell me how. Or why the kingdom had been cursed. What would they tell me, then?

"Why did the Beast…" A rustle sounded at my choice of name, but I ignored it. "Why did he call the Princess Tourney? Why did he seek a betrothal when he cannot even speak?"

*You'll have to ask the young prince that for yourself, Princess Sophia.*

"Princess Sophie," I said without thinking. "No one calls me Sophia." I took another bite.

A sudden roar, resounding through both my mind and my ears, made me wince and drop food into my lap.

*What is going on here?* The Beast's anger was far more intimidating now that I could hear him in my mind as well. I wiped up the spilled food before I looked up at him, giving myself a chance to regain my composure. Several of the servants were attempting to babble explanations, and I didn't try to separate out their words, although I did keep my mind receptive, curious to hear the Beast speak again.

*I gave clear commands that no evening meal was to be served except in the dining hall.* His voice vibrated with the same power and authority that he wore so easily on his misshapen body. It was even deeper than I had imagined, as if a growl lurked behind every word.

The servants fell silent while I looked at him as calmly as I could manage and took another large bite. His eyes narrowed, and his hand trembled slightly. *Answer me!*

Once again it was Matthew who took the lead. *Aye, that you did, young master.* He spoke with the same measured tones he had done before the Beast's arrival. *But the young princess ordered different. And who are we to disobey royalty?*

The Beast curled his hand into a fist. *It is* my *orders that will be obeyed in this castle. Do you hear me?* He took two long strides forward and swept his fist across the table, catapulting my plate against the far wall. I flinched, and he fell back half a step, a strange expression crossing his face.

*Don't you be forgetting that's your betrothed, there, young master,* said Matthew, and I admired his courage. I was still trying to calm my pounding heart.

The Beast whirled around to glare at where I presumed

Matthew to be sitting. *Not by my choice, as I need not remind you.* His words came out low and dangerous. *I allow you too much license, Stable Master.*

I shot to my feet. It was Matthew who had at least begun to answer my questions, and now he had stood up to the Beast for me. I could not allow him to be threatened in such a way.

The Beast swiveled to stare at me, and I met his eyes. "Then *I* will now remind you that I am your betrothed. And a princess of Arcadia. It is time for your imperious orders to cease. And if you make any further attempts to prevent me from eating, you will not like the consequences, I assure you."

His eyes widened as he realized I could hear and understand him. I held his gaze, my own icy, for just a moment longer and then swept from the room.

As I hurried back toward my bedchamber, I congratulated myself on my exit. Seeing him silenced by shock had been just as satisfying as I had hoped.

But before I reached the room, a heavy hand on my shoulder swung me around. I gasped to find myself confronting the hulking Beast. I hadn't even heard his approach.

*So, you can hear me now, Sophie.*

I flinched at the sound of my name without my title. It felt strangely intimate hearing his voice say it into my mind, here all alone in this dim corridor. I swallowed, trying to instill some confidence into my voice before I spoke.

"I meant what I said. No more orders."

*A request then?* The soft whisper still seemed to hold the hint of a growl. *We have much to speak of.*

I bit my lip, wanting to refuse but knowing he was right. I couldn't let my pride reject his request when I needed information he possessed. I inclined my head. "Very well, then, I will join you in the dining hall tomorrow evening."

His hand, still holding me close, didn't loosen, and his eyes searched my face. Did I imagine the barest hint of admiration in his gaze? I had expected anger at my defiance.

He lowered his face closer to mine and, somehow, I did not pull away. Instead, as his mental voice dropped even quieter, I instinctively swayed toward him, straining to hear with my physical ears. *Will you marry me in the morning, Sophie?*

I started violently, unprepared for his repeated request. He dropped his hand, and I stepped quickly back. For a moment, I was tempted to flee, but I stopped myself. "I will not agree to a wedding date until my twin is here at my side."

He cocked his head slightly to one side, a curious look passing over his face. Then a dark cloud seemed to settle over him. *It is not safe for anyone to travel here. The way is barred.*

"Then we shall have to wait for the curse to be lifted."

*Impossible.* He stepped toward me, and then quickly away again. *Remember, Sophie, that you won the Tourney. You are bound by the ancient laws...unless you wish to see this darkness cover your own lands as well.*

I trembled at the image his words conjured.

*You* will *marry me, Princess Sophia of Arcadia. You must.*

With that dark promise—or threat—he turned and stalked away into the blackness of the corridor.

I stood there for a full minute before stumbling the rest of the way into my room. I thought I was alone but issued a command for any servants to leave, just in case. As I blindly prepared for bed, my mind tumbled around and around in circles. The Beast had indicated to Matthew that he had not chosen the betrothal. That he did not want it. And yet he kept pushing for the wedding. I could make no sense of it. I needed more information.

It wasn't until I lay in bed in the darkness, that I thought of his younger sister, Princess Adelaide. No one had spoken of her fate, left alone in a kingdom with only her brother, and now gone without trace. I pulled the covers over my head and closed my mind. If any servants entered my room, I preferred inaudible whispers to any further words.

# CHAPTER 9

For the first time, I had remembered to close my curtains, so I slept late the next morning. When I woke, the room looked exactly as I had left it the night before. Obviously, someone had heard my demand to be left alone and had taken me seriously. I sat up in bed and hugged my knees. While I was grateful to see they had respected my order, I couldn't help feeling a tingle of discomfort to know there had previously been invisible people in my bedchamber.

I slid out of bed, wrapped myself in a robe I found draped over the back of a chair and padded to the door. Leaning out into the corridor, I opened my mind to hear the servants. Silence. Another difference between listening to the servants and to Lily —apparently distance made a difference. In truth, I felt grateful. I couldn't imagine having to sort through the conversations of everyone in the castle at once.

Looking around the room, I found a bell tucked away on a high shelf. Leaning out into the corridor, I rang it for several seconds. I then left the door open and retreated into the room to wait.

I had no way to hear the small incidental noises of the

servants such as the sound of footsteps, so for a while I was straining my mind to nothing but silence. When a voice finally did sound, I jumped.

*Your Highness?* A girl, possibly around my own age. *Did...did you ring?*

"Yes, I did. Thank you for coming."

*Of...of course.*

"What's your name?" Admittedly I didn't know the names of every servant back at home in our palace in Arcadia, but without the ability to see any of the Palinarans, I found myself looking for something to attach to them.

The girl didn't respond at first. Had I surprised her with the request? *It's Lottie, Your Highness.*

"It's a pleasure to meet you, Lottie. You sound a little nervous. Is anything wrong?" I hoped the Beast hadn't been rampaging around the castle while I slept punishing the servants for feeding me.

*Oh, no, Your Highness. I've just never spoken to royalty before. I'm only a chambermaid. But everyone in the castle has heard about how you can hear us after all, and there was no one else around, and I thought...*

"Yes, indeed. You've quite saved me." I smiled, trying to put her at ease. "It's a little hard to find anyone when everyone is invisible."

*It must be very strange.* She sounded fascinated. *I can't imagine such a thing.*

"It is a little odd, yes," I said, wryly noting my instinct toward understatement. "But I'm slowly getting used to it." I paused, considering. "You said you've never spoken to royalty before...I understand this is the Beast's own castle."

*It is Prince Dominic's castle, yes.* Her slow words clearly communicated her unease at my manner of referring to the castle's master. I couldn't help but smile a little, although it was probably childish of me. Every time I called him the Beast, it felt like a small defiance.

"Do none of his family or other nobility live here with him? What about before the curse?"

*Oh, no, Princess Sophie. Prince Dominic rarely invites others here. Even Princess Adelaide hasn't been here for over six years.*

"Princess Adelaide?" I jumped on her mention of the Beast's younger sister. "Do you know where she is now?"

*I...I couldn't say, Your Highness.*

I sighed. What did that mean? That she didn't know? That something was preventing her from saying? Or that she had been instructed not to give me any information on the curse and the missing royals? I changed direction, not wanting to discomfort her.

"So, there are no invisible members of court wandering around? It's just the Beast and the staff?"

*We are isolated here at the heir's castle. And Prince Dominic doesn't like for any of us to leave the protection of the grounds. Wastelands have sprung up across the kingdom, and the animals which roam it keep us in as well as others out. Rumor says that some of the court wanted to brave the danger and attempt to seek help from the other kingdoms. But Prince Dominic warned them not to challenge the boundaries put in place by the ancient laws, lest we brought more darkness on ourselves. The court has disbanded and the nobility have all returned to their own lands, to protect their people as well as they might.*

I must have looked concerned because she rushed to reassure me. *Don't worry, we are safe here, Your Highness. The godmother has placed a special boundary around the castle grounds.*

Another mention of how this godmother had helped the Beast. Only it seemed a strange kind of helping to me. If only I knew the whole story. I chewed a strand of hair thoughtfully. She had already been more communicative than most of the staff in the kitchen. And I suspected I was more likely to convince her to confide in me than I was a more senior staff member. I made a sudden decision.

"Are you one of the maids who has been cleaning my chamber, Lottie?"

*Yes, Princess Sophie. Is it not to your liking?*

"No, no, everything has been lovely." I paused, then leaned forward. "Lottie, in truth, it is a little unnerving to me to think of having someone in my bedchamber who I cannot see. I would like to requisition you for a special role."

*Me, Your Highness? Are you sure?*

"Yes, of course. It will not be so very different from your present role, although I hope you will be willing to assist me with dressing and such things."

*Me—a lady's maid?* She sounded more astonished than displeased, so I continued.

"Well, I will need the room cleaned as well. What I would like, Lottie, is if you would become my personal maid, and I will give orders that no other servants are to enter my chamber at any time." I considered. "And you must promise me that you will inform me whenever you enter or exit the room while I am present. I would like to always know if you are here or not. Can you do that?"

*Certainly, Your Highness.* She sounded a little breathless. *It would be an honor.*

I smiled. Lottie might not have experience as a lady's maid, but I already preferred her to whoever had attempted to dress me up for the Beast earlier. Hopefully, I would be able to ease her out of some of her deference. I was pretty sure I had heard my title more times in our few minutes of conversation than in the whole of the last week. It was a little exhausting.

A very different sort of personality sprung into my mind, and a grin spread across my face. "I wouldn't wish you to be exhausted, and of course you must have the chance to have a break from guarding my room. I will request a second maid. I met one yesterday, in fact. Tara, I believe her name was."

*Tara...the serving maid?* Apparently, I had shocked her enough to drop my title. I tried to suppress my earlier grin but didn't quite succeed.

"She seemed like a lovely girl," I said gravely.

*I suppose so, Your Highness.* Her disapproval was patent, but I ignored it.

"I haven't actually met the steward or housekeeper yet, so could you ask them to attend me here as soon as possible? I will convey my new orders regarding my chamber and request yours and Tara's services."

*Certainly, Princess Sophie. I'm certain they will come immediately.*

"Thank you."

There was a moment of silence, and then, *I am exiting the room, Princess Sophie.*

"Thank you, Lottie." It seemed my instinct had been right. Lottie would be a diligent personal maid.

A pang of hunger made me hurry to my feet and rush to the now closed door. Flinging it open, I called into the apparently empty corridor. "And please have a meal sent up as soon as possible!"

*Certainly, Your Highness.* Lottie sounded more distant than she had before. I sighed with relief at having caught her before she traveled out of earshot. I hadn't gotten to finish my meal the night before. In fact, far too many of my meals since I had arrived had been missed or interrupted.

I thought uneasily of the meal I had promised to eat with the Beast that night. Hopefully we would be able to keep our conflict in check long enough for me to eat my fill. But perhaps I should order some afternoon refreshments from Lottie or Tara, just in case.

The steward and housekeeper were respectful and obliging. If they found my requests odd or inconvenient, they hid it well. Not surprising, perhaps, if they were used to the Beast's fits and tempers.

I brooded darkly on his overweening sense of authority as I made my way down to the dining hall around sunset. I found it insufferable enough, and I was free to defy it. I couldn't imagine being one of his servants, forced to accept his ill temper without demur.

The table had been laid out in the same manner as previously, the Beast once again rising to his feet at my entrance. He seemed to have taken a little more care in his clothing, but the fine clothes still looked odd and out of place on his strangely bulky frame. I carefully avoided meeting his eyes, unwilling to deal with whatever intense emotion might be lurking there.

I took my place with a nodded greeting and waited politely for him to be reseated before beginning to eat. For the first couple of minutes neither of us spoke, and I was reminded of our first meal together. Except that this time I strained my mind beneath my calm exterior, forcing myself into a receptive state at odds with the tension I felt at his presence. My only purpose for being here was to gain information, and I didn't want to miss anything he might say.

*I hear you are already ordering my servants as you see fit,* he said at last.

"Do you have a problem with that?" I asked, finally looking his way.

*Certainly not.* He paused. *As it pertains to your own care.*

I drew a steadying breath, not wanting to start a conflict so quickly. "I am striving to make myself at home."

*An admirable goal. Although once we are married, we will unfortunately have to relocate to the capital.*

I ignored his reference to our wedding. "You do not like the capital?"

*I prefer my solitude.*

I refrained from retorting that I was sure everyone else preferred it that way too, and took the opening he had provided. "I have heard you disbanded the court. There cannot be many left living in the capital now."

He shrugged, an awkward gesture on his broad shoulders. *We are unable to trade with the other kingdoms which means much of our commerce and production has halted. And all of our diplomacy as well, of course. I could not guarantee my ability to feed the people if large numbers remained in the city. Plus, the estates needed their leaders in this uncertain time. Until the curse is released, we are all of us trapped, our kingdom unable to move forward.*

I blinked twice. I hadn't expected such a reasonable response. Emboldened, I pressed him further. "What is the curse, exactly? I couldn't get an answer from your servants."

The Beast had turned his gaze to the opposite wall as he spoke, and he made no response to my question. I waited silently. At last he turned his head to look at me, piercing me with his gaze.

*How is it that you can hear me? Can hear the servants?*

For a long moment we both sat frozen, our eyes locked. He was the last person I would ever tell about Lily and my connection. And, somehow, he knew it. Knew that I had secrets of my own. I ground my teeth together before breaking the stare.

I lifted another forkful to my mouth, only to change my mind and put it back down on the plate. "Why did you call the Princess Tourney?" I looked up at him, but he had already looked away.

Another long silence stretched out, and I sighed. Did he intend to tell me anything?

*I am the heir to Palinar.*

He hadn't turned to look at me this time, and I frowned at his profile. "That is one thing I already know. You haven't answered my question."

He glanced toward me. *Isn't it obvious? I am the heir. I need a royal bride, and I had no other way to find one.*

One of my hands tightened around my glass. "And now that I'm here, what do you intend to do next?"

He laughed, the sound unexpected and rough, as if from disuse. *Why, marry my betrothed, of course. I can arrange the ceremony for tomorrow morning, if only you will consent.*

"I have said it before, I will say it again: I will not marry you without my sister."

He gave another laugh, but this one lacked even the faintest trace of humor. *Then we will wait.*

"For what?"

*For the curse to be broken—I believe that's what you said last night, is it not?*

I stood to my feet, struggling to keep my voice calm. "That is all you have to say? You brought me here knowing you were cursed, knowing I would be trapped here like the rest of your kingdom. And now we are merely to sit around, both of us prisoners to this castle?"

The Beast leaped up, his chair clattering loudly against the stone floor as it fell behind him. *Not by my choice.*

"Well not a single part of this has been by my choice!" My hands balled into fists, my whole body trembling.

The Beast and I stood facing each other, so close I could feel the anger radiating from him.

"You have destroyed my life, Beast!"

He raised his lip, his fangs glistening in the firelight. I took a shaky step backwards, and he growled low as he had after our confrontation in front of the castle. But this time the sound rose in volume until it turned into a roar.

I stood my ground, shaking still, but determined not to run this time. Abruptly he fell silent, only to turn and stride from the room. I remained in place until my tremors stilled, staring at the door he had slammed behind him. Had I just won a victory? If so, it felt far less satisfying than I had imagined.

# CHAPTER 10

When I pushed open the door to my chamber, my head pounding from the recent tension, a vague whisper stirred my awareness. I rubbed my eyes and forced my mind into a receptive state.

"I apologize, could you please repeat that?"

*We are here, Princess Sophie. Tara and I.* Lottie sounded concerned.

"Thank you for letting me know. Have you had a chance to fill Tara in on my requests?"

*Yes. And I want to thank you so much for asking for me.* Tara jumped in to speak for herself. *I never dreamed of such an opportunity, and I want to assure you that you can absolutely rely on me. I will not allow another soul to cross your doorway. I will guard it with my life.*

I chuckled despite my fatigue. "I hope that won't be necessary, but I appreciate the sentiment."

*It will not be necessary, Your Highness.* Did I imagine Lottie's slight stress on my title? *The staff have all been informed of your orders, and none of them would defy you.*

Tara sighed. *But if they did, we would protect you.*

*We would not, however, wish you to feel unsafe.* Was it possible to hear a glare? *You need have no fear of the staff here.*

A bubble of amusement welled inside me, and I desperately wished I could see their facial expressions. They were as much of an ill fit as I had imagined, and I briefly felt guilty for forcing them together. But, the decision had already been made, and I suspected they would make a good team, even if they couldn't see it now.

*You look tired, Princess Sophie...* Tara sounded hesitant, and I suspected she would have liked to substitute the word tired for something stronger. Of course, Lottie wouldn't have commented at all.

"I will admit I have something of an aching head." I gently massaged my temples before smiling in their direction. "Your master is not the easiest person to talk to."

*Don't tell me he chased you off before you finished your meal again? Tara!*

Tara ignored Lottie. *Would you like me to fetch you some food from the kitchens?*

"There is no need, I ate enough." I sighed. "He does have a bit of a temper, doesn't he?"

*It's gotten ever so bad since the curse,* Tara agreed.

*But you're tired,* interjected Lottie. *Don't let us keep you up talking. We'll help you undress.*

As she spoke, I felt the laces at the back of my dress loosen, although I could not feel her hand. I had to suppress a shiver at the strangeness. I had made her experiment with me earlier, and nothing we tried had allowed either of us to make contact with the other. I could not see her, of course, but she had assured me that she was attempting to place her hand on my arm. And yet, each time she got close, her hand seemed to veer away, skimming just above the surface of my skin. I was just glad she could still touch my clothes.

On the other side of the room, a large jug of water lifted into the air and began pouring water into a basin. Tara's voice sounded from that direction. *I would love to see you tell him off one day. I can't imagine being brave enough myself.*

I snorted, and my laces jerked. I suspected Lottie would soon be losing some illusions about princesses and their elegant ways.

"Don't worry, my knees knock together so loudly he can probably hear them." I stepped away from the dress which now pooled at my feet.

Tara giggled, so I decided to push for a little information.

"How did he become a Beast? He was obviously a normal man once."

My dress, which had been floating away from me, paused, and a small splash of water missed the basin and landed on the table.

*Oh, how clumsy of me! I promise I'm not usually so careless.* Tara sounded breathless as the jug floated down to the table and a towel mopped up the spill.

Any lingering uncertainty disappeared. They had been told not to speak to me about the curse. Which meant I would need to be much less direct in my future attempts. And also, that it was time to resume my search of the castle.

The next morning, I woke to a fresh breakfast laid out next to my bed. No one answered my tentative morning greetings, so it seemed my new maids had already left the room. I ate quickly, eager to return to my explorations. By the time I had finished eating, Lottie had announced her arrival and stood ready to help me dress.

I considered asking her to be my guide, but I worried that such a task might make her uncomfortable. Especially given she was still adjusting to her new role as my maid. Plus, I wasn't sure that I could take a full day of being called 'Your Highness' every five words.

So, once again, I found myself wandering alone through the rooms of the castle. I soon found myself in a new section, one that seemed even more expensively decorated than the parts I had already seen. I shook my head. Such a large building to house only one prince. Yet another example of the Beast's selfishness.

I had managed to turn myself around in circles twice when I heard a small voice.

*What are you doing?* Gordon spoke from a shadowy back corner.

"I'm learning my way around the castle. What are you doing?"

*I'm hiding.*

"Hiding from what?"

*From Gilda. She wants me to scrub pots. She says it will be good for me. I don't see how.*

"That is certainly a little mysterious." He sounded just the way I had always felt when forced to study mathematics. "You seem very young to be working in the castle."

Gordon sighed as if he had the weight of the world on his shoulders. *That's what I always say. I'm only nine years old, after all. One of the grooms has a son, Michael, who's nine, too. And he's always running around outside. But Gilda says that if the prince is housing and feeding me, I must earn my way. She says I need to learn to be grateful.* He sighed again. *Sometimes it's hard to be grateful. Especially when I want a second sticky bun, and Gilda says no.*

I carefully kept any amusement off my face. "Does Gilda have the care of you? What about your parents?"

*I don't know my parents. Apparently, some of the grooms found me out in the stables when I was just a baby. I wish I could have stayed out there.* He sounded dejected.

"In the stables? You'd like to live with the horses?"

*With old Matthew. He's a right one.* A more energetic note entered his voice. *Have you seen the way he handles the horses? There's not a one anywhere in the kingdom he couldn't calm right down. Even the prince has things to learn from old Matthew.*

"It's a pity that I am unable to see him, then. He sounds like a fine stable master."

*Oh, that's right, I forgot.* He spent a moment pondering my predicament. *You would think it would be fun to be invisible. But it turns out it doesn't feel any different from usual. Plus, what's the use of it when Gilda can still see me?*

"What use indeed?" I bit my lip. "So, you would rather have been a groom than a kitchen boy?"

*Of course! Who wouldn't? But, apparently, they all felt that a baby needed a 'female influence'. Whatever that means. So here I am stuck with Gilda and all the scullery maids.*

I couldn't help feeling sorry for the boy, although he himself seemed much more interested in the horses than his lack of family. And as for the Beast...expecting a young child to earn his keep in such a way? I shook my head. It was despicable. Did he truly have no compassion?

Sudden inspiration struck me. "Gordon, would you like to leave the kitchens for a while and come to work for me?"

*Like Tara, you mean? I don't think I'd make a very good lady's maid...*

It was hard not to laugh at his doubtful tone, but I managed it. "No, I was thinking you could be my page boy."

*Does a page boy have to scrub pots?*

"Not a single one."

*Well, in that case I suppose I could give it a try. Do you have your own horse? I could look after her for you.*

He sounded so eager that I didn't have the heart to tell him that a page boy's usual roles didn't include horse care. "I do, indeed. Her name is Chestnut. But, for now, I was thinking that you could be my guide around the castle. If you grew up here, you must know it very well."

*Oh, I'm the best. I have to be—to keep finding new hiding places where Gilda can't find me. Did you know I once used the moving cupboard that takes the food between the kitchen and the dining room to hide from her for a whole day? She was watching the door of the kitchen, sure I would come back when I got hungry, but little did she know, I kept using it to sneak back in for food.* He sounded extremely proud of this accomplishment.

I paused for a moment as I imagined how easy a task he would find it to hide from me. "If you're going to be my page boy, Gordon, you must promise you won't hide from me as you do from Gilda."

*Oh, no, I would never,* he assured me. I expected to hear a comment about my royal status, but instead, he added, *You're letting me look after your horse. Chestnut, I should say.*

I grinned at being put so effectively in my place–which was apparently well behind my mount. Gaining a guide who seemed to have not the least filter on his words seemed well worth any small bruising to my ego. And, in fact, Chestnut was an extraordinary horse who had borne the trip into Palinar admirably. Perhaps Gordon had the right of it.

~

It turned out to be difficult to direct a guide when I couldn't risk telling him my true purpose. Not when the entirety of the staff had shown themselves determined to keep me in the dark. Gordon's easy chatter could work against me as well as for me.

Still, at least I no longer kept finding myself back in the same room. Gordon showed me all around this more lavish wing of the castle, except for one set of rooms which he blithely informed me belonged to "the prince".

*None of us are allowed in there. Which means it would make the best hiding place, of course.* His wistful tone made my lips twitch again. *But I daren't. The prince might eat me.*

"Eat you! I'm sure he would not."

*No, you're probably right. But one of the grooms told me..."*

I put up my hand to stop him. I had enough terrible imaginings about my betrothed running around my head without adding to the mix ridiculous horror stories made up to tease children. "No one is going to be eaten. But I dare say it is best if you don't attempt to hide in there regardless."

Gordon reluctantly agreed with me, only cheering up again when he remembered that he no longer had any need to hide from scrubbing pots. We had nearly made our way back out of the Beast's wing, when we passed a door that looked just like all the others. *Oh, and there's the gallery, of course. I suppose you've already seen that.*

I stopped. "The gallery? You mean a portrait gallery? This door?"

I pushed it open as soon as I heard his confirmation. As much as I tried not to let them, the Beast's eyes—so human in his otherwise terrifying form—haunted me. And I hadn't forgotten the overheard conversation of the scullery maids, who had called him handsome as well as scary in the days before the curse. His own castle should have a portrait of him, surely.

The door unexpectedly gave way into a cavernous hall, lined with portraits on every wall. High windows poured light into the space, illuminating the heavy paint and vibrant colors. I ran my eyes down the closest portraits, but could tell from the clothes that they could not be the Beast.

"Gordon? Are you here?"

*Yes, Princess Sophie.* He sounded like he was already a long way down the hall.

I raised my voice slightly. "Is there a portrait here of the current royal family?"

*Of course—it's that big one.* I suspected he was waving, having once again forgotten that I couldn't see him.

I scanned the walls, hoping to spot one significantly bigger than the others. And, sure enough, I soon found a painting easily twice the size of the others around it. It hung in the middle of the room, dominating the wall.

In the center of the portrait loomed an older man. He wore the crown of Palinar on his head and his hand rested against the hilt of his sheathed sword. I fell back a step as I gazed into his motionless visage. There was a hardness and a cruelty in the lines of his face and the tilt of his eyes that scared me more even than the Beast.

I took a steadying breath.

To the king's left sat his wife, her daughter standing behind her, posed with one hand on her mother's shoulder. The two looked so similar as to be startling, Princess Adelaide merely a younger version of her mother. Both appeared gentle from their painted expressions, a soft light in their familiar blue eyes. I remembered that eight-year-old Princess Daisy of Trione had reported that Adelaide had always been kind to her when they had met. Unlike Prince Dominic.

Thinking his true name drew my eyes irresistibly to the other side of the portrait, no longer able to resist the pull of seeing the Beast in his old form. The painting could not have been painted long before the curse—Prince Dominic looked at least seventeen, the age he had been when the other kingdoms lost contact with Palinar.

Once again, the painter had done a masterful work, the face in front of me looking almost frighteningly lifelike. Somehow the artist had even managed to capture something of the intensity of his gaze. Prince Dominic might have inherited his eyes from his mother, but they burned in him in a way they didn't in her.

The young prince stood slightly separate from the others and back a step. His expression looked distant and cold, but his hand on his sword hilt lacked the aggression of his father's stance. Once again, I marveled at the nuance the painter had managed to convey.

And I had to admit the scullery maid was right. Prince Dominic had been tall and strong, his face almost too handsome for comfort. The first time I had seen the other princes of these lands was when Lily and I had arrived in Marin and been presented to the court at the opening of the Princess Tourney. Only Dominic had been missing. At the time, I had found Daisy's older brother, Prince Teddy, cute. I even remembered using the word handsome at one point.

But I knew now I would never even have noticed the others if Prince Dominic had been there, too. Even as young as he must have been when he sat for this portrait, he made Teddy look like a boy. I couldn't explain exactly why, but it hurt me to look at him as he used to be, his face so closed and hard.

*I overheard someone say that King Nicolas wanted theirs to be the biggest of all the pictures. Did you know that they had four horses on the carriage that brought it here from the capital?*

How in the kingdoms would I know such a thing? But apparently the question was rhetorical because he forged ahead. *Four horses just for a picture. Can you imagine? I'd like to drive four horses, someday. I don't suppose you brought four horses with you? On your carriage perhaps?*

"I'm afraid not. I rode." I tried to steer the conversation back to the royals, eager to take advantage of the opportunity to talk to someone who didn't guard their words. "Did you ever meet King Nicolas?"

*No. The king never comes here. And I was only three the last time Queen Ruby and Princess Adelaide visited. Gilda tried to lock me in the kitchen the whole time.* He sounded scornful of such an attempt. *They were here for a week, and on the first day I climbed up to the cooling pies the chef had made for the evening meal. I ate so much I felt sick for days. They let me out after that.*

I could easily imagine the havoc a determined three-year-old could wreak on a busy kitchen and felt sorry for everyone involved. I wanted to ask him what had happened to the rest of the Beast's family but didn't want to rush into it in case he clammed up after all and refused to answer any more questions.

"Did the prince not get on with his father?"

Gordon snorted. *No one got on with old King Nicolas. He was a monster even without a curse. The adults are always sending me out of the room when they talk about it, so I have to listen at the doors. If you weren't a princess, I'd tell you some of the stories, but it doesn't seem right to tell a princess such awful things.*

I once again examined King Nicolas, the man who had wanted his own portrait to dominate the gallery. It wasn't at all hard to believe the man in the picture had done despicable things. His wife, on the other hand...

"And what of Queen Ruby? What stories have you heard about her?"

*I don't need stories, I met her myself.* He sounded proud. *Well, I was only three, so pretty much a baby, but I remember her, a little. And Princess Adelaide. The princess played with me every day after they let me out of the kitchen. And the queen gave me the biggest red ball you ever saw.* He fell silent, apparently dwelling on the magnificence of this gift. *I would still have it, too, if Michael hadn't 'borrowed' it and lost it. I tried to make him give me his ball, even if it wasn't as nice as mine, but he's a big bully.* He dwelt on the injustice of the situation.

"I'm sorry it was lost. If I get the chance, I'll try to find you another ball."

*Really? That would show up Michael! Make sure it's a red one, though. His is only brown.*

"I'll do my best. Perhaps I can ask the queen where she got the original one from."

*Ask her?* Gordon easily took my bait. *You can't talk to someone who's been dead for years! Really! Girls.* I could easily picture him shaking his head in scorn.

So, Queen Ruby was dead. I glanced between her and her terrifying husband. Did that mean King Nicolas was dead also? I felt guilty for hoping so, but I didn't think I could cope with both the Beast and his father—at least not if the king was anything like this portrait made him look.

A heaviness gripped me. I had suspected before I came that

the missing Palinaran king and queen must be dead, but I had still held out some hope. My eyes once again traveled to the prince. Could the Beast have had some hand in the deaths of his parents? I wouldn't have even considered the possibility if not for the darkness and misery of the Tourney—a reflection of the Beast himself. And I had now seen his temper first hand.

If he had killed them, would that have been enough to curse his kingdom? It was a chilling possibility, but hard to countenance in the face of his servants' support—and that of a godmother, supposedly. A godmother, despite the fact that the rest of the kingdoms hadn't seen one in generations.

But still the seed of doubt lingered.

# CHAPTER 11

*G*ordon suggested we move on, but I couldn't bring myself to leave the captivating portrait. I took several steps back, trying to get far enough to absorb the scope of the whole family at once. It was strange to see such similar features animated in such different ways.

*What are you doing here?* The now familiar growl sounded so abruptly that I jumped.

I put a hand on my racing heart and glared at the Beast. "I'm merely entertaining myself in your portrait gallery. I assume you didn't hang all of these works of art just so you could forbid anyone ever looking at them."

*I didn't hang any of them. And I would burn this one if it were not for...*

When he didn't continue, I frowned, sure he had been finally about to say something of interest. I glanced as surreptitiously as possible between the Beast himself and this portrait of Prince Dominic. He was recognizable still, especially the eyes. But his current face appeared even more misshapen against the image of what it used to be. Had I made a mistake by searching out his portrait—his previous humanity only highlighting his current beastly state?

*This wing is forbidden to you.*

I jumped again at the aggression in his tone after such a long silence. "Of course I shall not enter your chambers, but what reason can you have for barring me from this hall?"

*I do not need a reason.* Each word was punctuated by the ghost of a growl.

"You do if you wish me to continue to eat with you each night."

I waited while he weighed the two. What did he have in this wing that he felt such a strong need to bar me from it? Surely the answers I sought must lie here, somewhere.

He looked at the portrait, and I couldn't begin to read the storm of emotions that flashed across his face. But then, how could it not cause him pain to look on his dead parents and his old self? I wanted to call back my words. To tell him that I would stay away. But I thought of Lily and hardened my heart. He had already caused me great pain, and I could not allow myself to become weak.

*Very well,* he said at last. *I will see you tonight, Sophie.*

As before, in the corridor, his use of my name shocked me. The sound of it in my mind felt as intimate as a caress. I had to force myself to hold his gaze, and something in his expression told me he knew it.

I clenched my teeth as he gave me the shallowest of bows and exited the room. When would I stop being thrown off balance by his presence?

*Wow!* I had completely forgotten Gordon. *You stood up to him just as well as old Matthew does!*

I understood from our earlier conversation that this was high praise.

"Thank you." I sighed. "Could you show me the way back to my room?" If I was to eat with the Beast again, then I wanted a chance to rest first. And I would need Tara and Lottie's help with making arrangements for my new page boy.

As I ate the first few mouthfuls of my evening meal, I looked around the large, mostly empty dining hall. The far end of it was shrouded in shadows, the servants not having bothered to light all the candles for just the two of us. Only the crackling of the fire and the sound of cutlery clinking provided any noise. When had this become my life?

I remembered relaxed and happy meals with my family, who always ate at least the morning meal together. Even boring state meals had been enlivened by Lily's silent commentary. Many a time I had needed to suppress an oddly timed laugh after some humorous comment from my sister. Now I only fought to suppress discomfort, anger, and fear. And I could only imagine the state I would be in at this point if I hadn't learned the means of communicating with the servants.

I continued to chew listlessly, unable to summon up my usual enthusiasm for the delicious food. "How do you do it?" I asked, putting down my fork at last. "How have you borne it, trapped here alone for years?"

The Beast looked at me, surprise etched across his face. He probably hadn't expected me to initiate conversation after our confrontation in the portrait gallery.

*I am not alone,* he said. *Not since my godmother made the servants visible to me. And in truth I have never been alone.* His mental voice dropped almost to a whisper. *Unlike my sister.*

His sister? Curiosity burned, but I knew better than to ask for an explanation. I had barely eaten yet, it was too early in the meal for a conflict. I sighed. I shouldn't have expected empathy from him. The Tourney had shown me his implacable and merciless nature with the way it had driven us on through the events, regardless of illness or injury. Plus, he wasn't a prisoner here, as I was. He had chosen to retreat from the world.

I took several more bites, the resentment growing. Would it have been so hard for him to apologize? Even once? Was he truly without compassion of any sort?

"But what of your kingdom? You say it is not safe to travel outside the grounds, yet surely you must have some way to communicate with them?"

*My royal carriage is safe, as you saw. I send it to my lords on occasion with letters and missives. And as for the rest of the time...well, they know I watch them. They would not dare step out of line.*

That hadn't been exactly what I meant, although I could easily imagine the nobles fearing a royal family led by King Nicolas and now a cursed beast. But my mind caught on his earlier comment. He watched them? From here?

"Do you have spies among your own people, then?"

*Spies? No, of course not. How would they communicate with me if I did?*

I flushed at the note of derision in his voice. "How do you watch them then, Beast? Locked away in your isolated castle?"

The wrinkle of confusion had returned to his brow, as if he were honestly confused by my comments rather than merely contemptuous. When he spoke, his words were slow. *I brought my family's mirror with me, of course. I would never have left it unattended in the capital.*

"Your mirror?" I now felt completely lost, as if we were having two different conversations, each missing the other's point entirely.

*Yes. My family's mirror. It is the oldest and most powerful of the royal mirrors.*

I frowned at him, and a strange expression crossed his face. *Does your family not possess a royal mirror?* His tone turned thoughtful. *I know the Marinese duke does not. Do not tell me you knew nothing of their existence?*

"I have never heard of a royal mirror." I hated having to admit my ignorance to such an arrogant person. "I take it you are referring to a magical object of some sort. I had understood magical objects to be extremely rare in these lands, given the disappearance of the godmothers so long ago." Of course, if the Beast's own claims were to be believed, there had been a godmother here not so long ago after all.

*The royal mirrors are old beyond counting. They have been passed down from monarch to monarch in each kingdom for many generations. You truly had not heard of them?*

"No." I snapped the short word.

*Then I regret mentioning it.*

I ignored him. "What does this magical mirror do? Allow you to spy on your people?" It seemed a strange object for the godmothers to gift.

*It allows the viewer to see and hear events taking place far from them, certainly. But the mirrors also form a network with communication possible between each of them, or all together. It allows the monarchs of all the kingdoms to speak together at will.*

Now that sounded like a powerful and useful tool. "Why have you not used it to communicate with the rulers of the other kingdoms? You could tell them of the state of affairs in Palinar—ask for assistance."

A soft growl rolled over me, seeming to escape from the Beast without his noticing. *Palinar doesn't need their help.*

I rolled my eyes. "Don't be ridiculous. You need all the help you can get."

A soft sound, almost like a sigh, slipped from the Beast's mouth. *I have received no communications since the curse fell. And any attempts to call outwards have reached only darkness.*

Ah, that was the truth of it. The curse had cut off even magical communication. I considered his words some more.

"You can magically spy on anyone you like? Even the other rulers?" I could see lots of problems with such a situation.

*Not everyone. There are limits. The mirror will only show you your own people.* He watched my face. *Do not be concerned. There are... limits...to what the mirror will show.*

I tried not to let the relief show on my face. I had already been imagining the feeling of ghostly eyes on me at all times.

"So, you hole yourself up here, in your castle, and watch your kingdom from afar?" The disapproval was obvious in my tone, but I made no attempt to check it.

*For now.* He seemed impervious to my criticism.

We ate the rest of the meal in silence, my mind still considering all the ramifications of his revelation. When I had finished, I stood to my feet, proud to have made it through an entire meal with him.

He stood swiftly as well, stepping over to offer me his arm as if he meant to escort me to the door. I eyed it doubtfully but could think of no reason to refuse the uncharacteristically polite gesture from my betrothed. Had it been mere days ago that I had resolved never to let him touch me? It seemed an eternity ago.

Reluctantly I placed my hand in the crook of his arm. As we walked slowly to the door, I thought of the prince in the portrait. What if there had been no curse? What if I had come here to be his bride, traveling in a proper royal procession, Lily by my side?

I kept my eyes on the ground. With only the feel of his arm beneath my fingers, his muscles hard and strong, it was easy to imagine the tall young man from the painting. Would I have been pleased when I saw his handsome face? Or scared by his hard expression? I could no more decide the answer to that question than I could understand my own emotions when his all-too-human eyes pierced me through.

When we reached the door, I looked up into his face and couldn't help a start of shock at his beastly features. Whatever I might have thought of that prince, he was long gone. And if I wanted to break this betrothal, then I needed to outwit him. Which meant understanding the advantages he possessed.

"Will you let me see your magic mirror?" I asked him, abruptly.

His eyes narrowed. *The mirror is only for use by members of the royal family. If you wish to see it, you need only consent to our wedding taking place immediately. Will you marry me in the morning, Sophie?*

I flinched back, berating myself for being once again surprised by his apparently inevitable question. "Don't call me that!" I snapped unthinkingly.

He raised an eyebrow. *By your name, you mean? I thought you said Sophie was your preference. What would you have me call you instead?*

I flushed at having revealed myself in such a way. "Never mind," I mumbled. "Forget I said anything." I hurried out the door, not looking at him as he held it politely open.

I had wished for him to learn some manners, but they fit so uncomfortably on him that it didn't help. He remained an otherworldly creature, out of place in my life, and impossible to imagine as my future husband.

# CHAPTER 12

 $\mathcal{M}$ y sleep was fitful, disturbed by visions of a handsome prince with piercing blue eyes who looked down into an elaborate handheld mirror reflecting an image of me tossing and turning in my bed. Every time I woke, I found myself in a cold sweat, clutching my blankets around my neck.

As the hours passed, a new thought crept into my mind. I couldn't believe it had taken so long to occur to me. If the mirror could be used only by royals, and only to see your own people, would it not be possible for it to show me Lily? I might not be able to use it to communicate with her, but I could at least reassure myself of her safety.

But the Beast had already refused to let me see it. And if he considered it a bargaining chip, something to use to pressure me into agreeing to our wedding, I would never convince him to change his mind. Which meant I needed to find it on my own.

By the time the sun rose, I had given up on sleep entirely and was busy planning. After his attempt to bar me from his wing of the palace, I felt sure I would find the mirror there. But I would need to ensure that the Beast himself was absent before beginning my search. I hadn't seen him wandering around the palace except for when he had found me in his wing. I suspected he spent most of his time there.

The only other place I had seen him outside of meals was with his stallion. And Matthew, the stable master, seemed to have a privileged position with him. I would wait until he went to visit his stallion, and then I would find the mirror and finally see Lily.

I could see the corner of the stable building from my window, but I would need a clearer view to ensure I didn't miss his arrival. Which meant finding a better position somewhere in the castle. I tried to remember the many rooms I had visited on that side of the building.

Hours later I wistfully watched the sun shining on the flowers and reflecting from the snow. I still hadn't explored the gardens, and they looked much more appealing than the hard seat I had managed to drag over to the window of the unused chamber. But I didn't want to miss the Beast leaving the castle. I thought of my sister, and the emptiness in my mind without her familiar presence. It would all be worth it if I could get even a glimpse of her and be sure she was well.

As the angle of the sun crept around and the warm rays shone directly onto me, I found it hard to keep my eyes open and my mind alert. My lids kept drifting shut, my bad night's sleep catching up with me. I eyed the dusty bed longingly.

I had asked Lottie to deliver a midday meal to me here, carefully putting in the request when Tara wasn't around, to ensure I wouldn't be questioned for wishing to spend the day in a random, unused bedchamber. But even the food failed to completely dispel the sleepiness.

I had just finished pacing the length of the room to stay awake, when I returned to the window and noticed movement. Instantly all fatigue dropped away, energy coursing through me at the sight of the Beast's bulky frame striding toward the stables. I forced myself to wait until he had disappeared inside.

As soon as I was sure he had gone to visit his stallion, I raced from the room, my feet flying as I headed straight for the Beast's wing. As I twisted and turned through the castle, I felt proud of myself for remembering Gordon's tour. All of the corridors looked the same, and it made navigation difficult for anyone who had not grown up familiar with the building. I would have to arrange to have some tapestries hung and statues placed in available niches.

I had taken two more turns and was passing the portrait gallery when it occurred to me that for an unthinking moment I had been considering myself the actual mistress of this castle. Planning improvements to it for when I might host guests here. I shook myself. I could not allow myself to be lulled into forgetting this was a large prison, not a home.

I didn't slow as I raced past the door to the gallery. In the many hours since I had first conceived of this plan, I had considered all the options. The gallery hadn't contained any pieces of furniture—in fact there had been no place where a mirror could have been hidden. Instead I had become increasingly convinced that the only place the Beast would keep such a valuable magical object was his own chambers.

When I reached the door that Gordon had called forbidden, I stopped. I had accused the Beast, either aloud or in my mind, of almost every crime. And yet, only yesterday, I had assured him I would not enter his rooms, and today, here I was. I shook my head. The normal rules did not apply when a monster kept you prisoner in his home.

I pushed open the door.

I didn't know what I had been expecting, but it had almost certainly involved darkness and gloom. And probably dirt, since Gordon had said even the servants were barred from these rooms. But the Beast's chambers were large and surprisingly airy, filled with solid oak furniture, worn silken with age. The stone floor was covered with overlapping rugs of deep red and gold, and I could see no sign of filth or neglect.

I couldn't help crossing over to the large windows in his bedchamber, noting his extensive view which included most of the gardens and the stables. This would have been the ideal view-point for my morning's observations, except for the obvious issue. As I watched, the Beast appeared astride his black horse, walking toward an open field on the far side of the gardens.

The distant figure appeared to twist a little in the saddle, and I stepped back, jumpy. Had he been looking this way? I shook myself and added stern instructions not to waste time on foolish fancies. I needed to start my search.

The Beast had three interconnected rooms. A bedchamber, a sitting room and a dressing room. The sitting room seemed the most logical place for such an item, so I began there. As the minutes ticked by, my tension rose.

I moved next to the dressing room, observing the strange way his jackets hung when not on his shoulders, highlighting his misshapen frame. I saw no sign of a mirror, however.

Finally, I returned to his bedchamber, rummaging carefully through the drawers of his desk, attempting not to disrupt anything. I didn't want to leave any sign of my visit. I could feel the knot of discomfort in my center growing. I resisted the urge to run to the windows to check for any sight of the Beast. I reminded myself again and again that I had seen him leave for the beginning of a ride. I had plenty of time to turn all three rooms upside down if need be.

As I slid shut the final door, I gave a huff of frustration. Should I search the bed? Did he keep it tucked under his pillow? I hesitated, reluctant to climb onto his large four-poster or touch the place where he laid his head.

As I looked around the room, hoping to spot somewhere else to look, my eye fell on a curtain hanging against the wall shared with the sitting room. I frowned at the anomaly. A curtain on an internal, windowless wall?

I strode over and pulled it back, revealing a large oval mirror mounted on the wall. A simple, elegant frame met at the top to form the outline of a crown. The royal mirror.

I berated myself silently. I had allowed my search to be influenced by my dream, but now that I thought about it, I couldn't remember the Beast ever referring to it as a hand mirror. I had nearly missed it, when it should have been immediately obvious to me. I had already wasted so much time.

I stepped close to the mirror which reflected my own face back at me. Nothing about it gave any indication that it was anything but an ordinary mirror. But ordinary mirrors were not kept behind elaborate curtains. And the smooth silver of the frame was engraved with a single word: Palinar. If I had still possessed any doubt, it would now have disappeared. This must be the royal mirror of Palinar.

I stepped back, wondering how to activate it. Feeling a little foolish, I spoke aloud. "Show me my sister, Lily." After a second's pause, I added, "Please."

I focused on her face, identical to my own yet at the same time so different, and the feel of her voice and emotions in my mind. *Please, please, please,* I thought at the mirror. Slowly the surface began to fog, silver clouds obscuring my reflection. *Yes!*

As I waited impatiently for her image to appear, I couldn't help a small thrill of fear. I had assured myself that I would know if anything truly serious happened to her. But what if that wasn't true? I had received no news for days now. What if Cole had attacked her seeking revenge?

I tried to calm myself. Surely he had been recaptured. The whole of Marin was looking for him, and his family were all imprisoned so he had nowhere to turn for shelter.

The mirror distracted me from my fears, the fog clearing to reveal an entirely different scene from the bedroom it had previously reflected. I stepped forward, squinting at it in confusion. What was I looking at?

I could see no sign of Lily, or of any female. Instead I saw several horses racing across a landscape I didn't recognize. Men in long cloaks rode them, leaning low to encourage their mounts to speed. I could even hear the distant sound of hoof beats and the wind in trees.

I moved closer again, as if that could somehow bring clarity to the scene, and heard the one in front direct the others to veer to their left. As he began to change his own direction, he glanced back to check that the others were following, and I got a momentary glimpse of his face. I gasped.

Cole. As if my exhalation had broken the enchantment, the mirror began to fog again. So, Cole was still free. I wished I had been able to recognize his location and that I possessed some means of communicating it to Lily.

I chewed on a strand of hair. I had asked the mirror to show me Lily, but instead it had shown me Cole. What did that mean? I remembered the way my thoughts had veered from my sister to the man I feared might injure her. As the enchantment of the mirror had been at work, my mind had been fixated on Cole rather than Lily.

The fog remained in place, clouding the surface rather than returning it to its original reflective state. I turned my mind back to my sister, focusing on the feel of her and my own longing to see her. This time the fog cleared more quickly and, when it did, I rushed forward to place my fingers against the surface. Lily.

My twin looked pale and tired, her face creased with lines of worry. Given the first vision in the mirror, I didn't need to overhear a relevant conversation to know they had been unable to recapture Cole. And I knew she would be fretting about being cut off from me and what it might mean. If there was one thing Lily hated, it was being powerless to help the people she loved.

*Lily!* I projected her name as forcefully as I could, my hand pressed flat against her image, and my mind focused on the feel of our connection. She looked up, a confused expression crossing her face. For a brief moment, I felt a ghost of her presence in my mind. The sensation was too weak to form words, instead it was only a wave of grief and fear, tempered with love and hope.

I leaned forward to rest my head against the cool glass of the mirror, a single tear slipping down my cheek. Even in the midst of my longing for it, I had forgotten the feeling of peace and fullness that came from connecting with my twin.

Movement flashed across the mirror, and I pulled back to see what was happening. Lily had turned at the sound of an opening door, and her face brightened. I didn't need to see the new arrival to know his identity. Only Prince Jonathan, her betrothed, could bring that particular look of love to her face.

Sure enough, Jon moved forward into view and snaked an arm around her, pulling her against his chest. "I've only just managed to get away from the meetings. I feel like I haven't seen you in forever." He smiled down at her, and I couldn't help smiling myself. I loved the way he looked at her—as if she gave him strength and purpose. Lily deserved someone who would love her as much as Jon did.

But after meeting her eyes, a shadow passed across his. "Something's happened, I can see it in your face."

Lily buried her face in his chest, and I could barely make out her muffled words. "I thought, just for a moment, that I could sense Sophie. But when I called, I got no reply."

"Oh, love." He stroked her hair. "Perhaps she found a way to send you a message of sorts. What did you feel?"

Lily straightened and shrugged. "Just her familiar presence in my mind. Love, I suppose, and…loneliness, maybe?"

"You know what my father said. The ancient laws will protect her, and the Beast cannot harm her while they are bound together by their betrothal."

She sighed. "I know. I just wish I knew what happened to our connection. What if it's gone..." her voice dropped down to a whisper... "forever?"

Jon looked concerned. "Surely not. You just felt her then, did you not? I'm sure it is only that Palinar is blocking you somehow."

"Yes. Yes, I'm sure you're right." I could tell from Lily's face that she didn't completely believe it, but she was letting herself trust him as much for his sake as her own. "And I haven't even asked you how the meetings went. Was there any word on Cole?"

He shook his head, the tiredness creeping into his own eyes. "The captain of the guard believes he has somehow managed to flee across the southern border into Talinos. And he has not gone alone."

Lily frowned and opened her mouth, to question him, I was sure, but the mirror had begun to fog again.

"No!" I shook my head and stretched out my hand to touch the mirror again. "No! I want to see her again. Show me my sister."

But before the mirror could clear again, the curtain was ripped closed, almost pulling the material loose from the wall in the process. I staggered away from the Beast, tripping over my dress and toppling backwards to land on my rear. I expected to look up to see him towering over me, but he had returned to his door, which he was holding open, a thunderous look on his face.

*What did you tell me only hours ago? That you would not enter my chambers?*

I flushed.

*How dare you trespass in here!* His voice reverberated in my mind, and I winced. *How dare you use my mirror when I had forbidden it!*

# CHAPTER 13

*I* finally managed to scramble to my feet. "I didn't mean any harm." I spoke loudly, over the growl that now filled the room. "I only wanted to..." But my voice trailed off as the look in his eyes combined with my own guilt to send me running from the room.

I had meant to flee in the direction of my chamber, but my feet took me in a different direction. When I found myself in the entrance hall, I knew what had brought me here. I had taken enough. My guilt at breaking into his rooms had faded in the face of my anger at the way he treated me like an enemy. Or a possession, to be controlled.

I needed space. To clear my head.

But, more importantly, I needed to talk to my sister. To hear her voice in my mind and to reassure her that I was safe. The afternoon sun had started to set, and I wasn't wearing a cloak, but I didn't consider going back for one. Running down the outside steps, I turned toward the stables.

When I burst into the building, Chestnut nickered a greeting, reminding me that I hadn't visited her in a while. I whispered to her as soothingly as my shaking voice would allow, racing to strap on a saddle.

Within minutes the two of us cantered down the aisle of orange trees. The Beast had told me the gates would be locked, but they were ceremonial more than anything. No fence encircled the grounds. If I could not go through the gates, I would go around them.

Sure enough, the end of the aisle was now barred by iron, twisted into elaborate shapes. I turned Chestnut's head, and we trotted down the fence. As I had predicted, it soon disappeared into a large bush and failed to emerge out the other side.

I steered Chestnut around the foliage, urging her onward with my knees. Riding back to Marin wasn't an option, of course —and I wouldn't have tried it anyway, for all the same reasons that had brought me here. But I hoped the block on my connection with Lily might disappear as soon as I passed the boundaries of the castle grounds.

As we burst free, I strained my mind, more eager than ever to reestablish the link between us. I hit the wall, but felt it give way a little, as if it weren't entirely solid. I urged Chestnut to continue and thrust my thoughts forward, struggling to find a path through. My days of practice with the servants and the Beast had honed my mental capacity, and I felt a new force behind my attempts.

With a rush, I broke free of the block, my mind instantly connecting with Lily's. I almost fell off Chestnut from the sudden rush of shared emotion.

*Sophie!*

*Lily!*

*Oh, thank goodness, thank goodness, I've been so worried!* I could tell my twin was crying.

I drew a shuddering breath, fighting my own sob with a smile. *Of course you have. You always are.*

*Hey!* I didn't have to see her face to picture her watery chuckle. *I've made a lot of progress on that, I'll have you know. Jon's been assisting me.*

I laughed back at her, reveling in the moment. *Jon's as bad as you are, you know that, right?*

*Sophie, what happened? Where have you been?*

*The situation is bad here in Palinar, Lil. I wouldn't have made it through the wilderness if the Beast hadn't sent his royal carriage for me. But it seems his castle and grounds here are protected. Only I think the protection is blocking our connection somehow. It happened as soon as I arrived. And, seriously, it's hard to describe the magic here, but I've never seen anything like it.* I sent her a mental picture of the aisle of orange trees, full of both blossoms and fruit, the sun bouncing off the orange globes to strike the snow below.

*Is that...snow? In the middle of summer?*

*Among other things. The whole place is like this. And the servants are invisible, and the Beast can't speak, and I think the rest of his family is dead.* I blurted it all out, knowing it would make little sense to her, but needing to let it out. *And no one will speak to me about the curse. Oh, and the Beast has a magic mirror. Apparently, all the kings have one—ask Jon about it. I saw you in it, but I also saw Cole. He was riding with some other men.*

*What? Where?*

I tried to describe the setting, but it sounded as generic as it had looked.

She sighed. *He truly has escaped into Talinos like we feared, then. Nowhere in Marin looks like that. But never mind him. Are you all right? Has this Beast mistreated you? And did you say the servants are invisible?*

I could tell she had no more idea where to start than I did. I took a deep breath, no longer paying attention to Chestnut who had dropped to a slow walk. *Oh, Lily.* Tears leaked down my face. *It's so good to hear you again. I've been so lonely.*

*I knew it! I should never have let Jon convince me. I'm coming after you.*

*No! Lily promise me you won't. Not until I've learned more about the curse at least.* I wished I could reach out and shake her. *Didn't you hear what I said? Even I wouldn't have made it without the Beast's intervention. You'll be ripped apart by the wolves!*

A remembered echo of their howls sounded through my mind, so real that I shivered. And then I heard it again. I gulped. That hadn't been a memory.

*Sophie? Sophie, what is it?* Lily had instantly picked up on my change of mood.

*Uh, nothing. I just thought I heard something.* I turned Chestnut around and pointed her back in the direction of the castle. At least, I hoped it was the right direction.

*Heard what? Wait? Where are you now? How are you talking to me?*

*I had to leave the grounds to get through. But I'm heading back now. If our connection cuts off, you'll know why this time.*

*Heading back? Sophie...Sophie, can you hear wolves?* She sounded like she had started to hyperventilate, the sound creeping into her projections.

Another chorus of howls rang out, sounding much closer than the last ones. I urged Chestnut faster. Shouldn't we have passed back into the grounds by now? Why had I let myself be so distracted? I should have stopped Chestnut as soon as I connected with Lily.

The next howl seemed to come from in front of us, and I jerked backwards. Chestnut stopped altogether, pawing the ground, and neighing loudly. I tried to urge her on, but she wouldn't budge.

"Come on Chestnut, come on." I murmured, trying to keep the fear out of my voice. But my blood had now started to pound and my hands to sweat. Was that the pad of paws I could hear? And heavy breaths in the now darkening air?

As if to make things worse, a flurry of snow landed on Chestnut's mane. I brushed it off, and tried to soothe her with my hands. "Come on, girl, we can do this."

She danced beneath me, squealing now in fear. I looked up and straight into the eyes of a large gray wolf. I screamed and twisted to my right, only to be confronted by two more wolves. Spinning my head to the left, I saw another one. I was surrounded.

# PART II
# THE PRINCE

# CHAPTER 14

*S*ophie? *Sophie!* Lily was screaming in my mind, but I was too focused on the wolves to respond. Did Chestnut and I have any hope of outrunning them? Chestnut squealed again and half reared, flashing her hooves at the wolves. I gasped and hung on, knowing if I was thrown from her back I would have no chance.

When she landed back on the ground, she danced to one side, huffing and snorting. All the wolves were growling now, and I suspected she was about to make a dash for it whether I wanted her to or not. I felt naked and exposed on her back. If only I had something—even a sturdy branch—to defend myself. If a wolf leaped at us, I had no way to whack it away.

I shifted my seat, keeping my eyes on the wolf that seemed to be the leader. Leaning low over Chestnut's neck, I prepared to urge her into a life and death gallop. My eyes darted around looking for the clearest gap in the circle of the pack.

*Sophie!*

*They've got me surrounded, Lily.* I knew I must be terrifying her, but I was too scared myself to try to temper the fear that pounded through our connection. *Chestnut and I are going to make a run for it.* I gulped. *But I don't know if we'll make it. I love you.*

I slammed shut our link and dug my heels into Chestnut's quivering sides. "Go, girl!" I screamed as she leaped forward. I directed her between the two smallest wolves and, somehow, she managed to break through. The trees flashed past, the short barks of the wolves sounding behind us as they chased us down.

The snow flew up around Chestnut's hooves, and she kept having to swerve to avoid trees, preventing us from reaching our full speed. I could feel Lily trying to connect with me, a niggling feeling in the back of my mind as I kept myself closed to her. If the worst happened, I didn't want her inside my head.

Chestnut turned abruptly, and I grabbed at her mane, struggling to keep my seat. Our new path took us along an outcropping of stone, and I could see gray bodies running along the top, somehow ahead of us. Before I could turn Chestnut the other way, one of them leaped from the stone, flying above us and landing on our other side. Somehow, despite our earlier escape, we were once again surrounded.

A growl to my right pulled my eyes back toward the rock just as one of the wolves launched itself at me. I threw myself sideways, knowing it wouldn't be enough to avoid the deadly claws.

A familiar roar cut through the sound of the wolves as I half hung off Chestnut, unable to see. One of the howls turned into a whimper, and a heavy weight landed hard against my leg and Chestnut's side, sliding immediately down and away.

I swung myself back up, unable to believe my last-minute reprieve. Looking frantically around between the trees, I found the Beast. He sat atop his stallion, the two fighting as one, hooves and sword flashing. Already gray bodies littered the ground, staining the snow red.

Chestnut neighed and moved toward the safety of the stallion. But before she could place herself behind him, a wolf leaped toward us on the opposite side. I gasped, ducking once more in the saddle. For the briefest moment, as I dipped down, my eyes locked with the Beast's before his flashed across to the incoming wolf.

A second roar filled the air as, somehow, he swung himself up to a standing position on the stallion's back, launching himself from the saddle and over my hunched body to collide with the wolf.

I screamed, sitting back up and trying to pull Chestnut around so I could see them. The stallion neighed loudly, the sound a harsh challenge, as his hooves dispatched a final wolf. The last few members of the pack had now retreated. Only the one in a deadly embrace with the Beast remained.

Claws slashed out and red blossomed along one of the Beast's arms. At the same time the wolf sank its teeth into his opposite shoulder. The Beast roared and ripped the animal's head away, the muscles of his arms straining. The wolf made a final effort to lunge forward and the Beast let go with his right hand, swinging it up and around so fast that his fist smashed into the skull of the wolf before its teeth could sink in. The animal went limp and fell into the snow.

The Beast stared down at the pile of fur for a moment, swaying as red ran down both his arms. Then he looked up at me, his breath scraping harshly through his throat. *Why did you try to leave? You know it isn't safe out here.*

I stared at him. "I wasn't trying to leave. I was just..." I trailed off, realizing I couldn't tell him why I had made the excursion outside the grounds.

*Are you injured?*

I shook my head. "No...no, I'm unharmed."

A look, almost like relief, flashed across his face before his eyes rolled back, and he collapsed, falling to lie beside his defeated opponent. My eyes widened, and I drew a shuddering breath. I looked again for any more wolves but could see nothing.

*Sophie! Sophie!* I must have relaxed because, unconsciously, I had reopened the door to Lily. *What happened?*

*I'm all right. So is Chestnut. We're both unharmed.*

Lily gave a shaky breath of relief. *Don't you ever do that to me again! What happened? Did you manage to get back into the castle grounds?*

I sent her an image of my shaking head.

*Then what happened? Are you sure there's no more danger?*

*It seems clear. For now, at least.*

*Then you need to get back!*

I hesitated.

*Sophie? What aren't you telling me?*

I sighed and sent her an image of the forest floor around me.

She gasped. *Is that blood? What happened to the wolves? Wait—is that the Beast?* She sounded half-horrified, half-fascinated.

*Yes.*

*Is he...is he dead?*

I swallowed hard. *I don't know. He just collapsed.*

*Well he'll die if he remains there in the snow for long enough.*

Her words jolted me into action, and I slid down from Chestnut's back. Slowly I picked my way toward the Beast, trying to avoid fallen bodies and splashes of red. The stallion snorted behind me, and Chestnut huffed quietly in response.

*Sophie, wait.* Lily's soft projection made me pause. I could tell she had more to say, so I waited silently. *If...if he dies, you'll be free. And maybe Palinar with you.*

*We don't know that.* But I bit my lip, a shiver coursing through me. Free. Free to return home, no longer cut off and alone. My eyes strayed back to his still form, stark against the white snow. I could get back on Chestnut and lead the stallion back to the castle. I could walk away now, and no one but Lily would ever know. If I took his carriage, I could be back in Marin within three days.

He hadn't shown any consideration when he pulled me from my life; I owed him nothing. But still I hesitated. Because the scattered bodies of the wolves told me otherwise. An image of him, standing on the rearing stallion's back as he launched himself at the attacking wolf, filled my mind. He had not hesitated for me.

I drew a deep breath. *I can't do that, Lily.*

*He's a monster, Sophie. You were there with me in the Tourney. And just look at his face now.*

I sighed and projected again the mental image of the forest around me. *He may be a monster, but he also saved me. And you can only see the shape of his jaw, not his eyes.* My projection dropped to a whisper. *They're so human, Lily.*

I could tell she had started crying again. *But you could come home to me, right now.*

*You know I couldn't, not really. I would never be able to live with myself. And neither would you, if you were here.* A realization hit me. For the first time in my life I was having experiences my twin was not a part of and could not understand. I would have to trust in my own judgment. *I have to try to help him.*

She sighed softly. *You were always a better person than me, Sophie.*

I shook my head. *Not better, Lily. Just different.*

*Well, you know I'm here for you, no matter what you decide.*

*I know. But, right now, I'm the one who needs to give help, not receive it. I can do this, Lily. All of it. Only I don't think I can risk coming out to talk to you again. Not until I've found a way to break the curse.*

*I understand. I love you, Sophie.*

*I love you, too.*

For some reason, when the connection faded, I didn't feel the same sense of being alone and adrift that I had felt when I first arrived at the Beast's castle and discovered myself cut off from

Lily. I straightened my shoulders and hurried over to drop to my knees beside the Beast.

I tried to put an arm under his shoulders, but couldn't even reach all the way across, let alone lift them. I bit my lip.

"Wake up, Beas..." I stopped myself and tried again. "Wake up, Dominic. You'll freeze if you lie here in the snow, but I cannot possibly lift you."

He stirred, his eyes fluttering partially open before closing again.

I tried more forcefully. "Wake up! Now!"

His eyes snapped open. *Sophie.* Wonder sounded in his mental voice, but I didn't stop to analyze the situation.

"I need you to get up. Can you do that?"

He groaned and tried to rise before falling back into the snow. I looked at the height of his mount's back and realized there was no way he was getting up there. I frowned, wondering if it would take too long for me to go and fetch help. What if more wolves came while I was gone? Or a new snowstorm? What if I couldn't find my way back?

I crossed over to the stallion who snorted and danced but, when I crooned softly, let me approach. I found a coil of rope attached to his saddle. Working as swiftly as I could, I led the horse over to his master and then looped the rope under the Beast's arms. I attached the other end to the Stallion's saddle, apologizing to the Beast as I did so.

"I'm sorry, but it's the only way. The snow will cushion you, and your cloak will protect you a little. But I need to get you inside to the warmth."

He groaned again but made no protest, so I hurried ahead with my plan. Walking in the front, leading both horses, I attempted to pick the smoothest course through the trees, avoiding any rocks that broke through the snow. I kept glancing at the dark shape dragging behind us and wincing. I would never have attempted such a plan if I could think of any other option.

It seemed an interminably long journey, far longer than seemed possible given my short trip away from the castle. When I caught sight of the gardens in the distance, my knees wobbled, and I had to force a final burst of strength into them. As I closed the distance, I remembered the only other time I had tried to leave the grounds. Only now did I realize the motivation behind the Beast's actions in spooking Chestnut. Not that he had needed to be so imperious in his note forbidding me to leave. A little explanation would have been appreciated.

When we actually crossed into the grounds, I almost went limp with relief. But the Beast wasn't safe yet, the cold and blood loss were as great a danger to him at this point as a further attack.

"Help!" I screamed as loudly as I could. "Help!"

*Your Highness?* The unknown voice sounded confused. *Are you hurt in some way?* A tiny pause. *Why do you have His Highness' stallion?*

"It's not me who is injured, it's your prince." I pointed behind the horses to where he lay on the ground. "He's been mauled by a wolf. Call for the castle doctor, and gather some others, too—we need to get him inside as quickly as possible."

The man, whoever he was, launched into action, calling loudly for a great number of people. We were soon joined by a crowd of voices. I stopped trying to pick out the individual words and let myself be swept along, glad to hand over the responsibility to someone more qualified.

The horses pulled away from me, led toward the stables by a lead line that floated, taut, in the air. A particularly loud cacophony preceded the Beast lurching from the ground. I trailed behind him, trying to leave enough of a wide berth that I wouldn't run into anyone.

*Princess! Princess!* A familiar voice penetrated through the fog.

"Tara?"

*Yes, I'm here. What has happened? There's the most terrible story going around—oh!* From the shocked tone of her exclamation, I assumed she had just seen the state of the Beast. Her voice dropped to a hushed whisper I had to strain to hear. *So, it's true, then. You were both outside the grounds.*

I couldn't focus properly on her words, distracted as I was trying to keep track of the Beast from a distance. I had expected to see more signs of consciousness from him now that we had arrived back to such a hubbub of people. But he lay unnaturally still, only the rise and fall of his broad chest assuring me he still lived.

Our strange procession made it into the entrance hall, and the chorus of voices seemed to swell even louder. I decided to risk an invisible collision—if such a thing were possible, I wasn't even sure—and approach the Beast. But I had no sooner taken a step in his direction than warm heavy material settled around my shoulders.

I looked down to discover I was now wearing a cloak. As soon as the thought crossed my mind, a bone deep shudder rocked me. When had it become so cold?

*Oh, Your Highness!* Apparently, Lottie had joined us, and she sounded horrified. She must have seen the Beast's injuries, then. *Half of your dress is soaked, and your face looks blue. You'll catch your death! Come quickly, and we'll draw you a bath.*

Oh. Not the Beast, then. I looked down and discovered to my surprise that I was indeed wet and racked with constant shivers. Somehow in the excitement of talking to Lily and the fear of the wolves, I hadn't noticed the temperature, or my own state.

*You're in shock, I expect,* offered Tara. *I saw a similar thing when Gordon went skating on the small pond in the east gardens and fell through the ice.*

*Skating! Surely, he must have known it wasn't safe.*

*Well, he did after he fell through. That child is always stumbling into mischief, though he always means well enough. But the doctor told us to warm him up and to keep him awake.*

I had been certain of my intention to check on the Beast but, somehow, I found myself in my room, soaking in a hot bath, while Tara and Lottie fussed over me, instead. Night had fallen outside—the first night since my arrival that the Beast had not asked me if I would marry him in the morning. Would he even be alive come morning?

# CHAPTER 15

*I* slept long and deeply, exhausted on every possible level. I woke to several new aches and a couple of bruises and immediately thought of the Beast. What was his state this morning?

When I slipped out of bed, a sleepy voice greeted me.

*Good morning, Princess Sophie.*

"Lottie?" A sudden suspicion entered my mind. "Did you spend the whole night in my armchair?"

*I wanted to be here in case you needed anything in the night. You might have become ill after your ordeal.*

"That is very considerate of you, but now you need to go to your bed. Just, on your way out, if you could please let Tara know to bring me some food?"

*I couldn't possibly sleep during the day, Your Highness. Let me fetch your morning meal myself.*

I shook my head. "Absolutely not. You need your sleep and Tara can look after me well enough without you. That's why I have the two of you, remember."

*Very well—if you wish it.* I could tell from her tone that she doubted my assertion that Tara could manage on her own, but I pretended not to notice anything unusual in her demeanor.

I paced the room while I waited for Tara to arrive, alternating between staring out the window at the gardens and sitting on my bed chewing my hair. The previous morning, when I had been planning how to sneak into the Beast's chambers, felt like another lifetime. So much had happened since then. It was hard to process it all.

Tara must have arrived at a run because I was sitting down to a hot meal within minutes. I had planned to ask her what the kitchen gossip had to say about the Beast's condition, but she didn't need any prompting to start sharing.

*I'm so glad to see you well this morning, Princess Sophie. You gave me and Lottie a fright last night. I would have insisted on staying with you, except that Lottie assured me she preferred to take the night shift, and I didn't like to make her uncomfortable.*

It was the first sign I had seen of any such consideration, but I refrained from comment.

*And I think it turned out for the best anyway, since Lottie's absolutely hopeless at ferreting out news of any kind.* This airy conclusion made me snort and reminded me why I had asked for Tara in the first place. The ex-serving maid didn't feel the need to temper her view of reality.

*The doctor popped down for a bite to eat around sunrise, poor man. He looked exhausted and, of course, the kitchen staff all mobbed him. We'd already guessed from various requests sent down for supplies that His Highness must have a high fever, but...*

"So, the Beast is alive still?" I asked, unable to wait through her meandering story for that crucial piece of information.

*Oh, yes, certainly. We have an excellent doctor. It's the prince himself who's the problem.*

"What do you mean?"

*He's a terrible patient, he always has been. He can still barely stand but is apparently insisting on going out to check on his horse.*

I put down my fork and rose to my feet. "Where is he now? In his bedchamber?"

*Yes, for the moment at least.*

I threw a robe around my shoulders and headed for the door. Pausing in the doorway, I looked back into the empty air of the room. "You're not going to protest? Or try to stop me?"

*Well, I feel sure Lottie would tell me that I ought to do so.* Tara giggled. *Especially since you're wearing your nightgown. But to tell you the truth, I'm just planning to follow you and see what happens.*

I laughed. "I applaud your honesty and your spirit of adventure."

Hurrying down the corridor, I made my way to the Beast's chambers as I had done such an astonishingly short number of hours before. I had never had the same interest in healing as Lily, but I had tagged along for enough of her sessions with our castle doctors to know a few basics. For instance, that someone with a raging fever and significant blood loss shouldn't be stumbling around in the snow.

When I reached his corridor, I slowed and then came to a complete stop in the open doorway of his bedchamber. The sound of voices told me that the room must be full of people, but my view of the Beast was unobstructed. I assessed his appearance, hoping that, for him, a servant blocked his view of my rude stare.

He was naked from the waist up, white bandages covering the deep cuts on his arm and shoulder. I bit my lip at the sight of his bare chest, covered with a thick layer of hair, and then forced myself to look up to his face. He had propped himself up on one arm and was arguing with someone about getting up. His eyes looked glassy and strange, and his face flushed.

A low growl silenced the rest of the voices. *I am getting up, and there is nothing any of you can say to prevent me. So get out of my way.*

"Absolutely not," I said loudly.

The silence seemed somehow to grow deeper, and the hairs

on the back of my neck stood up from the certainty that an unknown number of invisible eyes were trained on me. But I maintained a calm facade as I moved forward into the room.

"It is quite apparent, even without the assurances of your doctor, that you are extremely ill. You will remain in bed until such time as he gives you leave to rise."

Still silence reigned, and I received the distinct impression that a large number of people were holding their breath.

*Princess Sophie.* The Beast remained propped half up in the bed, but he also made no further move to get up. *I must check on my horse.*

"Do not be ridiculous." I reached his bedside, trying to ignore the way his eyes stayed fixed on me, dressed as I was in only my nightgown and robe. "You have, I can only assume, a great number of grooms and stable hands, not to mention a highly competent stable master. You would only be in the way, as well as inflaming your wounds and your fever to no purpose."

*Indeed.* A mature, weary voice I hadn't heard before leaped in to back me up. *It is just as the princess says. You must listen to Her Highness, Prince Dominic, if you will not listen to me.*

I turned toward the sound. "I assume you must be the castle doctor. It is very nice to meet you, sir."

*Oh, no, I assure you the pleasure is all mine. I am Doctor Henshaw, and if you can convince His Highness to remain in his bed long enough to heal, you will be doing him and all of us a great favor.*

"Certainly, Doctor Henshaw. There can be no question of his getting up. Perhaps you can give me a brief description of your preferred care regime."

As the doctor eagerly outlined his recommended diet and wound care, a series of strange noises came from the bed. I ignored them.

When the doctor finished speaking, a final rumble sounded from the bed. I turned to face the Beast. "Yes? Did you wish to say something?"

The Beast was glaring at me. *My horse just fought a pack of wolves at my request. I will not rest until I have checked on him.*

An unexpected wave of shame washed over me. The Beast showed more care for his horse than I had done for Chestnut on my first night. The thought unsettled me, and confirmed my determination not to allow him to further injure himself.

I rapidly considered the best way to subdue him and then drew myself up to my full height, assuming an outraged expression. "Are you trying to insult me?"

Some of the anger dropped from his face to be replaced by confusion. *Insult you?*

"I was the one who walked your horse back to the castle and handed him over to your stable. I have just told you that he is unharmed and in good hands. Are you calling me a liar?"

A stifled snort of laughter came from beside me, and the Beast turned wrathful eyes on his doctor. I intervened quickly. "If everyone could please clear the room, His Highness needs the chance to rest. I will remain here with him and will call one of you if need be." I turned in the direction of the doctor. "Please have the kitchen send up a meal as you have described."

*I'm not eating that.* The Beast sounded more sulky than angry, and I knew I had won. I kept the triumphant smile from my face.

"I will ensure he eats it."

*I'm sure you will, Your Highness. We can all be grateful you're here.*

I felt a pang as the last of the servants made their way from the room, talking in whispers. If I hadn't been here, the Beast wouldn't be injured at all.

I turned back around to find him glaring at me, but most of the heat had gone from his expression. *Do you really mean to keep me prisoner here?*

I arched an eyebrow at him, and he actually had the decency to look ashamed, his eyes dropping away from mine. With a sigh, he lowered himself back onto the pillow.

"Would you like another pillow?" I asked, as I pottered around his bed, rearranging the tangled blankets. When he didn't answer, I looked at him with both eyebrows raised and discovered he was staring at me with fascination.

"What?"

*Are you always like this?*

"Like what? Right?"

He actually barked a laugh. I grinned back at him. "Don't worry, Your Highness, I've spent a lot of time with my three-year-old nephew. I know all about looking after sulky children."

He shook his head, but a smile lingered on his face, the first I had ever seen from him. *You seem different.*

I shrugged and continued pottering around the room. I could hardly tell him the truth. Something *had* changed; it had changed when I had stared down at him, dying in the snow and considered leaving him there. Before I had felt powerless—trapped, angry and afraid. But when I had chosen to save him, I had changed the balance of power. Even if he didn't know it.

I remembered now that I would never be powerless over my own actions, and choices. I was no longer here as his prisoner. I had chosen to be here because I believed—had always believed—that I had the ability to save others. And not only my sister and the younger girls of the Tourney, but also the people of Palinar who were caught in the curse. And last night, as the Beast had saved me from the wolves, it had occurred to me for the first time, that maybe Prince Dominic needed saving, too.

Now I just had to believe I was strong enough to do it. When I had lost Lily, I had temporarily lost my way, forgetting that I had been the one to win the Tourney despite her best efforts to stop me. Together we were something of an unstoppable force, but that didn't mean I was weak on my own. And last night I had shown it, making the decision I knew was right, despite every temptation.

This morning I found that the Beast's fitful temper didn't have the same effect on me as it had previously. He was simply another of the many puzzles I had to solve.

Several hours later, while attempting to force him into eating a second bowl of soup, I found my new positivity wearing thin. He had slept most of the morning, waking in a foul mood when he was still greeted with only soup. So, my morning had alternated between boredom and bouts of his disagreeable mood. It had taken all of my willpower not to pull back the curtain and ask the mirror to show me Lily while he slept. Only the fear that it would wake him had stopped me, but the exercise in self-control had put me in nearly as irritable a mood as him.

At last I snapped. "Stop! You are a grown man and a prince. You appear to have no consideration for anyone but your horse, and it is time you learned to think of others, and to act with restraint." We glared at each other, my chest heaving from my own loss of control. "You will eat the food the doctor sends and stay in bed until he gives you permission to leave. And I do not want to hear another word about it!"

I expected him to shout back at me, but the anger in his eyes slowly faded away. *Very well, Sophie.*

I eyed him suspiciously. "That's it?"

*Were you looking for some other response?*

I narrowed my eyes, still wary of his capitulation.

*Perhaps you would be willing to read to me?*

"Read?"

He barked another laugh. *Yes, you know. Books. Words. Stories.*

"You like to read?"

*Don't sound so surprised. I lost my ability to talk, not to read.*

I glanced at him, surprised at his light-hearted mention of the curse. How would he react if I asked him about it? Reluctantly I decided not to test it. I didn't want to ruin the first moment of almost-rapport we'd had.

"What would you like to read?"

*There's a book in the drawer of that table next to my bed. You can start back at the beginning, if you like.*

I pulled it out and examined the cover. "Large Scale Economics?" I groaned. "Mathematics—my favorite."

*You're a princess, aren't you? Aren't these sorts of things compulsory in Arcadia?*

I sighed and sat again. "Yes, unfortunately. That's the problem." I opened to the first page and then looked back up at him. "I'll read you this one if you promise that you'll find me a volume of fairy tales to read next."

*Fairy tales?*

I raised an eyebrow, and he shook his head. *Fine. You can choose the next one.*

And despite the boring topic, reading turned out to be an inspirational move. It gave us both something to focus on other than our frustrations, and the Beast even ate his simple evening meal with minimal complaint. As had happened earlier when we discussed his nobles, the Beast surprised me with his intelligence and balanced perspective on governance.

I had never forgotten that he had once been a regular prince—his arrogant attitude made such a thing impossible—but I hadn't considered that he had been a prince trained to rule the largest of these kingdoms. Apparently, his lessons had included more than just ordering his subjects around.

The sour note of the evening came just before the doctor arrived to relieve me. I had stood up, ready to leave, when the Beast reached out from the bed and grabbed my hand. I stilled, realizing his intention a second before he spoke.

*Will you marry me in the morning, Sophie?*

I ripped my hand away and hurried from the room without speaking. Obviously, I had been foolish to think that anything had changed between us. But in the doorway, I paused and looked back. "Can I recommend that next time you go with

'Thank you, Sophie'? You might find it's better received." I didn't wait to see his response.

# CHAPTER 16

*T*he next morning, I was still fuming and considered abandoning the ungrateful Beast to do himself whatever harm he wished. But the thought of ingratitude made me hesitate. While it was true that he had neither apologized for driving me from the castle with his temper, nor thanked me for saving his life and then spending my day nursing him, the same could be said of me.

The day before we had carefully avoided all discussion of the cause of his injuries, and I had neither apologized for trespassing in his room after I had assured him I would not, nor thanked him for coming to my rescue in the forest. If I truly believed that I had power over my own actions and choices, then my apologies and thanks couldn't be conditional on his.

The thought made me squirm all the way through the morning meal, and I changed my mind about which gown I wished to wear so many times that I had to apologize to Lottie. The truth was that I did not want to do it. He may have saved me, but the Beast was still an arrogant, imperious, thoughtlessly cruel…

*Princess Sophie?*

I jumped. "I'm sorry, Lottie, I wasn't paying attention."

*You have no need to apologize to me, Your Highness. I merely wished to know if you wanted your cloak.*

I shook my head. "I won't be going into the gardens this morning." As painful as apologizing would be, it was still the right thing to do. And my family had taught me that it was the role of royalty to do the right thing regardless of how much it might cost.

*You seem...distracted this morning, Princess Sophie.*

The mild comment was the nosiest Lottie had yet been, so I tried to think of a way to not answer her question, but in an encouraging way. I might have admitted my struggle to Lily, but I didn't wish anyone else to know about my internal tantrum.

Thankfully, before I could think of something, Tara burst into the room, already talking at full volume. *You've won a friend for life in Doctor Henshaw, Princess Sophie. The servants are saying you kept the prince from the stables and got him to eat the broth the chef prepared. The poor man was terrified of sending it up.* She giggled. *I think he was afraid the prince might bring it back down himself and throw it in the chef's face. But the doctor made him prepare it, anyway, assuring him confidently that the 'plucky young princess' would see he ate it.*

I flushed at this evidence of the doctor's belief in me. My remaining hesitation fell away. My gratitude for his rescue was not contingent on his gratitude for my rescuing him back. The Beast might not deserve my good attitude, but *I* did. I wanted to be a royal who earned respect, not one who demanded it.

When I arrived in the Beast's chambers, however, a murmur of low voices greeted me.

"Good morning." I walked into the room but stopped short when I saw the bed. The Beast lay against the pillow with his eyes closed and a sheen of sweat across his face. His body was rocked by spasmodic shivers, but he never opened his eyes. The murmurs stopped at my entrance.

*Your Highness.* The doctor's greeting sounded polite but distracted. One of the white bandages began to unwrap itself and I saw a fresh splash of red across it.

"What happened?" My mind raced frantically through the previous day. Had I done something wrong?

*I'm afraid the fever has taken hold. And his wounds have resumed bleeding.*

"But he stayed in bed the whole day yesterday, I swear it."

The bandages paused for a moment and then continued to move. *And I have no doubt he would be in a much worse situation today if he had not done so. The situation now was unavoidable.* I thought he meant to continue, but he fell silent.

Unavoidable? It didn't seem like a natural progression of an illness to me. I frowned. "Does he have a weak constitution?" It would be surprising given his physical strength, but curses could work in strange ways.

*Weak? No, indeed, he is exceedingly strong. And so we must hope he will recover from this setback.*

I bit my lip. I had often daydreamed through Lily's healing lessons, perhaps I was wrong about his illness. The doctor must surely know better than me.

"Is there anything I can do to help?"

*We have sufficient nursing staff at the castle to attend to his needs, there is no reason for us to trespass on your time, Your Highness.*

I hesitated, and he moaned. Stepping forward without thinking, I dropped to my knees beside his bed. He moaned again, and I placed a hand on his forehead. "You must be strong, Beast," I whispered.

He stilled instantly beneath my touch, and some of the tension seemed to leave his face. A soft whisper passed through the servants in the room that I did not try to decipher.

*Well. It seems you have a soothing effect on the patient. Perhaps we could do with your services, after all, if you are willing. For a short time, at least.*

"I am at your disposal for as long as you have need of me, doctor." I had made the decision to help him live, and I didn't intend to see him die now.

For the next three days, I spent most of my waking hours in the Beast's chambers with the doctor and nurses. He was delirious, moaning and growling and writhing in his bed. Sometimes he had to be forcibly restrained so that he didn't hurt himself. Only my touch and voice seemed able to calm him, so I hated to leave the staff to cope without me. Even when the doctor ordered me to my bed for some rest, I hurried back after only the smallest amount of sleep possible to allow me to keep functioning.

Their care and concern for their master never abated, and it both impressed me and piqued my curiosity. It was almost as if I wasn't the only with reason to be grateful to him, and yet I had only seen him treat them with brusque disregard or outright anger.

If there was any part of them that felt, like I had done in the woods, that his death would be a freedom of sorts, neither their actions nor their words ever even hinted at it. They seemed, instead, truly concerned about his condition.

Occasionally I would be left alone with him while they rested or fetched new supplies, and when that happened, I would sit there and stare at his disturbed face. What was going on in his fevered dreams? Without audible words, he didn't murmur or cry out.

On the third evening, during one such occasion, it occurred to me that he might not survive, and that I had never given my apologies or thanks.

It felt foolish, speaking to an unconscious person, but it also might be the only opportunity I had. Perhaps some part of my words might penetrate into his dreams.

"There's something I've been wanting to say to you." I took a deep breath. "I'm sorry for entering your room without your knowledge after telling you I would not." He stilled as he often did at the sound of my voice. "And I never took the chance to thank you for saving my life from the wolves. You put yourself at risk for me, and I appreciate it."

He stirred and for a moment I thought his eyes would open, but they did not. When I left his room that night, it was with a heavy heart.

But the next morning, when I rushed back in, I could sense a change in mood, even without listening for the exact words. I hurried to the side of the bed and saw that the Beast slept peacefully, his face calm and no longer coated in sweat.

*Good news*, said Doctor Henshaw, a smile evident in his tone. *The fever has broken and the wounds have stopped seeping. I believe we are now on our way to recovery.*

I smiled and sank into a nearby chair. A tension in my chest that I hadn't realized was there eased. A blissful vision of my own bed flashed through my mind. Next time I lay down, I intended to sleep for twelve hours.

*You should go and get some more rest, Princess Sophie*, said Henshaw. *You deserve it, and I don't want to find you getting sick next.*

"Are you sure?" I joked, having become comfortable with him over the last few days. "You might need me more than ever if he's going to wake up at any second."

Henshaw chuckled. *Even the prince is not strong enough to get out of bed today. So you should take your rest while you can.*

I grinned. "I've been warned, hey?"

I stood up to leave, but a hand gripped my wrist, holding me in place, and a weak voice said, *Sophie.* I looked down into clear blue eyes, free from the sheen of fever. *I thought I heard you in my dreams, but I wasn't sure if...*

*She has hardly left your side, Your Highness*, said Henshaw. *She has been truly tireless.*

He frowned as if confused by his doctor's words, and I pulled away, stung. Was it really so unbelievable that I would assist in a dangerous illness?

"You must excuse me, I was just on my way out."

He said nothing further, but his eyes followed me as I moved to the door, and when I looked back from the doorway, I saw a hint of the pleading I had seen in them the first few times we met, before we could communicate.

But I had given everything I had to help him through his illness, barely sleeping for days. What more did he want of me now? My relief from earlier gave way to a deep weariness. He had been unconscious for days, I didn't know why I had thought he would wake up with a different attitude. I left without speaking. I should have known better than to expect gratitude.

It felt good to do nothing for the day, other than take a short stroll through the garden. I considered resuming my search of the castle but couldn't muster the energy. Tara and Lottie took it in turns to keep me company, and I found Lottie's quiet presence and Tara's constant chatter equally welcome. I invited them both to stay while I ate my evening meal, though they both refused to actually eat with me.

In retribution, I made them entertain me instead with accounts of each other's physical appearances.

Tara volunteered to go first. *Lottie is tall, and...um...willowy.*

*Skinny, you mean,* said Lottie with a depressed tone. *Without a single curve.*

*Willowy,* said Tara firmly, sounding more supportive of Lottie than I had yet heard her. *The trick to beauty is having confidence in yourself. Start thinking of yourself as willowy, and you'll soon find everyone else does, too.*

*Only if I announce it loudly at every opportunity,* muttered Lottie.

*See!* said Tara. *You think you're wounding me, but I take ownership of my outrageous statements—I'm refreshing and fun.*

"I couldn't agree more," I said. "And I'm forming a tall and willowy impression of you as we speak, Lottie."

*She has pale blonde hair,* continued Tara. *And gray eyes. And very long, elegant fingers.*

*Oh! Thank you,* said Lottie, and I instantly wondered if the tall, shy girl had always been secretly proud of her elegant fingers. My heart warmed to Tara for noticing.

*Now it's your turn to describe me,* said Tara.

*Well...Tara is short, much shorter than me. And slim, but with a large...bosom.*

I could almost hear her blush in the word, and Tara and I both burst into laughter.

"She's blushing, isn't she?" I asked.

*I think she's heating the whole room.*

*You would, too, if you had this horrid pale skin that turns red at the least emotion,* said Lottie, roused almost to defiance. She ran the rest of her description together in her rush to get it out. *She has golden-chestnut hair, brown eyes and toffee colored skin—lucky thing— which only seems to blush when she wants to look coquettish.*

*Coquettish?* exclaimed Tara. *What an excellent word!*

By the time I had finished eating, I considered my efforts a great success, because Lottie had warmed up considerably and had actually entered into a conversation about Tara's latest beau, a good-looking groom.

*But doesn't he always smell like horses?* I imagined Lottie's nose wrinkling in disgust, though her tone was mild enough. It amused me to picture outrageous expressions on the faces I had crafted for each of the servants I had come to know. Just one of the ways in which I kept myself from going crazy while trying to interact with a large number of invisible people. I longed for an ordinary conversation, without the extra strain that came from communicating without body language.

*He does sometimes,* admitted Tara. *But he's so perfectly delicious to look at, that I'm willing to overlook it.* She giggled.

*I think I would prefer a footman or, or a gardener, or something.*

*Oooh.* Tara almost dropped the blanket she was busy folding. *A particular footman or gardener perhaps?*

*No!* Lottie rushed to deny the suggestion, but Tara laughed triumphantly.

*She's blushing again,* she informed me. *I think there is someone. Come on, Lottie, tell us. We promise we won't breathe a word to anyone, will we, Princess Sophie?*

"Oh, absolutely not." I shook my head. "Who would I tell anyway? It's not as if I would even know if I bumped into him in the corridor."

*Or the gardens,* said Tara. *Although I think he's a footman. I've never seen Lottie lingering around the roses in her time off.*

*I don't linger anywhere,* said Lottie with dignity, but Tara ignored her.

*I'm trying to think where I've seen you when you're not here. Wait! I've seen you around the entrance hall a few times.*

"What does that mean?" I found her flow of logic rather fascinating.

*The footmen all have different areas of service.* She sounded distracted. *Three of the footmen in that section of the castle are already married, so that leaves...* She trailed off, presumably to run through the remaining footmen in her mind. *Connor and Robert are the best looking. I know several serving girls who are sweet on them, but Robert is so loud, it's hard to imagine our Lottie being interested in him.*

*Goodness, no,* interjected Lottie. *He's obnoxious.*

"Well, that's definitive. What about Connor?" I frowned. "And why does that name sound familiar?"

*I think he was in the kitchens that first night,* said Tara. *Probably acting surly and suspicious of you.*

"Oh yes, I remember now. Surely he's not the one, Lottie."

*I think it's Samuel,* announced Tara. *He's cute but not too good-looking, if you know what I mean. Sort of friendly-looking and really sweet.*

"He sounds perfect!"

*Stop it, you two,* Lottie mumbled. *He's not perfect.*

I laughed. "Just perfect for you?"

*Maybe.* Her whisper was so quiet I could barely hear it.

Tara laughed again. *She's blushing even harder now. I think you'd make a wonderful couple. Is he sweet on you back?*

Lottie sighed. *I don't think he even knows I exist.*

*Well, we definitely need to change that!*

Lottie gasped. *Don't you dare!*

*You're too shy to speak two words to him, aren't you? But if he could just get to know the real you, underneath, I'm sure he would like you.*

They began bickering light-heartedly, and I smiled to see how Tara had managed to break through Lottie's reserve. It occurred to me how easy I found it to listen to them, and to separate their voices. I no longer had to strain to make my mind receptive. With practice, and possibly trauma and stress, my mind had adjusted to this new form of communication. Now all I wished was that I could see them. And that Lily could be here to share in the fun.

Eventually they both insisted I go to bed and, sure enough, I slept for a solid twelve hours. When I awoke the sun was shining, and I knew my first stop of the day would be the Beast's chambers. It had been strange to spend an entire day so disconnected from his recovery after being so absorbed in it previously.

# CHAPTER 17

$\mathcal{I}$ arrived at the Beast's chambers to the sound of raised voices. I sighed, closing my eyes for a moment before stepping in through the door.

*Oh, thank goodness,* said Henshaw. *You've arrived.* He raised his voice. *Everyone else out.*

I frowned. Did he have some terrible news to impart to me? I looked over at the bed, afraid I would see the Beast had regressed. But he was sitting up in bed, glaring at me.

*Well it's about time.* He sounded sour.

I raised both eyebrows at him, and he looked away.

"Being troublesome, is he?" I asked, not bothering to lower my voice. His shoulders twitched, but he didn't look back around.

Henshaw's quiet voice sounded in my ear. *He hasn't been what I would call pleasant, no. I've seen the magic you can work, so I'm hoping you can calm him if I just give you some space. But call me if you need. I won't go far.*

"I'll do my best," I promised, and he murmured a farewell.

Walking slowly over to the bedside, I glared at the Beast. His eyes skimmed the presumably now empty room and fixed on me.

*When I woke up, you were here, and old Henshaw told me you had hardly left my side. Where have you been?*

"Excuse me?" I put as much icy outrage into the words as possible.

He frowned at me. *I wanted to speak to you, but Henshaw refused to let anyone fetch you. He defied me—all of them did! My own servants, in my own castle, during a momentary weakness!* He ground his teeth together.

"Well, good for them," I snapped. "I didn't know they had it in them."

He growled quietly, so I picked up a heavy book from a small table beside him, lifted it over my head and let it drop back onto the table. It landed with a loud bang, and he fell instantly silent.

"If you act like a wild animal, *Your Highness,* I will treat you like one. If you wish to have me here, at your bedside, I will not endure roars, growls, or abuse of any kind. And I will also not listen to any insults toward your servants. For three full days and nights, we attended you tirelessly, nursing you through an illness that could have been deadly. And you dare to criticize me for finally resting once you are out of danger? Or them for placing the well-being of another person before your every whim? You are arrogant, entitled, and self-absorbed. They may put up with you as their employer and prince, but I can assure you that I will not."

I stopped, sucking in huge breaths as I tried to calm myself. It was the second time I had exploded at the Beast, and it felt good to express my true feelings. I thought he might order me from the room, but he did not. I sank down into a chair, and for a moment we both sat in silence.

Eventually he spoke, his voice cold. *I have a memory from when I was fevered. I thought it was real, but it must have been merely a dream. I thought that you were here, and that you thanked me for saving you.*

"You remember that?" I flushed slightly.

*You did say it? Even though I am...what was it? Arrogant, entitled, and self-absorbed?*

I sighed. "You are all those things. But you also saved my life. Both can be true at the same time, you know. And I behaved badly breaking into your room. I can acknowledge that without taking away the endless list of ways in which you have behaved badly."

*Endless list?* He huffed, irritated, but I stared at him with a stony face until his cheeks turned the faintest pink. His next words were more hesitant. *When I awoke I saw you, and I remembered what you had said. I thought you would want to see me.*

"And when Henshaw told you I was resting?"

*In the middle of the day? Ridiculous! It's not as if you were ill.* His voice became hard again. *They were trying to keep you from me, and I do not appreciate disobedience.*

"Trying to keep me from you?" I shook my head in disbelief. "Has your illness made you delusional, too? You might consider listening to and believing your servants from time to time. I can't imagine what makes them so loyal to you."

*I am their prince.*

I stared at him, my brow furrowed. "No. You are a monster, locked away in a remote castle."

He froze, such a stricken look in his eyes that I felt guilty. I had meant to shock him out of his prideful attitude, not to truly wound him. But then he opened his mouth, his row of sharp teeth glistening, and growled. I immediately stood up and strode from the room without looking back.

He stopped abruptly and called after me, *Sophie, Sophie!* but I ignored him. I had been clear that I would not allow him to growl at me. He needed to know that I had meant what I said.

A discreet cough alerted me as I walked past Henshaw. I briefly slowed my steps. "I'll be back later today. In the meantime, I recommend leaving him entirely alone, although what you do is your own business, of course." There was no reason for his servants to endure his displeasure in my place.

The Beast's growl rumbled from inside his room, and Henshaw sighed. *I think you make an excellent suggestion, Your Highness.*

I sighed as I walked away. The Beast would be furious, but I didn't regret my suggestion. I had warned him, so he had no one to blame but himself. And I needed him to see that I was a person of my word.

But as I walked away, a memory floated to the front of my mind, a small detail that had obviously been noted by my subconscious but not processed at the time. The book I had slammed against the table had not been the book on economics we had previously read together, it had been a volume of fairy tales.

He had remembered our deal and must have asked a servant to search one out for us. Had he been waiting all day yesterday for me to come and see the book he had prepared? Perhaps it had been his attempt at an apology. My steps faltered, but then I shook myself and hurried on. I had endured more at his hands than could be atoned for by a single book. The Tourney alone had made me ill twice, and that was to say nothing of Celine's leg or of poor Marigold.

And this morning he had showed no willingness to change his ways. I had challenged him on being an animal, hoping to call out the man who remained. But it seemed he wasn't ready to relinquish the monstrous part of himself.

And yet, as I wandered aimlessly through the castle, my thoughts kept returning to the fairy tales and to the memory of the Beast flying above my head as he leaped to wrestle a wolf with his bare hands—for me. There was something here I did not understand. A missing piece. He wasn't the prince he had presumably once been, but he wasn't completely the monster I had expected, either. Perhaps if I could unlock the secrets of the curse, I would be able to understand him.

My steps gained some vigor. There was so much of the castle I still hadn't searched, and here I was with the perfect opportunity.

It took me a little bit of time to find Gordon, my unofficial guide, but I eventually tracked him down. He had already proved useful as a page boy, keeping station just outside the Beast's bedchamber and running errands or messages as needed. He was enthusiastic about going on another exploratory mission and spent the first ten minutes trying to convince me that we should start with the dungeons. Eventually he admitted that he wasn't allowed down there on his own, and his fascination instantly made sense.

However, I stood strong in my veto. The dungeons repelled me for the same reasons they attracted a young boy. I hoped I could discover the secrets of the curse in a part of the castle not likely to be infested with rats.

We soon found ourselves exploring yet another wing of the castle. *This is the king and queen's wing,* explained Gordon. *No one much has come here for years. Just the maids who do the dusting. Some of us play hide-and-seek here sometimes, though. It's the perfect spot because the adults never come here. And I usually win because of all the practice I've had with Gilda.*

I shook my head in sympathy with the long-suffering Gilda.

When we reached the king's chambers, I stood for a long time, staring at another portrait of King Nicolas. This one depicted him alone and was considerably smaller, yet it still managed to dominate the room. Certainly nothing about this image changed my impression of the Beast's father.

"Why does no one come here?" I asked, hoping to push him into revealing more information about the royal family.

The lid of a golden canister on the dressing table lifted into the air and then resettled into place with a clink. *I already told you. He was a bad man. No one liked him. Plus, he cursed us all, so I guess that made people hate him worse.*

I froze, my mind racing, and my mouth going dry. King Nicolas had cursed his kingdom? Not the Beast? If I had been wrong about him in this, what else had I misunderstood?

Half way across the room, the lid of a chest rose into the air and then dropped back down.

"What..." The word came out too quietly, so I tried again. "What do you mean? About King Nicolas and the curse?"

*I already told you,* Gordon sounded stern. *I don't think I should be telling terrible stories to princesses.*

I rolled my eyes. "That's very considerate of you, Gordon, but completely unnecessary. I'm pretty tough, you know. How about you tell me the story about the king and the curse, and then I'll tell you how the Beast fought off a pack of wolves, and how I got us both back to the castle."

Gordon crowed. *Really? That'll show up Michael, all right. He's been full of stories about how he saw you arrive back.* His face glowed. *I wish I could have seen him fight. I once saw him sparring with some of the guards, and he was so strong.*

"You go first, though," I said.

Gordon grumbled for a moment but began his tale willingly enough. He clearly didn't understand everything he was relating, a by-product of his having heard the stories by listening through doors, I supposed. But he knew enough to paint a frightening picture, and I found myself wishing I had asked the question in a room that didn't contain a life-like picture of the king glaring down at me.

King Nicolas had used his position and authority to amass wealth and power, repressing his people and taxing them heavily. He made constant use of his mirror to spy on his people, ruthlessly crushing the merest hint of disloyalty. The nobility were afraid to question him, even in the privacy of their own homes, and the people dared not rebel. But conditions in the north of the kingdom became so bad, that a small group of rebels did develop.

Eventually the king rode out himself to find and kill them. He chased the leader of the group to a small, remote village. Whether the people were really sheltering the man, or whether the king merely thought so, no one would ever know. Because, the king had descended on the town with a troop of guards. He had called out all the villagers, and when they claimed no knowledge of the rebels, King Nicolas had slaughtered every single one of them with his own hand. From their oldest elder to their smallest child.

I gestured with my hand for us to leave the room and hurried out without waiting to hear if Gordon had seen me. I was struggling to breathe, too choked up to speak. The monstrosity of it! What sort of sickness lived in such a man, that he would do such a thing, and with his own hand? He had violated the most sacred tenets of a ruler, and I no longer wondered at his bringing down a curse powerful enough to destroy a whole kingdom. The High King demanded love and sacrifice from his rulers. The king of Palinar had shown nothing but hate, greed and selfish ambition.

I found my voice. "And so, the kingdom was cursed for his despicable act?" I had always understood the importance rulers had for the well-being of their kingdoms. When true love governed, prosperity followed for all, after all. But it seemed an injustice to see it working in the opposite way.

*Well, no, not right away,* said Gordon. He had led me into the queen's chambers, and this time I didn't see any of the objects scattered throughout it move. In fact, his voice sounded from right under her portrait, as if he were gazing up at it. *He returned home to the capital. And then Queen Ruby died, and that's when we were cursed.*

"How..." I stopped to clear my throat, afraid to hear the answer. "How did she die?"

*Dunno. No one ever really talks about her. I just know that everything changed after that. I never felt any different, though.* He paused. *Are you really sure you can't see me? Who would have thought being invisible could be so uninteresting?*

I shook my head, unable to focus properly on his prattle. Stumbling backwards, I sank down to sit on the bed. I was filled with an absolute certainty that—one way or another—King Nicolas had killed his wife. It turned out that a king violating his responsibility to his people was not enough to bring down a curse. But a king that broke trust with both his kingdom and his own family? Apparently, that was enough.

In my shock, I reached out to Lily, meaning to share the horrible revelation with her, and her now familiar absence hit me yet again. I wished desperately for some sort of comfort in the midst of such evil, and I had not even suffered the worst effects of it.

It still seemed strange to me that the very people to suffer under King Nicolas were the ones to also suffer the effects of the curse. Hadn't Matthew even told me the royals had been originally excluded from it?

As I pondered this thought, an explosion took place in my brain. I thought back over all the pieces of the puzzle I had been told or had managed to cobble together myself. What if I had been thinking about it wrong all along? What if the servants even had it wrong? What if the people had not been cursed, exactly, but had instead been saved? Moved en masse to another realm where their royal family could not touch them.

And now it seemed that the Beast was the only royal who remained. Was it possible I had chosen wrongly in the forest? Could Lily have been right, and if I had let him die, the whole kingdom would have been free to return to the normal world?

My stomach churned at the thought that his death might be the answer. And that, if it was, defeating the curse might be beyond me. Because I would not have a hand in killing him.

# CHAPTER 18

*a*s I walked numbly back to my chamber, Gordon still chattering obliviously beside me, I fought to control my rebellious stomach. I could not accept the idea that I should have let the Beast die. No part of it felt right. Death was not the answer—surely the story of the Beast's father demonstrated that.

As my mind continued to cartwheel furiously, further questions appeared. So much still hadn't been explained. It seemed that King Nicolas' monstrous acts had brought the godmothers back to Palinar earlier than they had returned to any of the other kingdoms. But they had come with wrath, not assistance.

And yet something had then changed. A godmother had helped Dominic. Another confirmation that my role here was not to bring about his death. But I had yet to hear even a hint of what had caused his beastly transformation. Or when. And the two stories were so hopelessly intermingled, that it was hard to make sense of one without the other. If the original curse had actually been to protect the people against their royals, then giving their prince fangs seemed rather counter-productive.

Or had the later godmother, the one who assisted him to see

his people, also been the one to give him his own curse? Giving with one hand and taking away with the other.

I tried asking Gordon about the Beast's transformation, but he had no idea. *He forbade everyone from mentioning his family or from speaking of his curse.*

"Then how have you overheard conversations about the king?"

*Oh, that was before he returned. We had been cursed for two weeks before he appeared back at the castle.*

"And you are not afraid to speak of it, then?"

*It's only the servants he forbade. You're not a servant.* My eyes widened at his strange logic, but I didn't correct him. I had already benefited more than once from his strange misunderstanding.

*Will you tell me about the wolves now?* He sounded far too excited about my having been attacked by wild animals.

"Uhhh…" I tried to gather my thoughts together. "Well, I decided to go for a ride on my horse, and I ended up outside the castle grounds." A less than complete version of events, but enough information for Gordon to possess.

As I told him the story, I lived it again, only this time I had a new perspective. I imagined the Beast not as the villain who had cursed his kingdom, but as a misguided boy, raised by an evil father, who had lost his entire family. Had King Nicolas also killed his own daughter? It was incomprehensible—but no more so than any of his other actions.

Could I wonder that a prince raised to power and privilege with only selfish ambition as his model had become arrogant and entitled? The real wonder was that any good instincts remained. I couldn't imagine that King Nicolas had ever risked his own life to save another.

Some of the attitude of the servants made more sense now. Did they retain hope that their prince would grow to be more like his mother than his father? With Princess Adelaide gone, what other hope could they have?

When I returned to the Beast's chambers that afternoon, I still hadn't decided if I should mention my new knowledge to him. How would he respond if I asked him about it?

I had no idea what to expect on my arrival. I felt a pang of guilt that the servants might have left him alone as I had recommended. What if he had worked himself into such a rage that he set back his recovery? But I shook my head, rejecting the thought. Whatever his past, he was a grown adult who must take some responsibility for his own health.

I was listening extra hard as I approached, but I could hear no sounds at all. No one spoke to me in the corridor, and I wondered if that meant Henshaw was now stationed inside the room. Walking slowly in, I saw to my surprise that the Beast was in a light doze, his eyes closed and his chest rising and falling with his soft breaths. I stopped part way into the room, unsure if I should leave, and he opened his eyes.

For a long silent moment, we stared at each other. Could he read the conflicted emotions in mine? Was my new knowledge written across my face? I felt myself flush at the intensity of his gaze. I had never been looked at so intently in my life.

*You came back.*

I drew a deep breath, breaking the uncomfortable bond between us. "Of course."

He frowned, and I felt a pang somewhere in the vicinity of my heart that he had been thinking I had truly left.

*No one has ever said such things to me before.* I opened my mouth to reply, but he held up his hand to silence me. *No one has ever dared. And I have never apologized in my life. 'A prince of Palinar doesn't apologize to anyone.'* His words were slow, obviously causing him pain to say. *But I have been thinking while you were gone. Perhaps...perhaps I have been wrong.*

I waited for more, but he seemed to be finished. I wanted to roll my eyes. That was it? He didn't intend to actually apologize? But I reminded myself of what I had just learned about his family. This was progress for him.

"We are all of us wrong sometimes," I said gently. Hadn't I just discovered I had been wrong about his role in the curse?

Sitting beside him, I picked up the book which still rested where I had dropped it earlier. I began to read. "Once upon a time in a faraway kingdom…"

The doctor insisted that the Beast remain in bed for another week. I suspected that he would have liked it to be longer, but he must have recognized that such a span was already a small miracle. My voice was hoarse from the hours I had spent reading aloud, and my mind strained from trying to think of ways to pacify a man who usually spent his days on horseback.

I tried to keep him talking about the systems of governance in Palinar, and I surprised myself at my interest in the differences between his kingdom and my own Arcadia. He often seemed impatient with me, but I kept reminding him that I had not been raised to rule Arcadia as he had Palinar. And if there were gaps in my education, I couldn't blame my family. I had been the one sneaking fairy tales into my lessons to read instead.

At Dominic's insistence, I visited Chestnut and his stallion, who turned out to be called Spitfire. His love for his horse seemed like the least beastly thing about him and, as I entered the stable, thoughts of him filled my mind. Perhaps I could gain some insight into him here.

I took the animals handfuls of treats, pleased when Matthew emerged not long after I arrived and settled in for a long conversation.

*I hear you've got things well in hand up there in the big house,* he said at one point, a hint of humor behind his placid words.

"I'm doing my best." I sighed. "But it isn't easy."

*No*, he said. *The young master has never been what I would call easy.*

"It must have been difficult for him," I said, as I brushed Chestnut's mane, "with a father like that."

Matthew remained silent for a long time, and I held my breath, hoping I hadn't silenced him.

*I used to be a senior groom in the capital stables,* he said at last. *I was tasked with teaching the young prince to ride. When he first started spending time out here at his own castle, he brought me with him and installed me as the stable master.*

He was silent for another moment, and I kept quiet, as well.

*When the prince is with the horses, I see a true ruler in him. Firm but gentle, authoritative but loving. I have been waiting many years to see him learn to view other people in such a manner. But perhaps such a day will never come. Still...we cannot live without hope.*

"No," I murmured. "We all of us need hope."

I put down the brush with a sigh. "I should be returning. The prince will be anxious to hear news of Spitfire."

*One day you must return and tell me how he looked in action. He is one of the most magnificent stallions I have ever had the care of.*

I agreed, hiding a smile. I hadn't expected to hear the calm old stable master sound so much like Gordon. Apparently, the boy never quite disappeared, no matter how many years passed.

But as I left the stables, my smile dropped away. The smell of horses reminded me so forcefully of Lily, it felt like an actual pain in my chest. We had spent so many hours with our ponies and then our horses over the years. I couldn't even see one without thinking of her. And my new-found independence didn't change how much I missed her, both in person and in my head. She would have kept me laughing throughout the trying hours of the Beast's recuperation.

On the first day that Henshaw permitted him to leave his bed, the prince insisted that he visit the gardens. Henshaw hemmed and hawed but eventually agreed. I could tell he would have preferred the prince restrict himself to his sitting room, but I could understand his desire for fresh air. I felt it myself.

When I went to leave the room so that Henshaw could get him up and help him dress, the prince held out a hand to stop me. I looked at him inquiringly, noticing that he looked a little pained.

*Would you...would you like to come to the gardens with me?*

"Is that a request, Beast, rather than an order? I'm shocked."

*I can rephrase it if you'd prefer.* He glared at me, and I laughed.

"No, indeed. It suits you better than I would have supposed."

He growled deep in his throat as I chuckled my way out of the room, but I decided to overlook it. I couldn't expect miracles, after all.

We met half an hour later in the entrance hall, and the prince offered me his arm. I accepted it, remembering the only other time we had walked that way. So much had changed between us since then. I had spent so many hours gazing at him on his sick bed that his features no longer shocked me, for one. And for another, I had discovered that we unexpectedly shared some interests—I would never have predicted he could love gardens as I did.

But some things had not changed. He still asked me every evening if I would marry him the next morning, a question that had started to seem more ridiculous than insulting while he lay ill in bed.

The Beast walked slowly, his breath more labored than usual, but he did not lean on me. I marveled at the strength that had allowed such a quick recovery after such significant wounds and such a prolonged illness.

He led the way, and I followed silently, both of us apparently happy just to be free from the sick room. When we turned the corner of a tall hedge, I gasped. He looked down at me with a look of satisfaction. *It is beautiful is it not? I thought you might like to see it, since you mentioned that you love roses.*

I dropped his arm and ran forward, both hands pressed against my heart. The rose garden, which I had previously only glimpsed from afar, was unlike any I had seen before. Snow covered the ground, as it did everywhere in the castle grounds, and the deep colors of the roses stood out against the stark white. The bushes had been arranged in two concentric spirals, twisting around each other without touching, leading me deeper and deeper into the roses until they entwined in the center. On one of the spirals, the roses darkened as it coiled inward, on the other they lightened, so that in the center, brilliant crimson blossoms coiled around pure white ones.

I stood staring at them, overwhelmed by the beauty of the design and the color of the roses, complimented by the dark green of the leaves and stems and set against such a pristine backdrop. I heard the Beast approach more slowly behind me.

*So, you like them?*

"I've never seen anything so beautiful. Truly."

*My mother designed it many years ago, when my grandfather was still alive, and my father was the crown prince. She was fascinated by the tower staircases.*

I watched him out of the corner of my eye. So, the roses reminded him of his mother, then. Did he have the same feeling of comfort and security here in the garden that I felt inside a library?

"They are very beautiful," I repeated, not knowing how to put my feelings into words.

We strolled slowly from bush to bush, and the Beast told me the names of the different species, many of them ones I had never encountered before. *My head gardener here is very skilled. He has adapted remarkably well to the...unusual conditions.*

I snorted. Unusual conditions, indeed.

Rather than growing more tired, the Beast seemed to be energized by the walk and the cold air. His stride grew surer and his breathing easier. He looked incongruous amid the beauty of the garden. A monster who had wandered from his territory.

Looking at him standing there among the roses, I had a sudden flashback to my time in the carriage traveling here. I had been unable to imagine the Beast surrounded by flowers, and yet here he was. What would I have thought if I had known then what I knew now?

He looked back at me quizzically, and I shrugged at him.

*We can come again tomorrow, if you'd like.*

"I would like that, very much," I said, surprising myself by the truth of my words.

We went to the rose garden every day for two weeks, and every day the Beast gained strength. He still had not thanked me for nursing him, or keeping him company, but sometimes I thought I could read gratitude in his eyes. He had become almost mellow as a patient, although the servants reported that he was more restless whenever I was gone. I was merely relieved that he had stopped haranguing them constantly.

By the end of the second week he seemed back to full health, and I marveled at his recuperative powers. Lily would have found him a fascinating patient, I was sure. I mentioned it to Henshaw, but he said the prince had always been like that, even as a young boy. Hearing that made me even more impressed since I had assumed it was a side effect of the curse.

*We can all be glad of it*, Henshaw had said. *He might well not have made it if not for his strong constitution.*

I longed to ask him why that would be such a terrible thing for the servants, but couldn't think of a way to phrase it that didn't sound awful.

As the Beast regained his physical strength, I had been afraid he would also resume the full force of his arrogance, but on the day that Henshaw declared him able to return to regular activity, he seemed unusually genial.

Eventually I couldn't resist commenting on it. "Should I ask Henshaw to give you another examination?"

*What do you mean?*

"I think that was your second joke. Have you ever joked before…in your life? Maybe your fever has returned."

The Beast growled, somehow turning the sound playful, and bent over a rose bush.

"What are you doing?" I asked, warily.

He glanced up at me, and I realized he had pulled the bush back and was about to release it, catapulting the snow covering it in my direction.

"Oh no. Oh no, you don't." I backed up, almost tripping in my hurry.

He grinned at me, exposing his fangs, as he took time to draw it even further back. I squealed and ran for it, my skirts tangling around my legs in my hurry. I didn't quite make it around one of the bushes when icy shards exploded across my back, some of them managing to slip down the back of my neck.

I groaned and whipped the rest of the way out of sight in case he had a second bush already prepared.

*You can't hide forever,* he taunted, a laugh sounding in his voice. *You're surrounded by snow covered bushes on every side.*

"But I can hide a pretty long time," I called back, before creeping behind a different bush. I peered through the leaves, and when he strode over to where I had disappeared, I quickly wove through another two bushes, keeping myself out of sight.

He didn't seem to be in any hurry, and after watching him for a moment from behind yet another bush, I realized he was following my footprints. I grabbed a whole armful of snow and began to run, crouched low so as to stay out of sight. I used the spirals of the garden to curve back around and come up behind him.

I must have made enough noise to give myself away because he began to turn. But before he could get fully around, I flung my snow into the air, dumping it over his head. He growled and shook himself, ice flying in all directions, but enough of it stuck to his hair to start dripping down his neck. I crowed in triumph.

He looked over at me, his eyes narrowing. *Oh ho! You think you just won, don't you?*

I saw his intentions in his eyes a moment too late. Scooping up a handful of snow, he grabbed my arm and pulled me close. Taking his time, he placed the ice on my head and began to crush it into my hair.

I squealed again. "Dominic!"

He froze, a look of shock crossing his face, and then he dropped his hand, allowing most of the snow to fall away. A single icy trickle down my back made me shiver, and he grabbed my other arm and pulled me closer to him, as if to warm me.

*You've never used my name before.*

I flushed and wished I could tear my eyes away from his. But something in their blue depths seemed to hold me in a different sort of captivity. I remembered the way his mere presence used to unsettle me when I first arrived—the raw power and intensity so different from anything I had encountered before.

And then, suddenly, he was the one to break away, striding away from me without a word. I watched him disappear between two hedges and took a deep breath. Because my heart was pounding as if I had just run through the garden, and I couldn't quite convince myself it was from fear.

# CHAPTER 19

*W*e had been eating the evening meal in Dominic's room while he was still recuperating, but that night we were back in the dining hall. The prince made no mention of our interaction in the garden, talking calmly throughout the meal about our latest book. But I noticed his eyes seemed to hold additional warmth whenever they rested on me.

When he escorted me to the door, I dreaded what I knew would come next. When he asked if I would agree to marry him in the morning, his eyes glowed as they bore into mine. I grimaced.

"I don't know why you insist on asking a question to which you already know the answer. When you break the curse, we will set a wedding date."

I expected anger, the curse was a topic we always carefully avoided, but not the flash of pain that crossed his face, as if I had slapped him when he expected a kiss. His face settled into lines of cold anger, and it was the first time I realized how much his usual expression had changed since my arrival. This was like the Beast I had seen then.

I sighed and left the room. There was no point talking to him in such a mood, and I preferred to leave without a fight.

The next morning, he wasn't in the entryway at our usual meeting time. I waited several minutes and then hurried to his room, afraid he had suffered some sort of relapse. But his chambers were empty.

For a moment, I glanced longingly at the curtain that covered the mirror, but I resolutely turned away. I was determined not to make the same mistakes twice. I returned instead to my room, hoping that I would find Tara still there tidying and could send her out on a reconnaissance mission. I was certain she could find information in much less than half the time it would take me.

But when I reached the room no one answered my calls. Even Gordon had apparently disappeared from his usual post outside my door. I frowned and crossed over to my window, wondering what I should do next. Had Dominic said something about not walking today that I had forgotten? Or was this because of our interactions the day before?

As I gazed outside, not really taking in what I was seeing, I noticed a flash of movement. Looking more closely, I saw a familiar figure riding along the front of the castle on Spitfire. I should have guessed he would go riding, now that the doctor had finally cleared him to do so. But why had he not invited me to join him?

I watched him until he disappeared around the corner of the building. Why did I feel hurt? When had I started desiring Dominic's company? I stopped, catching myself on his name. When, in fact, had I stopped calling him the Beast in my mind?

After wandering listlessly around my chamber for nearly an hour, I gave myself a good shake. This castle still held many unanswered questions, and I wasn't going to find any answers here. If the Beast had found other activities to fill his day, I could certainly do the same.

I headed straight for the kitchen, hoping to find Gordon and possibly to requisition a sticky bun. The servants knew by now that I liked them to announce themselves in my presence, so I was greeted with a round of cheery good mornings when I entered.

*Princess Sophie, I'm sorry, were you looking for me?* Lottie sounded contrite.

*We wouldn't have both come down here except that we thought you meant to spend the morning in the gardens,* chimed in Tara.

*It was quite thoughtless of us,* said Lottie. *It won't happen again.*

"Oh no, you're both fine," I replied. "There's no point you sitting around all day in my chamber doing nothing when I'm otherwise occupied. I was actually looking for Gordon. Is he around here somewhere?"

*That scamp!* Gilda sounded flustered. *I hope he hasn't taken to hiding from you now, Your Highness. I'll be sure to give him a piece of my mind when I see him next.*

"Oh goodness, please don't do so on my account," I smiled in her direction. "I dare say I gave him the morning off and then forgot all about it. He has been extremely diligent, I assure you."

*Oh. Well then. In that case, I'm glad to hear it. He's a well-meaning lad, with a good heart, but he can be mighty thoughtless at times.*

*He's probably out regaling the stable boys yet again with the story of your fight with the wolves.* I could almost hear Tara's eye roll. *He's been getting excellent credit off that one.*

Gilda sighed. *Those boys! They're nothing but a bad influence. But I can hardly keep him away, not when they're the only lads his own age.*

"No, indeed," I agreed. "It seems quite wrong to keep a child of his age locked up in a kitchen."

*It was a fortunate day for us all when you arrived Princess Sophie,* said Gilda, apparently overcome by my sentiment. *A fortunate day, indeed.*

"Well thank you." I laughed. "But you all seem to have been managing tolerably well without me, so I dare say you would have continued to do so."

*Aye, for now,* said a voice I vaguely recognized. *But time's running out, isn't it?*

*You hold your tongue, Connor!* snapped Gilda, allowing me to place the voice—the surly footman who we all agreed would not do for Lottie.

Tara quickly jumped in. *We can help you, Princess Sophie. With whatever you wanted Gordon for.*

*Oh yes, of course!* said Lottie.

I agreed, figuring I would have a better chance of getting an explanation for Connor's strange comment if I interrogated them alone rather than in a kitchen full of servants. As we all made our way out of the room, I stole a sticky bun from a nearby tray, calling out a thank you to the general hubbub since the staff seemed to have taken my exit as a cue to resume their usual chaos.

I munched as I walked along, following Tara and Lottie's voices as they debated which part of the castle to show me next. They eventually decided on the theater, and we started off down one of the wings. I licked the last of the sweet icing off my fingers, as I tried to come up with a strategy. No brilliant ideas presented themselves.

"What did Connor mean? About running out of time?" I asked eventually, hoping to surprise them into an answer.

But from their silence, I guessed they had been expecting it.

*What does Connor ever mean?* said Tara after a long pause. *He's always looking for a reason to be sour.*

Her attempt at prevarication was so blatant that I could see there was no point in pursuing the matter directly. "What were you both doing in the kitchens?" I asked instead. "I didn't know you spent much time there, Lottie."

Tara giggled. *She didn't used to. But then I let her know that Samuel always spends his mornings there if he isn't on duty. I dragged her along with me because I have this brilliant plan to—*

*Embarrass me.* Lottie sounded glum. *You know that's all that's going to happen, right?*

*Don't be so pessimistic! You're nice and you're pretty, too. I'm sure Samuel would like you if you gave him the chance.*

"And if he doesn't, he'll have to answer to me."

I peered around in confusion. "Is this the right way?"

*Oh, no, sorry we were supposed to take that corridor back there.* Tara's voice was moving away, so I followed it.

"You know I should make you both carry a candle or something, so I know where I'm going," I said.

*That's a good idea!* said Lottie. Two candles detached themselves from the nearest sconce and floated to a spot just ahead of me. One of them dropped slightly and then moved away from the other.

We started off again, and I watched the bobbing candles in fascination. "This really is one of the strangest things I've ever done."

*Only one of?* Tara sounded amused. *If this castle isn't the strangest thing you've ever encountered, your Arcadia must be a very odd place indeed!*

"You're forgetting that competing in the Princess Tourney was what got me here in the first place. And I don't know if anything could top some of the things that happened there."

*What was it like?*

*It must have been terrifying!*

I shrugged. "I had my sister with me which helped. As for what it was like…" I looked down. "We're forbidden to talk about it."

*We know what that feels like.* Lottie's quiet words sounded sad.

I bit my lip. It wasn't really fair of me to be trying to coax the servants into talking about something that might get them into trouble. But I was helpless, lost in the dark without information, and I didn't know how else to get it.

I cast around for something I could say to brighten the mood.

"You know, something has just occurred to me. When you carry candles, or bowls or blankets, I can see them, floating through the air. Why can't I see your clothes?" My eyes grew wide. "Please, please tell me you're not all naked in this other realm?"

*What?*

*No!*

Tara dissolved into giggles. *Oh, can you imagine!* She drew a deep breath and then went off into another round of laughter.

*Definitely not,* said Lottie in a more dignified tone. *Our personal possessions, like our animals, came with us. Only the communal items belonging to the castle remain with you, able to be touched by either of us.*

"It was a rather ingenious solution," I murmured quietly to myself.

*Solution, Your Highness?*

"Never mind. Are we nearly at the theater?"

*Yes, it's just here.* Both candles stopped outside a nearby door, and then the door itself swung open. Stepping inside, I saw a reasonably sized room with several rows of tiered seats. A small platform at the front of the room was framed by red velvet curtains, and gilt statues lined the edge of the room.

"Goodness!" I blinked several times.

*It is a little gaudy, isn't it?* said Tara.

*It's certainly not much fun to dust.*

"What use is there for such a room in a castle that hosts so few guests?"

*Oh, that's just Prince Dominic. Apparently, some crown princes in the past used to like to bring large groups of nobles down here with them. They would have readings and recitations, and even small plays on occasion.*

I certainly could not imagine Dominic sitting in one of the spindly chairs. It would probably collapse beneath him. I walked down the series of broad, shallow steps and stood on the platform facing the chairs. I tried to imagine them full of brightly dressed nobles and had to blink again. If the room was over-whelming now...

Still. "It seems a pity for the room to sit unused."

*Oh, it isn't unused,* said Lottie. *The servants use it all the time. Some of the maids can recite beautifully, and the pastry chef can sing the most incredible opera. Even the stable boys sometimes put together humorous routines.* I must have looked shocked because she hurried to reassure me. *Only on our half days off, of course. Usually we all have different days off, spread across the week. But once a month we have an extra half day all together. The kitchen leaves out a cold meal for the prince, and they clean up the scraps the next morning. I suppose you would have missed it since the last one happened while the prince was ill. Naturally the medical staff would not have considered taking time off in such a situation.*

"How considerate of Prince Dominic."

*Oh yes,* agreed Tara. *Several of the maids started out working in the capital, and they said they never got an extra day like that there. But it's been the way here for several years.*

"But he always seems so...well..."

*Terrifying, you mean?* asked Lottie.

I nodded, but my mind flew back to the time when Dominic had been ill in bed. I had wondered then if despite his brusque behavior to them, the servants had a reason to be grateful to him.

*His ill-humor was bad enough before...well, you know, before,* said Tara. *I'm sure I couldn't speak to him without my knees knocking together. But he always makes a point to set up systems for his staff that are more than fair.*

Lottie murmured her agreement. *As long as you stay out of notice, you don't get roared at, and then he's an excellent master.*

"What was he like before?" I asked, following Tara's lead in not mentioning the curse. "I can't imagine it."

*Well...*Usually Lottie was the cautious one, so Tara's hesitation made me dread what was coming next. *He was a little less angry, I suppose.*

I stared in their vague direction. "That's it? A little less angry? His parents die, his kingdom is cursed, and he's transformed into a beast, and he only becomes a little angrier? What in the kingdoms was he like before?"

Tara giggled. *When you put it like that...*

*It's true that he was angry and proud and rude before the curse,* said Lottie, surprising me with her honest speaking. *But he wasn't nearly so bad. My family has worked at this castle for generations, and they told me about the good years here after King Nicolas was crowned. After he became king, Queen Ruby used to come down here alone, except for the children, for long visits to work on her rose garden.*

*None of us servant children were allowed to play with them, but they used to have a merry enough time together apparently. The prince never minded playing with his sister, even though she was four years younger. My older brother said he sometimes used to spy on them, and the prince always let his sister win when they played games together.*

*Only they stopped coming after a few years. And then His Highness grew old enough to come alone. As the years passed, he came more and more frequently, and he seemed more and more ill-tempered.* She hesitated. *I know it is none of my business, but I've always felt as if he came here to escape the capital. And whatever it was he wished to escape, it was having a bad influence on him. I'm glad I have never had to live in the capital.*

The portrait of Dominic's father loomed in my mind. I would have attempted to escape such a man, too. I only wished I knew what had happened to Princess Adelaide. I could no longer imagine Dominic would have done anything to harm her.

I wandered over to one of the chairs and sat. The last time I had spoken to my sister, Lily had called Dominic a monster. And I had even agreed with her—mostly. In the weeks since then I had started to question that assumption. But then something would happen to cause him to revert back to his beastly self—like he had the night before.

Each time it happened, I was forcefully reminded of the trials and terrors of the Princess Tourney, a competition shaped by his twisted nature. And of the way he had ordered me here alone, without the least consideration, and proceeded to treat me contemptuously.

And yet then I heard stories like this from the servants, which confirmed the picture of him I had started to build in my mind. A picture of a man who was more prince than monster. But was I fooling myself? What was the truth?

I wished desperately that I had some way to discern his true nature. I would have called my godmother and begged her to tell me, but she had yet to respond to either Lily or me in these lands. Apparently, the brief but earth-shattering appearance of the godmothers in Palinar had not opened a door to their return.

I had come to the conclusion that our godmother had already gifted us in preparation for these adventures, knowing she would not be able to reach us here. But, then, perhaps Lily had been more successful in Marin since I had left. After all, they had defeated the darkness there already, and done so with the assistance of a godmother.

If I could only discover why Dominic had been made into a beast. What evil had he committed to deserve such a fate?

*Would you like to continue the tour?* Tara's question interrupted my musings, and I agreed to move on, knowing the answers I needed didn't lie in my own head.

"What happens to you all when the prince travels to the capital?" I asked them as we made our way through a series of unused guest chambers. "Do most of you travel with him?"

*Back to the capital?* Tara sounded confused. *The prince never travels back to the capital.*

"Surely he does not stay here all year round? He must make at least short trips back now that he is the only remaining royal."

*But he cannot.*

*Tara!* Lottie whispered, warningly.

I stopped. "What do you mean he cannot?" Both girls remained silent. "Tell me!"

Lottie sighed. *Prince Dominic cannot leave the castle grounds, or he will die. It is part of the enchantment, and why he nearly died after he went out after you.*

I leaned against a nearby wall, my head spinning. So that was why his injuries had resulted in such a severe illness, and why it had progressed so strangely. He had not merely responded to the attacking wolves in the heat of the moment. He had left his sanctuary alone to come find me, knowing there was a good chance he would die.

# CHAPTER 20

*I* returned to my chamber before the evening meal, wanting a bit of space to process my thoughts. I asked the girls to be back in time to help me dress, but when they returned it was with a large tray. Steam drifted off the various plates of food, and my heart sank.

"Don't tell me I'm free to eat on my own this evening?" I asked, pretending to them and myself that I was glad to eat alone.

*His Highness must have been exhausted by his ride,* said Lottie, but she sounded uncomfortable. Everyone knew the prince was back to full strength.

I looked away, hiding a flush. It stung a little to have a whole castle full of people witness my rejection. When I had regained my composure, I turned back to them with a smile. "I think I'll take the opportunity to have an early night. If one of you can unlace me now, you can both take the rest of the evening off."

But my early bedtime led to a disturbed night of fitful sleep. I kept dreaming I was back in the woods with the wolves and woke up countless times to the sound of howls.

When I got up in the morning, I felt tired and out of sorts. I missed my sister and the rest of my family, and the various activities that had made my life productive at home. And I was sick of invisible people and strange magic…and a beastly man who did nothing but confuse my emotions.

After being abandoned the day before, I had no intention of showing up for our usual garden stroll. But my decision to visit Chestnut led me through the entrance hall only twenty minutes later than our usual meeting time.

To my surprise, the prince waited there, one foot propped up on the stones in front of the fireplace as he stared blindly into the unlit cavity. At my entrance, he started and looked up.

*You came. I had almost concluded there was no point waiting any longer.*

I bit my lip; I felt too tired for a fight.

He cleared his throat, and I frowned at how uncomfortable he looked. *I'm sorry for yesterday. I needed space and a chance to clear my head, but I should not have gone riding without first informing you of my change of plans.*

I stared at him, temporarily robbed of words. Had the Beast just…apologized for something?

He grimaced, as if embarrassed by the justice of my shock. *I would like to make it up to you, with a surprise of sorts.*

"A surprise?"

He held out his arm. *I promise it is a pleasant one—or at least I have tried to make it so.*

I shook my head, still in shock, but placed my hand on his arm. Today had taken an unexpected turn, and my emotions were scrambling to catch up. As Dominic led us through the castle, he talked casually of his pleasure at riding again and of Spitfire's excellent condition. Every now and then he glanced at me, concern lurking in his eyes, as if he feared I might take offense at the topic.

I responded as minimally as politeness would allow, trying to work out from our path where he might be taking me. But we seemed to be moving deeper into one of the few parts of the castle I had yet to explore.

Finally, he pulled me to a stop in front of a double wooden door, arched and carved with flowers and woodland animals. I eyed it. What lay behind such a door?

*Will you close your eyes? I'll lead you in.* The anxious uncertainty in Dominic's eyes seemed out of proportion to the seriousness of the question. Looking up at him, I realized he was asking something deeper. He was asking me to trust him.

My breathing hitched and then sped up as I considered the question. Could I trust someone with such wild swings of emotion and behavior? But his earlier apology still echoed in my mind. After the past month, I knew how big a step that had been for him and, somehow, I couldn't bear to reject him immediately afterwards.

"Of course." I closed my eyes, keeping them shut even when he moved away from me.

I heard the doors creak open, and then he returned and took my hand. A small shiver shook me. It felt far more intimate than my hand in the crook of his arm. Or perhaps it was just because my eyes were closed.

He pulled on my hand, and I stepped tentatively forward, resisting the urge to stretch out my other hand to feel for obstacles. We walked forward several steps before he stopped and dropped my hand. *You can open your eyes now.*

I opened them and looked around. For several seconds, I couldn't make sense of what I was seeing. I appeared to be looking down on a wonderland—an internal garden that mimicked the one outside. For a delirious moment, I couldn't determine if it grew flowers or books. Then I blinked and the scene came into clarity. I stood inside the doorway, at the top of a small flight of stairs, looking down on the most unique library I had ever seen. Wooden bookshelves formed spiral passageways that wound around each other into a distant center. And every one was filled with books. Tall arched windows flooded the space with light, and chairs nestled within the curves, carved in the same patterns as the door.

It would have been a beautiful room just from its design and contents, but someone had transformed it into something magical by covering the entire room with roses. They wound around the chairs, covered the book shelves and had even been stuck between the books themselves.

Without conscious thought, I stepped down the stairs and began to wind through the books, running my hands along the spines and breathing in the smell of them. As my eyes caught on titles, I saw books on mathematics, economics, history, politics. I walked past them, memories of home and my family over-whelming me. My sister-in-law, Alyssa, would love it here.

But as I curved around, new memories came as well. Memories of reading aloud to Dominic as he recovered from his illness. As the spiral tightened, I felt utterly enclosed by the safe and familiar. And yet, at the same time, the room was so unlike any library I had ever encountered. This mirror of the magical rose garden outside felt as much like my new home as my old one.

I made a final turn and found myself in the center, where the spirals met. I could hear Dominic's soft footfalls behind me and began to turn toward him, but gilded pages caught my eye. I stopped to examine the books more closely, before looking up at him in wonder.

"Fairy tales," I murmured. "The fairy tales are all in here."

*I made this for you, so what else would be at its center?* The smile looked awkward on his face, his fangs getting in the way, but the light in his eyes more than made up for it. *I know that you would have wanted to share your birthday with your sister, and..."* He paused, looking almost as awkward as he had done during his apology. *"...and I know that it's my fault you cannot. So, I wanted you to have something special for your birthday. In Palinar, a princess' eighteenth birthday is usually celebrated with a ball. But I hope that you will be able to enjoy this anyway.* He gazed into my eyes. *Happy Birthday, Sophie.*

I drew in a sharp breath. My birthday. Today was my eighteenth birthday. And Lily's. I had completely lost track of the days in this strange life, so removed from my normal one.

Flushing, I looked away. The center of the spiraled bookcases formed a round nook where two comfortable chairs flanked a small table. A vase of roses and a chocolate cake had been placed there. I walked over to it, slowly shaking my head, still in shock.

But perhaps some part of my mind had remembered, and that was why I had woken dissatisfied and with my family on my mind. Two tears slipped down my cheeks. I had never imagined that I would spend this day apart from my twin. We had spent years dreaming up different plans for our eighteenth birthday, many far too outrageous to ever come to pass.

I swallowed and wiped at my face. Somehow Dominic had known and had gone to all this effort for me. My grief didn't erase my gratitude to him for marking the day, and I didn't wish to show him a face full of tears. When I was sure I could smile, I turned around.

"I could not have imagined such a thing," I said. "Thank you." He hadn't moved from where he stood, but at my words he strode over to join me. "But how did you know? I didn't think I'd mentioned anything about it?"

He glanced away, his face tightening and my curiosity rose. "Dominic?"

He looked back at me. *I don't want to make you angry with me on today of all days.*

"Angry with you?" I put my hands on my hips. "Well now I'm really curious. And it's my birthday so you have to tell me anything I ask. And do whatever I say, too," I added for good measure.

Dominic raised both eyebrows. *Is that how birthdays work in Arcadia?*

"Oh, absolutely," I said. But I couldn't quite restrain my smile, and I could read in his eyes that he knew I was teasing.

*Well, in that case...* But the amusement dropped from his eyes as he continued to speak. *When I returned from my ride yesterday, I knew I had behaved badly. I returned to my chambers, but my thoughts of you had made me curious. I wanted to see your sister, this other Sophie who might have won the Tourney and come in your place. So, I asked the mirror to show her to me.*

I gasped, but he didn't stop.

*Its logic sometimes works strangely, and I thought that, given our betrothal, it might see her as one of my family, despite her not being Palinaran. And it worked.* He paused. *I didn't expect her to look so much like you. But at the same time, she seemed different, somehow.*

*She was with Prince Jonathan of Marin and another girl I didn't recognize. They were discussing how the other girl had decided to delay a visit to Princesses Emmeline and Giselle of Eldon.*

"Celine! So, she's still with Lily? I'm so glad!"

Dominic looked at me questioningly.

"Princess Celine of Lanover," I explained. "One of our allies from the Four Kingdoms. She and the Lanoverian delegation came on the same ship we did."

He looked at me curiously. *You're going to have to tell me more about your home and how you came to be a part of the Tourney. It still seems like a great mystery to me.*

I bit my lip. We had avoided talking about our families previously, keeping our conversation to less personal ground. Did his sudden interest mean he also intended to finally tell me what had happened with his family?

"But how did you know about my birthday?"

He shifted uncomfortably. *This Celine apparently doesn't want to leave while you're still in danger. Your sister was pleased that delaying the trip meant Celine would still be there for Lily's birthday ball the following night. Tonight. She was angry...*" He coughed. "*...with me. That you couldn't be there.*

My tears welled again at the thought of Lily and my shared grief. But I also felt a tiny pang as I thought about the sorts of things Lily had probably said about Dominic. Still…if he hadn't been spying on my sister, he wouldn't have heard horrible things about himself. How else would she be likely to feel?

*I realized that it was your birthday today, and that you would be sad without your sister and your family. So, I spent the night setting this up. I thought forgoing sleep was the least I could do after all the rest you lost for my sake during my illness.* He frowned. *There wasn't enough time to set up a ball, but I wanted to mark the day for you. And we can still have a belated birthday ball on another occasion.*

I felt such a swirl of emotion that I didn't know what to say. Grief to be parted from Lily and denied the celebration I always expected to have. Pleasure at this beautiful room. Anger that Dominic had seen my sister only yesterday while I was not permitted to see her myself. Embarrassment that I had been upset when he canceled our meal the night before. Astonishment that he had gone to such lengths. I kept trying to remember when I had ever seen him show such understanding and consideration toward another's feelings. Weeks had passed now, and yet he kept surprising me.

I swallowed and looked down at the table. "How about we have a slice of cake? If it's anything like the pastry chef's other creations, I'm sure it will be more than delicious."

Dominic looked almost as torn as me, and I suspected he felt relieved I wasn't angrier but also disappointed I wasn't more whole-heartedly happy at his gesture. But he only nodded his agreement.

So, we sat down together, a Beast and a foreign princess, in a flower-filled library and discussed the smallest and most inconsequential of things while we ate the most incredible cake I had ever tasted. For all Lily and my wild ideas, I could never have imagined such a birthday.

# CHAPTER 21

*I* spent the rest of the day in the library, determined to enjoy it as much as possible before the roses wilted. Dominic kept me company, more accommodating than I had ever seen him before. He showed me a whole section of fairy tales and even, for the first time ever, read to me instead of the other way around. His deep growly voice turned out to be surprisingly perfect for the task.

After a delicious lunch which the servants set up on the table that had held the cake, I even dozed off in a large padded armchair. I woke disoriented and experienced the wonder of the room all over again. I had intended to ask Dominic if I might see Lily in the mirror as a birthday present—I desperately wanted at least a glimpse of her birthday ball—but he was gone when I awoke.

Tara waited for me instead. *What do you think, Princess Sophie?* She sounded as if she were bursting with excitement. *Is it not the most beautiful thing you've ever seen? And the most romantic.* She giggled.

I smiled uncomfortably. There was no question of romance between Dominic and me despite our betrothal. The prince was hardly the thoughtful, romantic type. Or, at least, he had never been before. And surely everyone knew I wasn't here by choice or with any dreams of love. I was still determined to break the engagement and return to Lily. The only change was that now I knew Dominic needed rescuing along with his kingdom.

Tara didn't seem to notice my discomfort, continuing to chatter away. *I was so worried that Lottie would give it all away last night. She's* terrible *at keeping secrets. Did you notice how awkward she seemed?*

Oh. I didn't want to tell Tara that I had noticed but attributed it to a different cause. "Where is Dominic now?"

*He's down at the stables. He left me here to ask if you would join him. He wants to take you on a sunset ride.* I could tell from the way she said the final two words that she considered this more evidence of romance.

I grimaced slightly. But I had to admit it was another unexpectedly thoughtful gesture. Some fresh air and time with Chestnut would be an ideal accompaniment to my day spent indoors.

Dominic already awaited me in front of the castle, walking Spitfire and Chestnut up and down. The ride was beautiful, the oranges, reds and purples reflecting off the clouds to color the snow beneath.

By the time we returned to the castle, the evening meal had been laid out in the dining hall. It was the most magnificent meal we had yet eaten, with a full ten courses followed by an even more extravagant cake than the one we had eaten in the library. I insisted that all the servants I knew join us for the cake, including Tara, Lottie and Gordon, and they all sang for me so enthusiastically I blushed. Dominic didn't seem comfortable with their presence or the casual way I made them share the cake, but he restrained himself admirably.

When they all finally left, he walked me to the door of the dining hall, and my heart sank as I anticipated the inevitable question. But when he stopped in the doorway and looked down into my eyes, he merely whispered, "Happy Birthday Sophie".

I had meant to take the opportunity to ask to see Lily as a birthday gift, but Tara's earlier comment about romance flashed through my mind. I couldn't ask to visit Dominic's bedchamber after dark. I just couldn't.

That night I lay awake for a long time reflecting on a great many things. I had already had more adventures in my eighteen years than many people had in a lifetime. And I wished, as I had many times, that Lily and I had never left Arcadia. Only, this time, when the thought ran through my mind, I couldn't quite decide if I meant it.

I could no longer imagine a life where I had never left home. Who would I be? Who would Lily be?

Mornings walking in the rose gardens, afternoons reading in the library and sunset rides became part of our daily life. Dominic still ordered me around thoughtlessly at times and occasionally growled or roared at someone who attempted to cross him, but I could see he was making an effort. And a month after my birthday he even laughed when Matthew remonstrated with him, which I took as a sign of progress. It wasn't only toward me that he had softened.

Every now and then I would ask him about my ball, but I mostly did it to tease him. I suspected he kept putting off setting a day for it because he didn't like dancing and knew I would have no one else to dance with.

When Dominic had business to attend to, I spent time in the kitchens, just listening to the servants going about their day, or I continued my tour of the castle with Gordon. Despite my explorations, I could find no further information on the curse, and—

incredibly, unbelievably—I might have begun to feel complacent about my life here if it were not for two things.

The first was the niggling emptiness always present in the back of my mind. The place usually occupied by my awareness of my sister. Somehow, as the days progressed, it never seemed the right moment to ask to visit Dominic's bedchamber, and so I had not even seen her for many weeks. I knew that no matter how comfortable I became, I would never fully adjust to a life without my sister.

The second was a change I began to observe in the servants. An underlying tension started to permeate the castle, and I often heard snippets of cut off conversations that reminded me of Connor's comments from before my birthday. Time was running out.

Every question about their meaning, however, no matter how direct, was deflected. Even Gordon remained quiet on the subject. After overhearing several comments, I tried asking Dominic, but he shrugged it off as some nonsense of the servants. I couldn't help questioning his disinterest and dismissal, but I didn't want to break the trust we were building by calling him a liar.

He had returned to asking me every night if I would marry him in the morning, and I still said no. But he had started bringing me a rose from the garden each evening and presenting it with his question. And despite my refusal, I accepted the flower. It sat in a thin vase beside my bed, and every night I saw it as I drifted off to sleep and as I awoke, its perfume flavoring my dreams. I told myself I accepted it because I did not wish to see such beautiful blooms go to waste.

But gradually this predictable life began to change. Looking back, I realized that it was a month after my birthday when Dominic and I first began to notice a change in the weather. At first, we merely commented to each other on the pleasantness of the conditions as we walked and rode. The balmy days seemed almost idyllic among the wintry landscape, and we noted it only as an enjoyable variation. It wasn't until a week later that I noticed, with shock, a wilted flower. It was the first blemish I had seen in this magical garden.

Two days later I rode along the orange grove and saw that all of the fruit and many of the blossoms had fallen to the ground. Several days after that we were riding through mud, the melting snow turning the ground into a churning brown pit that splattered across the stomachs and flanks of the horses. One of the stable boys groaned when we returned them, and I could sympathize with his sentiment.

Soon most of the plants in the garden had wilted and withered. And yet, even now they didn't look natural. Impossibly, they had taken on a bleached look as if wilted by the summer heat rather than killed off by frost. Each day the weather grew warmer, too, as if the castle and grounds were returning to the proper late summer season. Only the rose garden seemed untouched, the melting snow doing nothing but making the ground there damp and springy.

Dominic and the servants all professed astonishment at the change, but I still couldn't shake the feeling that everyone knew something they were carefully avoiding telling me. Was this what the servants were referring to when they talked about time running out? Did this signify the enchantment around the castle was breaking down and, if so, what did it mean for us all? I only hoped we weren't going to be left unprotected against the wolves.

Dominic told me repeatedly that I had nothing to fear, but considering he also claimed not to understand the change in the state of the grounds, it was hard to take his assurances seriously. And yet, when I was actually in his presence, I found it almost impossible to be afraid.

Although the mud soon dried, we began to limit ourselves to the rose garden, the only part of the garden that still retained its old vibrancy. As I walked there one morning, the wolves once again crept through my mind, and I looked up, almost reflexively, to be calmed by the sight of Dominic beside me. But I could see only the top of his head, several rows of bushes away. He must have wandered off to look at something while I was distracted.

I took a single step toward him when a strong arm encircled my waist, jerking me backwards. A hand clamped down over my mouth. I struggled wildly against the unexpected restraint, my mind racing. None of the servants were capable of grabbing me in such a manner.

As my unknown assailant dragged me backwards, I kicked at his legs and tried to wrench my arms free. Nothing I did broke the iron hold around me. I tried to bite at his hand, but couldn't get a good grip. My attempts to scream for help came out so muffled as to be almost inaudible.

Terror coursed through me at the unexpected attack, all sorts of horrible scenarios running through my mind. I tried to think of anything I had ever been told about escaping such a hold, but nothing I tried worked.

A sudden roar broke through the air. I went limp with relief, and a moment later was pulled from my captor's hands and shoved into the safety of a bush. For a moment, all I could see was green foliage as my ears filled with the sounds of a scuffle.

The arms of the shrub proved less challenging than the arms of my assailant, and I managed to fight my way free to face the source of the chaos. The sounds of struggle had died away, and only the low rumble of Dominic's growl remained.

The man he gripped looked small in comparison to the hulking prince, so it took me a moment to recognize him. When I finally did, I gasped. Dominic's hands tightened at the sound, his prisoner wincing.

*You recognize him?*

I nodded. "It's Cole." I had long ago confided my fears about the escaped nobleman's son to Dominic and told him what I had seen in the mirror. It had just never occurred to me to fear for myself.

"I don't understand, how did he get here?"

*And more importantly, what was he trying to do to you?* I had never seen such a deadly expression on Dominic's face, and I shivered.

"Princess Sophie! Please!" Cole's face looked confused and a little desperate, but less calculating than I had remembered. "I meant you no harm. I came here to rescue you."

*By abducting you?* Dominic's low background growl rose in intensity as he shook the other man, who seemed powerless to resist the prince's strength.

"Stop!" I held up my hand, glaring at Dominic until he stilled. "I won't have you shaking him senseless or losing your temper and killing him or something." Cole paled at my words. "You have him in custody, and now he must be secured somewhere. Do you have a prison cell of some sort here at the castle?"

*He snuck in here and attempted to snatch you from the garden. He does not deserve your consideration.*

I put my hands on my hips. "Perhaps not. But we need to know how he got here. Or have you forgotten that last time we checked we were surrounded by an impenetrable wilderness full of vicious animals?"

Dominic's expression changed, and I could read the reluctant concession in his eyes. I looked around, wishing yet again that I could see the servants. Surely Dominic's roar had brought at least a few running to our location.

"Let the servants know where you intend to put him. I will go to the kitchens and have them prepare some food for him. I'm sure news of his location will have made it there by the time they have a tray ready."

*Food?* Dominic sounded outraged, but I shook my head.

"He must be fed. I shall tell them to keep it to bread and water, if you prefer?"

*I prefer to throw him out and let the wolves find him.* Dominic's words were punctuated by another, deeper growl.

"He made it here, didn't he? For all we know, such a course of action might allow him to go free. Or return to attack us again."

Dominic's eyes widened at the suggestion, and for a moment I feared he meant to dispatch Cole on the spot. I held his gaze, however, and his grip slowly loosened again.

"Matthew," I called without taking my eyes from the prince.

*Aye, my lady.*

So someone had fetched the stable master, just as I hoped. "Could you please assist Dominic in getting this man to a suitable location?"

*I don't need assistance, from Matthew or anyone.* Dominic almost spat the words.

"You need assistance in keeping your temper." I knew I should probably stay with them myself, but I needed a moment to myself to think through this astonishing development.

*You can rely on me, Princess Sophie,* said Matthew, and I smiled gratefully in his direction.

"I'll see you soon." I turned to leave but stopped short when Cole called my name.

"Princess Sophie!" When I wheeled back around to face him, he met my eyes, his own warm. "Thank you."

I stared at him. "Don't mistake good sense and common compassion for a short memory," I snapped. "I haven't forgotten what you attempted to do a moment ago, or what you did in Marin, either. I will bring you some food, but I will expect some answers in return."

His face fell, and he said nothing. After eyeing him warily for another moment, I hurried toward the kitchens. As I strode into the castle, my mind raced. What did Cole mean by coming here? And how had he managed it? Surely this must be evidence that the changes we had observed in the grounds stretched further into the kingdom.

When I arrived, I found the kitchen abuzz. Clearly someone had beaten me here with the news. Questions bombarded me from every direction, but I shook my head until silence fell. "I need bread and water for the prisoner. I won't know the answers to your questions until I have a chance to interrogate him."

*Interrogate? Are you going to beat him?*

I frowned, unsure from Gordon's voice if the prospect excited or repelled him. "Of course, I'm not going to beat him. It's a cruel and ineffective means of obtaining information. I will merely speak to him. If he ever wishes to be let out of whatever cell Dominic has found for him, he'll answer me."

*I hope you're right, Your Highness,* said Gilda. *I don't like this situation, not one little bit.*

I forced myself to smile, attempting to lift the mood of the room. "There is no need for so much pessimism. This may be a chance to gain valuable information. And, at the very least, we have evidence that it is now possible to cross the wilderness unharmed. Such a thing should be a cause of rejoicing."

*For you, maybe,* muttered a voice I recognized.

I rounded on Connor. "Do you never work, Connor? You seem to always be here, in the kitchen. Perhaps I should speak to the steward about increasing your duties, since they are clearly so light?"

He didn't respond and I rolled my eyes. "No? Well, see if you cannot work on a change of attitude. I have done nothing to deserve your constant snide remarks." If I wouldn't let a cursed prince speak to me in such a way, it was high time I stopped allowing a footman to do so.

*Yes, indeed! Be gone with you, Connor,* said Gilda. She said nothing else, so I assumed he must have complied.

A tray floated toward me with a rather stale looking hunk of bread and a small wooden cup of water. I eyed it skeptically but sighed and accepted it. Apparently, the servants shared Dominic's perspective.

*They've got him down in the dungeon,* burst out a puffed voice moments later. It sounded young, one of Gordon's sometimes friends among the stable boys, perhaps. *I can show you the way down there, Your Highness.*

*Don't be ridiculous, Michael,* said Gordon, confirming my guess. *I'm the princess' page boy, so I'll show her the way.*

I hid a grin at the proud note in his voice. "Thank you, Gordon. And thank you for bringing the message, Michael. Perhaps the chef might have sticky bun to give you by way of thanks."

*Thank you, Your Highness!*

I hoped the treat might go some way toward soothing his disappointment as I followed a bobbing, unlit candlestick out of the room. Gordon and I had long since adopted the use of a candle to make our trips through the castle easier.

Gordon seemed bursting with excitement as we hurried down toward the dungeon, and my remonstrances only served to calm him for short bursts. Given his long-standing fascination with the place, I could hardly be surprised at his current excitement at finding it occupied.

My fears, which had revolved around rats, darkness, and terrible smells, turned out to be unfounded. The dungeons were lit by a plethora of brightly burning torches, and the worst smell was that of stale air. Neither the corridor, nor the couple of cells that I peeked into, even appeared particularly dirty. The cold stone was certainly not appealing, but it was a great deal more pleasant than I had pictured.

Gordon's excitement seemed to dim somewhat, and I wondered if he felt the same. Perhaps Gilda should have allowed him down here long ago. She might have found the location soon lost its appeal.

Several guards called out their presence as we walked past, and we found Cole in the furthest cell. Dominic stood outside, his body tense, shooting frequent glances toward the closed door.

When we approached, he frowned, first at the tray I carried and then at me. He held out his hands as if to take it from me, but I shook my head and tightened my grip.

"I'm taking it in there, myself."

*I don't want you anywhere near him.*

"We need information. Do you really think he's likely to say anything to you?"

I raised my eyebrows, and Dominic looked away, the frustration clear on his face.

*Well, I'm coming with you.*

I shook my head again. "No, I need to speak to him alone if I'm to have any hope of getting the answers we both want. But by all means stay right out here, ready to rescue me, if need be." I smiled as winningly as I could, and he seemed to soften a little.

*Fine. But the door remains open.*

I nodded, turning to face the cell door and ordering the invisible guards to open it for me. When I stepped inside, I was pleased to see that Cole had been left untied, and that someone had even managed to strew fresh straw across the ground.

He looked up warily at my entrance, but his face relaxed at the sight of me standing there alone, and I knew I had made the right decision. He glanced past me to the open door and Dominic standing out in the corridor, but I didn't even attempt to close it behind me. I had no desire to be shut in a small cell with Cole.

I placed the tray down on the ground and retreated several steps away from both it and him. He looked as if he meant to approach me but stopped at the expression on my face.

"I'm sorry, Princess Sophie." He kept his voice low. "I didn't intend to harm you. I came to rescue you, and merely wished to get you away from that monster as quickly and silently as possible."

I frowned at his reference to Dominic and had to remind myself that I had once thought of him the same way. It seemed an increasingly distant memory.

"Why should I believe a word you say after what you did in Marin?"

"You mean what my father did." He ran a hand through his hair and sighed. "No, you're right. I bear some responsibility, too. I didn't know the full extent of his plans, but I knew enough, and I shouldn't have gone along with them."

He shook his head. "At the time, I thought it was the best hope of saving Marin." He paused uncomfortably. "And I'll admit, I didn't mind the idea of seeing my family elevated in such a way."

He met my eyes, his look open and honest. "But I've had plenty of time for reflection since then, both on my conduct and on my heart. I've racked my brains for a way to atone for my behavior. I knew no one else had dared to come after you due to the dangers, but I had no right to value my life so highly. If I died in the attempt, then perhaps it was only what I deserved."

I regarded him with furrowed brow, trying to read the truth in his eyes. "Why should I believe anything you say?"

He shrugged, holding his arms out wide. "I would understand if you did not. But please consider. I made no attempt to free my father or sister when I made my escape. And then I risked my life by coming here, which I did not have to do once I was free."

I stared at him, my mind troubled. Could he be speaking the truth?

# CHAPTER 22

*J* was almost silent during the evening meal, turning Cole's words over and over in my head and trying to glean his true purpose from them. He had answered all of my questions openly, but somehow had provided no real answers. He didn't know how he had made it through the wilderness. He had heard wolves in the distance, but he had carried firewood with him and lit a fire each night which he believed had kept them away.

His horse had managed to escape its ties on his final night, however, and had fled. He had expressed remorse and sorrow that looked genuine, fearing that the animal must have since fallen afoul of one of the wolf packs or of a bear.

*You cannot believe such a ludicrous tale!* Dominic at least seemed to share none of my feelings of confusion.

I shrugged. "We can no more prove it to be false than he can prove it to be true. It is not entirely implausible. And he seems genuinely repentant, as much as such a thing can be judged from protestations alone."

*I don't trust him.*

I sighed. "No, neither do I. I wish I could talk to Lily."

*It isn't safe*, Dominic was quick to squash the suggestion I hadn't made. *Whatever he has claimed, you cannot risk leaving the castle grounds.*

I chewed on a ringlet, afraid he was right. After what had happened last time, it was too risky. Especially when Lily was unlikely to have any more insight than we did.

I glanced up at Dominic. "He claims to regret allowing himself to be carried along by his father's evil schemes." My voice dropped to a whisper, amazed at my own boldness. "Do you have no sympathy for such a situation?"

Dominic froze, such a stricken look on his face that I instantly regretted my words. Memories of his father could cause him nothing but pain, and he had shown he didn't deserve to be compared to Cole. I held my breath, hoping he might finally tell me something of his curse, but he remained silent. In fact, neither of us spoke for the rest of the meal.

When he asked me at the door if I would marry him in the morning, his voice seemed to hold a greater urgency than ever before. I refused him with a heavy heart. Cole might well be hiding the truth from me—but, if he was, he wasn't the only one in the castle doing so.

I spoke to Cole again the next day and the next, always with Dominic lurking just outside in the corridor. His story did not change, and he remained surprisingly accepting of his imprisonment in the dungeon cell, his manner humble and open.

On the third night after his arrival, I tossed and turned in my bed, too perturbed by the unanswerable dilemma to sleep. Finally, I threw off the covers and got up, wrapping my thickest robe around me.

I couldn't shake the feeling that Cole was hiding something from me. But each time I had visited, his uncomfortable glances in Dominic's direction had increased. I would never convince Dominic to let me see Cole alone, but I might never get the truth from him with the prince looming nearby glaring murder.

I crept from my chambers, listening intently for any sound of voices. Hopefully it was late enough that all the servants were in bed. As I passed by the entryway, a small sound caught my ears, and I stopped to peer carefully inside.

Dominic paced back and forth in the large space, a fire burning low in the fireplace despite the warmer turn in the weather. So, I wasn't the only one unable to sleep then. I watched him for a minute, captured by the strength in his long stride and the concern etched across his face. I knew he was motivated only by consideration for my safety, and I hated going behind his back in such a way. But our situation could not continue as it had.

When I arrived in the dungeon, a confused sounding guard hailed me, but I put on my most royal face and ordered him to take me to the prisoner. When he hesitated, I raised a single eyebrow, and he stammered an apology and bid me continue on. Calling after me, he ordered one of the other men to open the cell door for me.

When I stepped inside, Cole climbed slowly to his feet from a small nest of straw. I flushed at the poor conditions, although he had never complained. If he had come to rescue me, this was a sorry way to treat him.

He had clearly just awoken and looked confused, glancing behind me. "Princess Sophie! This is unexpected. You are alone?"

I ignored him, ordering the guard to close the door. I didn't think Cole would tell me the truth if he thought a guard might overhear us. When the man hesitated, I snapped, "Now!" He complied, the door swinging slowly closed, a mute protest against my order. I knew there was some risk, but I didn't think Cole was likely to harm me, even if he was lying. Not locked in a cell with guards outside.

"I wanted to speak with you alone. I think there's something you're not telling me."

Cole shook his head. "You're very perceptive, Princess. You're right, I didn't tell you the truth before."

I stepped back hurriedly, and he amended his words. "I didn't tell you the whole truth, that is. I couldn't, with the...prince standing there." He had noticed my reaction to his previous references to Dominic as the Beast, then.

"Well he is not here now. I will have the truth, if you please."

He sighed and rubbed his face. "It's hard to know where to begin. I escaped the prison in Marin with the help of some true friends, who did not wish to see me imprisoned. But I knew that I couldn't simply walk free. As I told you, I needed to atone for my past conduct."

He paused and glanced at me, ruefully. "I will admit that rescuing you did not immediately occur to me. However, a party of guards sent from Marin caught up with me, somewhere inside Talinos. Prince Jonathan and Princess Lily were with them."

I gasped at the mention of my sister. It did sound like her, though, to go chasing off after the escapee herself. Especially when she had been forced to sit idle in Marin while I came here. Although she hadn't mentioned it to me when we had spoken in the forest. But that had been many weeks ago. Perhaps my clue from the mirror had directed their search.

"I had as little luck convincing them of my change of heart as I have had with you. But it quickly became apparent to me that they were far more concerned about the darkness in Palinar than they were about me. They seemed to think I was spreading the curse around the kingdoms or something."

He shrugged as if confused by such a concept, and I narrowed my eyes in thought. Once again that sounded like something Lily and Jon would have said. It was, in fact, exactly what we had feared. But I knew more now than I had known previously. The curse on Palinar, if it could even be called that, was far more complex than we had assumed. It wasn't the whole of the kingdom that had been cursed, only the royal family, and then Dominic separately—possibly, that part was still conjecture.

Jon's godmother had been clear that the darkness twisting

Dominic had found its way through him into the Tourney, and that the Tourney must therefore be destroyed. But we had merely assumed that the same darkness infected Cole and his family. Perhaps it had been pure greed that motivated them after all?

Cole had paused, as if aware I was considering his words, but when I said nothing, he continued. "I could also see how concerned Princess Lily was about you. So, I offered to prove the truth of my words by rescuing you. And all of Palinar, if I could manage it. They didn't like the idea, of course, but I was their only option. And I suppose they considered anything better than you remaining betrothed to a cursed monster who would keep you prisoner here."

I opened my mouth to tell him that I wasn't a prisoner, but closed it without speaking. In every way that mattered, I was one. And I could no more deny that Dominic was cursed than that I was trapped here. I didn't need Cole to tell me how much Lily hated the situation.

"The question is whether you know about Palinar's succession laws." Cole's abrupt change of topic caught me by surprise.

"Succession? No, I don't think it's ever come up." Uneasily I wondered why it had not. I knew the king was dead—why had I never asked why Dominic remained a prince? I suppose I had just assumed that everything was frozen while the curse remained.

"I'm not surprised." Cole's voice sounded dark, his eyes expressing anger and disgust that I somehow knew wasn't directed at me. "I'm sure he has done everything he can to conceal the truth from you."

I wished I could deny it, but it was exactly what Dominic had done, even ordering the servants to silence.

"Palinar has rather unusual succession laws. The heir doesn't automatically inherit on the death of the previous monarch. Instead, the throne is considered vacant and the heir a regent, until such time as he—or she—speaks the binding words of the coronation in the great throne room in the palace of the capital."

I frowned at him. Why would Dominic not have been crowned?

Sudden realization broke through. While the curse continued, he could not speak. There was no way for him to speak the coronation oath. So, I had been right that the whole kingdom was trapped in place until the curse was lifted.

"But," said Cole, immediately dispelling my wrong impression. "There is a limit. The heir must speak the oath within three years, three months, three weeks and three days of the death or abdication of the previous monarch."

I stared at him, my eyes widening. When exactly had King Nicolas died? *Time is running out*, the servants had said.

"But…what happens if the heir does not do so?"

Cole took a deep breath. "Then the heir forfeits his position, and the crown goes to whichever Palinaran royal is the first to make the oath. Of course, usually that would be whichever royal had the most support from the nobles, people, and guards. Especially the guards. I believe it has only ever happened once before, and they barred the entrance to the throne room to all except their preferred royal."

My mind raced. "But what if there are no royals?" None who could speak the oath, anyway. The entire kingdom was as incapacitated as Dominic.

"What, indeed. We fear it means the whole kingdom will remain forever cursed."

I leaned back against the stone wall, clutching my robe around me. "But what can we do?"

Cole leaned forward. "It's clear you have some sort of softness for the prince, you even seem able to understand his growls, somehow." He paused as if hoping I would explain, but I remained silent. "But it is equally clear that he cannot—or will not—fulfill the coronation requirements. The allocated time must be getting close. Do you know the date King Nicolas died?"

I shook my head, and he looked disappointed. "Well, we will

need to find out, somehow or other." He took a deep breath. "Because it's up to you—to us—to save Palinar."

I had come to this castle with exactly that aim, but I still wasn't sure how I could do so, or what role Cole thought he would play. "What do you mean?"

"We must marry."

I jerked backwards and bumped my head against the stone wall behind me. Rubbing the spot with one hand, I glared at him. "You must be mad. Even if I had any desire to do so, I am already betrothed. I will not break my engagement and risk destruction on my own kingdom." Was I never to cease receiving strange proposals?

Cole looked apologetic. "I know it's not what you would have hoped for. But we cannot see any other way. Your engagement is not with Dominic, exactly. It is with the heir of Palinar. And when those three years, three months, three weeks, and three days pass, he will no longer be the heir. And there will be no Palinaran of royal blood to take his place. But if, as soon as that moment has passed, we are married, then our marriage will make you Palinaran. You can then claim the throne. And you will have indeed married the future king of Palinar. We believe it will be enough to satisfy the ancient laws."

"We?"

"Prince Jonathan, Princess Lily and me."

I was still almost too shocked to process his words. "You're trying to tell me that Lily wants me to marry *you*?"

Cole chuckled darkly. "Oh no. She hates the idea. But they had no other Palinaran to hand. Certainly, no other who was willing to brave the dangers and attempt to reach you. And the only thing she hates worse than the idea of you marrying me, is the idea of you being trapped here forever by the curse with only the Beast for company."

I frowned. As incomprehensible as it seemed, his words made

sense. If we broke the curse, at least Lily and I would be reunited, however distasteful my husband.

But I could not accept such a thing. I was already betrothed. I stared across at him.

He sighed. "Am I really such a terrible prospect? I know I've made mistakes in the past, but I honestly want to make restitution for them."

I tried to look at him through objective eyes. His manner did seem to have changed since I had last seen him in Marin. He wasn't much older than me and, physically, he was attractive. Perhaps I might even grow to love him. My mind recoiled from the thought. But I couldn't reject his words out of hand, not if it truly was the only way to save Palinar.

While I stared at him, the door crashed open, and we both flinched violently. The Beast's roar exploded in the confined space as he burst into the cell. Cole leaped toward me and, for a moment, my confused mind wondered if he meant to protect or attack me.

He had barely brushed against me, however, before Dominic leaped forward and thrust him away. He flew through the air and smashed against the far wall. Sliding to the ground before slowly pushing himself back up, he faced the growling Dominic with surprising bravery.

I looked between the two of them as my mind registered what my hand was telling me. Cole had thrust a piece of parchment into my fingers, unseen by Dominic.

*What were you thinking?* yelled Dominic, his eyes still on Cole, but his words clearly directed at me.

"I needed to speak to him," I said, wishing my voice weren't so shaky after the many unexpected turns of the night.

*It isn't safe!*

"I'm fine, aren't I?" I pushed away from the wall and slipped from the room. When the prince didn't follow me, I called his name sharply.

He backed out of the room, his eyes not leaving Cole until the door swung shut, pushed by one of the guards. Then he turned and grabbed my arm. I let him tow me out of the dungeon and away from the listening guards. But as soon as we were out into the main part of the castle, I dug my heels in, pulling him to a halt.

He turned to me and the angry words dropped from my lips. I had never seen him look so desperate or so frantic. *Promise me you won't try that again.*

"I cannot promise you such a thing. And you should not ask it of me. I am not your servant or even your subject. And I will never get Cole to talk if you are always there glowering at him."

*He talked then, did he?* Dominic sounded disparaging, and I bristled.

"He would have, if you hadn't burst in so abruptly and interrupted us." The lie tasted like ashes in my mouth, bitter and all too light. It had been far too easy to say. But I could hardly tell Dominic the truth of what Cole had said, he would rip him limb from limb. And I was desperate to get away from him so I could read the parchment. I needed time alone to think.

Dominic pulled me closer. *Please, Sophie,* he whispered, his desperate eyes holding mine. *Please. I only want to protect you. Don't you see the way he looks at you?* He shivered and his voice went hard. *I will not let him touch you again.*

When I said nothing, refusing to give him the reassurance he wanted, he abruptly dropped his hand and stepped back from me, his face becoming angry and hard. *You may not be my subject, but this is still my castle. I will order the guards to deny you entry should you try such a thing again. You can save yourself trouble, and them embarrassment, by not making the attempt.*

I sucked in an angry breath and glared at him. "I have never forgotten that this is your castle, or that I do not belong here. Believe me, I am always searching for a way to leave."

He jerked back as if I had struck him, hurt flashing across his face almost too fast to see. I immediately regretted my hotheaded words. I had lashed out in my anger and spoken more harshly than I had intended.

I turned and ran toward my room.

I made it inside before I thought to look down at the parchment still clutched in my hand. I could see my name written across the outside in an all-too-familiar handwriting. I swayed, almost collapsing. A letter for me. From Lily.

# CHAPTER 23

*I* climbed into bed and sat there, a branch of lit candles on a table nearby, stroking the single word. Seeing my name in her hand made me feel near to her, and I wanted to enjoy that feeling for a moment. Because I feared that once I read its contents, my emotions would be once again thrown into turmoil.

Finally, I could delay no longer.

---

Dearest Sophie,

I miss you every day. Jon tells me to have trust in you, and I do! It is the Beast I do not—and cannot—trust. I cannot rest easy while you are helpless in his grasp. And I am determined that you be freed from your betrothal. I know that you left with such high hopes of breaking it yourself and coming back to us...but so much time has passed. I am becoming desperate. You were never supposed to be there alone!

Neither of us were ever supposed to have to be alone. I feel that I have failed you, and I don't know what to do.

Oh dear, Jon is telling me off for writing such a depressing letter. I just wish I could speak to you. Could know that the Beast did not blame you for those wolves injuring him…

I love you, Sophie!

---

She hadn't signed her name. She must have known I would easily recognize her handwriting. I cried as I read the words over and over. It seemed strange that she made no mention of Cole, but I could not deny her desperation to free me from the Beast. It was surprisingly easy to see how even Cole would seem a better option to her.

And I had just been treated to yet another display of the Beast's arrogance and temper. So why didn't I feel relieved to be offered a way out?

I didn't attempt to visit Cole the next day. It felt weak of me not to defy Dominic's order, especially when Cole might have been injured in the confrontation and need medical care I knew Dominic would never provide. But I needed more time to consider his plan.

He had made it this far on his own; if I could free him from the dungeon and requisition two horses from the stables, perhaps he truly could get us to the capital. We wouldn't even really be stealing the animals since, once we were crowned, this castle and all its possessions would belong to our future child.

I shuddered at the thought. I had no desire to have children with Cole. Or to attempt the flight to the capital, even if I now knew Dominic himself would be unable to pursue us.

I told myself I hesitated out of fear of the wolves, but part of me knew it wasn't true. I just didn't want to marry Cole. I still wanted to believe there was another way to free Palinar.

But when I asked Tara for the date the king had died, her answer shocked me. She was clearly reluctant to answer, but obviously unable to think of an excuse not to. And it turned out Palinar had been cursed for three long years before I arrived. And I had been here for over three months. Time truly was running out for Dominic to claim the throne.

When I realized how close we were to the deadline, I pleaded with her to tell me the truth of the curse, but she merely burst into tears and ran from the room.

I could only assume she reported our conversation to the rest of the servants, because they all began to act strangely. Every single one of them seemed almost as antagonistic toward Cole as Dominic was. But unlike Dominic, who stormed around the castle avoiding me, they all seemed unnaturally cheerful.

Tara soon told me this was because they had finally chosen a date for my birthday ball. I suggested this was hardly the time, but Tara insisted defiantly that they were all extremely excited about it and had planned it for their upcoming monthly shared half-day. I had long ago insisted that the ball must include all the servants—since it would hardly be a ball with only two people—so I could hardly tell them to cancel it now.

Plus, I was informed that preparations were already well underway.

Every time I tried to go somewhere quiet to think, a servant would appear with questions about the ball. I felt as if I had somehow stumbled into a farce. I wasn't even safe in my own chamber. My attempt to retreat there was foiled by the arrival of Tara and Lottie with a bevy of castle seamstresses. They all chattered loudly as they measured me for a ball gown, not leaving any openings for me to speak.

As soon as they removed the last pin, I fled, determined to

find somewhere where I could be alone. But I had barely settled myself in an unused room than Gordon appeared saying I was urgently needed in the kitchens. I sighed. Clearly Gordon's expert hide-and-seek skills were now going to be used against me.

I considered ordering him away, but I couldn't bear to send him to face the wrath of the other servants for having failed to bring me. So, I followed behind as slowly as I could, tuning out his constant stream of talk in an attempt to think.

I complained to Dominic at the evening meal, but he just shrugged and said the date had been none of his choosing. I huffed in frustration, but considering it was his first comment to me of the evening, I could hardly be surprised at his curt response.

"Why are you so determined to keep me from discovering the truth?" I exclaimed.

*That man doesn't hold any truth!* Dominic gripped his wine glass so hard, I thought it would shatter. *I am your betrothed, and I am responsible for your safety. If you refuse to see his true intentions in his eyes, I will have to ensure you never see him again. Cole will never leave that cell.*

"Never?" I almost growled myself in my irritation. "One day, when Palinar is freed, we will need to return him to the Marinese prisons, at least. Or are you trying to say you believe your kingdom will always be cut off and cursed?"

He stared at me. *The curse has nothing to do with it. I would not be returning him to Marin, even if the way were clear.*

I frowned. "What do you mean? He is their prisoner, not ours."

Dominic shrugged and looked down into his wine glass. *He may have been their prisoner. But now he's mine. If they wanted to keep him, they should have made sure he didn't escape.*

I stood to my feet. Indignation burned at this suggestion that Jon and Lily had been negligent. He spoke of Marin so disparagingly, as if only he knew how to correctly rule. As if Palinar was an example of a well-managed kingdom. "Why must you be so stubborn? So sure of yourself? Perhaps if you had worked with the other kingdoms in the first place, none of this would have happened!"

*You know nothing of what happened.*

"No, I don't." I almost yelled the words at him. But then I sighed and my voice dropped low. "And that is precisely the problem. How can I help you when you won't be honest with me?"

Dominic also stood to his feet, and for a moment I thought he meant to yell back at me. But when he spoke, his words were a quieter whisper than my own had been. *If I was honest with you, you wouldn't wish to help me.*

Then he turned and strode from the room. I stared after him in dismay. Just when I had found some measure of peace here, my whole world had once again been turned upside down.

I could almost feel the hours ticking by as I tried to make up my mind about what I should do. I could understand now the urgency that had made all the servants so tense. But their continued refusal to tell me anything made me want to scream. How could I begin to know how to rescue them, when I didn't even know the full story of the curse?

If I couldn't find another way to break the curse, then I was left with only two options. Marry Cole and break the curse, or leave an entire kingdom cut off from the rest of the lands. But if I broke the curse this way, what would happen to Dominic? If he missed his opportunity to be crowned, would he simply remain a silent beast forever? The possibility haunted me.

Dominic himself, however, continued to avoid me. Perhaps his absence should have made it easy to tell Cole I would agree to his plan but, somehow, whenever I tried to make myself return to his cell, my feet refused to carry me there. I could not bear to speak the words of agreement and turn my back on any hope of rescuing Dominic. Despite his current attitude toward me, I knew that he truly believed himself to be protecting me. Could I condemn him for that?

I missed our walks and our rides and our reading. I had only entered the library once since Cole's arrival, and I hadn't returned to the rose garden at all. I couldn't bear to be reminded of all the happy hours Dominic and I had passed in those places. How could I build myself yet another life in the capital with Cole? If we did break the curse, how could we possibly rule a kingdom in which we knew almost no one? Did Cole still have some contacts in the capital from before his family had moved to Marin?

Or perhaps we could find Princess Adelaide. She might still be alive. And then we could abdicate in her favor. It was the best plan I had been able to come up with, despite relying on the shaky premise that we could actually locate the missing Adelaide.

When I awoke one morning, only four days from the coronation deadline, I told myself that as unpalatable as the prospect was, I needed to do the right thing by the greatest number of people. I needed to save Palinar.

As Lottie dressed me, the occasional tear slipped out, despite my best efforts. After several long minutes, she tentatively spoke. *Do you...do you love this Cole, Princess Sophie?*

I jerked and she lost hold of my laces. "Love him? Of course I do not!"

She hesitated. *We have all been afraid that you might like him better than the prince, despite your betrothal. Some of the maids saw him when he was being taken to the dungeon, and they said he was very handsome.* She paused again. *We do not want to lose you.*

My heart squeezed as their strange behavior began to make sense. "He is handsome enough, I suppose. But, in Marin, he and his father and sister plotted to kill the ducal family and to take over the duchy. His father even burned a rival's warehouse, to advance his plan. A warehouse that held essential supplies for the people. Plus, the fire spread to some nearby homes and a baby nearly died."

Lottie gasped.

"Cole was going to marry my friend Celine and become a prince of Lanover. They would have succeeded, too, if we hadn't stumbled on a solution at the last possible moment. So, I guess all of that is to say that, no, I don't like him at all."

*Oh.* Lottie sounded relieved, and I felt guilty for reassuring her when her fears were actually legitimate. I was about to leave. Only I was doing it for her—her and the rest of her kingdom.

But as she laced up my dress, my mind wandered back over my words. There was something in the story I hadn't considered, and my mind kept circling back to it now. Sir Oswald's plan to overthrow Marin had involved Cole marrying Celine and becoming a prince. And now Cole's new plan involved his marrying me and becoming a king.

Dominic had been so insistent that he saw something in Cole's eyes. I had dismissed it as irrational fancy, but I suddenly remembered an old conversation Lily had once had with the young Princess Daisy. What was it Daisy had said? That Cole had a funny look when he watched Celine. Something like that.

If this plan succeeded, Cole would go from condemned prisoner to king. He had been willing to risk a lot to go from minor nobility to prince. How much would he be willing to risk for this?

I sank into the nearest chair, hardly noticing when Lottie announced she was leaving the room. Carefully I examined the evidence and considered my own true motivations.

He had given me a letter from Lily. But while the sentiments of the letter rang true, it didn't actually endorse Cole's plan. I had always found it strange that it didn't mention him specifically.

What if Cole had somehow stolen it from Lily? It seemed far-fetched, but hardly more so than his story.

He had given me the information on the Palinaran succession laws, facts I had confirmed in my single visit to the library but, surely, they were general knowledge within Palinar.

He had risked his life to come here, but then he had risked much in Marin, too. And with the snow melting and the flowers dying, something about the state of things in Palinar was changing. Perhaps the danger had lessened.

I turned my mind to my own motivations and was unhappy with what I found. I had been so busy telling myself I was making a sacrifice for others, when in reality I merely wanted to be free. I had been so grieved at the loss of my friendship with Dominic since Cole had arrived, and so afraid that I would never see Lily again, that I had convinced myself having her back would be enough.

And I had used the excuse that Lily wanted me to do it. But it wasn't Lily who was here. She didn't have the whole story, and she wasn't the one making the decision. Whether Cole had lied or not, he was not the right king for Palinar.

I shook my head in disgust with my own self-delusion. Who knew what further cage I had nearly condemned myself to? Or what harm I might have brought to this kingdom. They had already suffered from one terrible monarch, I wouldn't be responsible for saddling them with another.

I would see Dominic in the evening at my birthday ball. I would just make him tell me the truth about the curse, and then together we would come up with a plan to save Palinar. In the next three days. I groaned. But I also knew going with Cole could not be the right decision.

I sat at my small table and wrote a letter. The guards might be forbidden to let me in to see Cole, but I doubted they had received any orders about letters. I knew I had no real need to tell him of my decision, but I wanted to, if only to keep myself accountable. If I kept an escape plan in the back of my mind, it might prevent me from putting my full mind into finding a better solution.

Sure enough, when I delivered Cole's letter, the guards hemmed and hawed, but eventually agreed to thrust it through the slot usually used for food delivery. I watched the floating letter disappear, and then left the dungeon with a lighter heart.

# CHAPTER 24

*I* had expected to feel nothing but frustration for the ball, but a new sense of hope had entered my heart, and I couldn't quite resist getting sucked into the excitement of the preparations. Tara and Lottie had recruited several more maids to assist them, and the atmosphere in my chamber was light and festive.

They speculated about what Dominic might wear, giggling as they declared him handsome despite his beastly features. I raised an eyebrow but didn't dispute their claims. I wouldn't have called him handsome exactly, although he was certainly compelling, demanding your attention in a way that couldn't be denied. And he had most definitely been handsome before the curse—at least if his portrait was anything to go by.

They all made me close my eyes while they brought out my dress and carefully placed it over my head. It slid across my skin, as soft as silk, and settled around me with considerable weight. I was led to a mirror and then told to look.

When I did, I gasped. Tight fitting across the bodice, the gown flared out at the waist into the biggest skirt I had ever seen. But that wasn't what had elicited the reaction. The entire dress glowed. Shimmering in the candlelight, it shone like…"sunshine," I whispered. "And moonbeams." When I looked closer, I realized the entire dress had been woven out of actual gold thread, mingled with silver.

"However did you create such a thing? And so quickly." It must be worth a small fortune.

They all laughed and assured me their seamstresses had been more than up to the task. *I think they were merely relieved to have something more challenging than servant's clothes to work on*, said Tara. *It's been years now since any ladies visited this castle.*

They arranged my hair so that it was only half up, the curls cascading over one shoulder, and then declared me perfect. I actually blushed at their extravagant compliments. I couldn't help wondering what Dominic would think when he saw me.

The ballroom had somehow been polished in the short time since the servants had announced the ball, and the rose garden had managed to provide enough blooms to decorate the large space. I stood at the top of the shallow flight of stairs that led down into the room and took a deep breath. I tried to tell myself my nerves were due to the roomful of invisible people, and not to the one person I could see.

As I descended, light hit my dress from every direction, the chandeliers reflecting in the tall mirrors that lined the walls. Now I truly did shine like the sun.

The effect of the mirrors made the room seem much larger than it truly was, a gorgeous riot of silver and gold and crystal, punctuated with the red of the roses. I reached the bottom of the stairs and looked up into Dominic's face. He stood several steps away from me, dressed in a long jacket that matched the deep red of the roses and was embroidered with gold and silver thread that glowed like my gown.

His piercing blue eyes were locked on me, and the expression in them made me swallow nervously. He strode forward, stopping far too close for comfort.

*You look...beautiful.* He held out his hand in a silent request for a dance.

I dipped down into a slight curtsey before placing my hand in his. "And you look very dashing."

An invisible orchestra struck up a waltz, and his hand encircled my waist, pulling me against him more firmly than the dance strictly called for. I didn't protest. He twirled me around the room as effortlessly as if I were flying, leading us through the other dancers who I couldn't see. My heart soared at the beauty surrounding me and the exhilaration of the movement, and for a moment I forgot the way time pressed in upon us.

Apparently, Dominic felt the same way, because when the music paused at the end of the song, he whispered, *Can we forget everything else, just for now, and dance?*

I nodded my agreement, ready after the last few days to be free from the pressure and stress for one evening. We danced, clasped close together, as if in an embrace, for song after song. Dominic's strength made even the most difficult of moves simple, and he twirled me through the air as easily with one hand as with two.

This whole strange summer had been like a dream, removed from the normal realities of life. But never so much as during this ball, when I danced through a ballroom that appeared empty, but was filled with the sound of other dancers. Sometimes I forgot that Dominic and I weren't the only ones there, and then Tara or Lottie would call a greeting as they, presumably, swung past in the dance, and the illusion would be shattered.

Every few songs we paused to seek the drinks and refreshments that had been set up on a long table to one side of the stairway. Tara sidled up to me at one point to let me know that Samuel had danced the last two dances with Lottie. She sounded triumphant, and I wondered what she had done to bring the two together.

At one such break I saw an entire pile of sticky buns leaving the table, and caught Gordon in the act of sneaking out of the ball. He assured me that he wasn't up to any mischief and would, in fact, be on his best behavior—he just needed me to refrain from letting Gilda know he had disappeared. He assured me earnestly that he wouldn't have dreamed of doing so, except that one of the stable boys had found a lizard longer than his forearm out near the stables, and if he didn't go now, he might miss it.

I laughed and swore myself to secrecy, and then Dominic swung me back into the dance. I could feel his silent chuckles, and I wondered if he had been fascinated by lizards as a boy, too. I remembered how uncomfortable he had been when I included the servants in my birthday cake on my actual birthday. He showed no discomfort now, to be dancing with them all. I couldn't pinpoint a moment when his attitude had changed—it had been as gradual as the warming weather.

When I smiled to myself at the thought, he looked down at me quizzically, but I just shrugged, not wanting to put it into words. We danced for dance after dance, but eventually I grew weary enough to welcome a rest. He offered me his arm and led me through a curtain and onto a balcony which looked out over the gardens. I leaned on the stone balustrade and stared up at the stars. Here I could truly believe that we were all alone.

"I keep asking myself what is the strangest thing I have experienced since coming here, but I cannot decide." When I looked sideways at Dominic, I saw he was watching my face. I flushed, glad the darkness hid the color in my cheeks.

*I have been thinking that I have never experienced such an evening. I had always considered balls tiresome before this.* He shook his head as if unable to believe his foolishness.

"Ha! I knew you were delaying this one." I smiled. "Although, in truth, I also thought I was sick of balls after the endless number we endured during the Tourney."

*Ah, yes. The Tourney.* Darkness closed over his expression. *Will it always stand between us?*

I straightened and spun around to lean backwards against the stone rail. "How can it not? It's the reason for our betrothal and for my presence here."

*I never intended to use a Tourney to choose a bride. But what other choice did I have, trapped here as I am?*

I bit my lip, not wanting to ruin the evening with a fight. "You could have chosen not to seek a bride at all, could you not?"

*That was...not an option.*

I frowned, willing him to go on, but he fell silent. I clenched my teeth, sick of his silence and secrecy. "My good friend Celine broke her leg in the first trial and had to compete anyway, for weeks and weeks. And another girl, barely old enough even to participate, nearly died. Was that what you wanted in order to find a bride strong enough to withstand you? They say each Tourney reflects the man who called it..."

His face went still, his hand clenching into a fist. *I did not know it would be like that.* He leaned his hands against the stone and looked out into the night. *But I can understand why you want nothing to do with me. A twisted psyche like mine does not deserve a bride as beautiful as you.* He barked a laugh. *Each of our outsides reflects our insides, do they not?*

My anger melted away, and I had to hold back tears. "When I entered this evening, I thought that I had never seen you look so handsome."

He shook his head dismissively. *I did look handsome once. But it did not serve me in the end. Good looks could not prevent my curse.*

"Please tell me what could have done so," I begged. "There is still time. Let me help you!"

A spasm ran across his features, but he did not turn to look at me. I moved closer and reached my hand up to cup his face. Gently I turned him toward me, angling his head down so that I could look into his eyes. "Tell me what I can do to save you, Beast," I whispered.

His breath stilled, and I realized how close his face was to mine. He moved fractionally toward me, and my own breath hitched in my throat. I felt the warmth of his skin beneath my hand and smelled the musky scent I had come to associate with him.

A tingle of anticipation filled me as he moved closer still, and all rational thought was overwhelmed by a sudden desire to feel his lips pressed hard against mine. He moved even closer, and I felt the faintest touch, no more than an impression of warmth, before he pulled abruptly away.

I fell back, gulping deep breaths of the cold air in an effort to cool my cheeks, flushed with embarrassment. I risked a small glance at him, but he was looking out into the garden once more, his hands gripping the stone so tightly I feared he might crush it.

*I owe you so many apologies, Sophie, that I know words could never be enough. But I will show you my regret with my actions. No longer will I take advantage of the fact that you are trapped here. You are free to move through the castle, and to come and go, as you please. You may order your evening meal in your room, if you wish it, and you may order me away from you. I will obey.*

I stared at him, my mind trying to keep up with the change of subject. "I may go anywhere I please?"

A pained look crossed his face, but he seemed to brace himself. "Yes. I will tell the guards to let you pass freely."

Oh, he thought it was Cole on my mind. But I was thinking of someone far more important. "And what of your bedchamber?"

His head whipped around to stare at me, and I flushed again. I hurried to explain myself. "Am I free to visit the royal mirror?"

*Oh.* He relaxed slightly. *Yes, you are free to visit it whenever you please. Consider it a very belated birthday gift from me.*

"It is just the gift I was hoping for." I smiled at him, giddy with excitement. Not only at the prospect of seeing Lily but also of feeling connected to the other kingdoms again. Who knew what wisdom I might receive from my family?

Spontaneously I flung my arms into the air and twirled

around and around. When I stopped Dominic was watching me with an expression half of amusement, half of sadness. *You want to go right now, don't you?*

I froze. "Oh! Can I?"

When he nodded, I actually jumped up and down before rushing over and placing a kiss upon his cheek. "Oh, thank you, thank you."

I ran from the room, holding my huge skirts out of the way so they wouldn't hamper my progress. At the door of the ballroom, I looked back. He stood where I had left him on the balcony, one hand pressed against the place where I had kissed his cheek. I bit my lip, but the pull to the mirror overwhelmed everything else, and I ran on.

Thoughts not only of my twin but of my parents and my brother and sister-in-law filled my mind. And my adorable little niece and nephew. I couldn't wait to see them again, even if I could only view them from afar.

I was too distracted by my thoughts to pay attention to where I was going, so I didn't see the dark figure in the corridor until I collided with him. I would have fallen if he hadn't gripped my arms. My mind raced, full of confusion. I had just left Dominic behind, but no one else was visible and solid like this.

And then my eyes adjusted to the darkness, and I remembered there was one other person in the castle who could present such an obstacle.

"How? What?" I sputtered, trying to get out a coherent question. "How are you here?"

Cole smirked. "How did I escape from the Marinese prison? That's the question you should have been asking. Really you royals are all the same. Complacent."

"Let me go right now, or I'll scream," I warned him.

"Oh, I wouldn't do that, if I were you," he said. I took a deep breath, preparing to yell as loudly as I could, despite his words, and he hurried on. "Not if you value your sister's life."

I shut my mouth instantly, the blood draining from my head. Lily. "What do you mean? Tell me immediately."

He shook his head. "You really should have agreed to come with me. We could have kept everything perfectly pleasant, you know."

"I will never marry you!" I spit the words at him, almost too enraged to speak.

"Oh, I think you will. And you'll speak the words of the coronation and make me king. Otherwise you can watch your sister bleed out in front of you."

"Why should I believe you?" I asked, scrambling to think clearly in the midst of my panic.

He shrugged. "I assume the Beast brought the Palinaran royal mirror with him? Ask it to show you Lily. You'll see soon enough that I have her in my custody. She's waiting in the Palinaran capital with friends of mine who know what to do if you attempt to defy me."

I tried to slow my frantic breathing. If he was invoking the mirror so casually, he clearly did not fear what it might show me.

"And don't think of turning to that Beast of yours for help," he continued. "If I don't return, my friends know what to do. Don't think you could get to her in time."

Tears filled my eyes, though I fought against them. "You cannot think he will just let me leave with you."

Cole shrugged. "That's up to you to figure out. Tell him any tale you like to convince him to let you go and not to follow you. Feel free to be as astonished as you like when my escape is discovered. I'm going to the capital immediately—I've had enough of this creepy place with its floating objects. But I have no desire to travel the whole way with an enraged Beast on my tail, so I'm leaving you here for now. Check my story in the mirror, if you like. Then you spin that monster a convincing story and follow me within a day—alone—or you won't see your sister, or her betrothed, alive again." He shivered. "I don't know how you've been able to stand this filthy place. I think when I'm king, I will order it razed to the ground."

I stared at him in horror. "But what about the wolves, and… the bears?"

He shrugged. "You can't imagine I would really have risked my life riding here through a dangerous wasteland, do you? The wasteland and the animals are gone, they've been slowly disappearing for weeks. The rest of the kingdoms will figure it out soon enough and start sending parties in. But we'll have taken the crown by then, and none of them will be able to dispute the legality of it."

He let me go and stepped backwards, shaking his head. "I nearly had you, too. I could see it in your face before that creature burst in on us in the dungeons." He shrugged. "Oh well, maybe this way is better. Acting is exhausting."

I trembled uncontrollably as he faded away into the dark. All I could think of was Lily. I had to rescue Lily.

# PART III
# THE CAPITAL

# CHAPTER 25

*I* must have stood there, frozen in place, for several minutes. And then my legs were moving of their own accord, and I was running toward the Beast's chamber. I burst through the door and ripped back the curtain, my mind fully focused on Lily.

"Show me my sister, please," I said, running my words together in my haste. The fog appeared almost instantly, and I held my breath, knowing there was no use in hoping Cole had been lying.

Sure enough, when the mirror cleared, I saw Lily, lying with her head in Jon's lap. Both of them had ties around their hands and feet, and Jon was glaring at a guard I could just see in the corner of the room. I placed my hand against the mirror, tears filling my eyes. How had he got hold of them?

He must have stolen the letter Lily was part way through writing me. Which would explain why she hadn't signed it, and why it didn't mention anything specific about Cole. He had probably been afraid that if he forced her to write a fake letter, she would find a way to include a coded message to me.

I stepped back and pulled the curtain across the mirror, not wanting to see any more of the scene. At least they were together and looked healthy enough for the moment. I could only imagine how angry they must be, however.

I left the room and slowly made my way back toward the ballroom. Would the Beast still be there? It was a place to start, at least. The raging part of me wanted to tell him the truth and send him after Cole. But I knew I couldn't do that. It was all too likely he had spoken the truth, and his men had instructions to kill their hostages if he didn't return.

Another thought hit me. I couldn't send Dominic after Cole, even if I wanted to. He couldn't leave the castle grounds. Because, while some aspects of the reverse curse on the kingdom itself were lifting, Dominic's curse remained firmly in place.

And yet I felt an utter certainty that if he knew what was happening, he would insist on accompanying me, despite the risk to himself. Which meant I had to make sure he didn't even suspect the truth. I decided on a convincing story and rehearsed it in my mind.

When I reentered the ballroom, I found Dominic still standing on the balcony where I had left him. He turned, clearly surprised at my reappearance. But his surprise quickly turned to concern, and he strode forward to meet me.

*What is it? What has happened? What have you seen?*

I felt grateful my story didn't require me to hide my grief and fear. "I saw Lily." An unplanned sob broke through.

Dominic took both my hands, holding them in a firm grasp. *Tell me.*

"She...she's sick. Really sick." I lowered my voice. "She might die. And she's calling for me." I focused my gaze on him, filling my expression with desperate pleading. "You said earlier this evening that I was free now, that you wouldn't keep me trapped any longer. Did you mean it? I have to go to her."

Dominic took a deep breath and dropped my hands, turning

away. Did he mean to take back his words? To tell me I couldn't go?

"Cole has shown that the passage is safe now," I said. "Everything is changing—like the snow melting and the flowers dying. Please! I have to go."

He turned back to me, his face a blank mask. *Of course, you must go. My carriage will take you to ensure your safety.* He took another deep breath, as if to steady himself. *I did mean what I said. I should never have kept you prisoner in the first place. How could a marriage between us ever have worked in such circumstances? I release you from our betrothal. Go, be with your sister. And only return if you wish to do so.*

"I...I...don't know what to say," I whispered. He had just given me what I had been seeking since my arrival, but I couldn't feel any relief or pleasure.

He laughed, no humor in the sound. *I must truly be a monster if my attempts to make some small retribution for my misdeeds meets with such astonishment.*

I shook my head. "No, I didn't mean..."

*Just go. You need to pack and get some sleep before your journey. I will have the carriage ready for you at dawn.*

My body responded to his order, leaving the room while my mind still struggled to think of the right thing to say. When I reached my chamber I cried deep, heaving sobs. I wasn't sure if I cried for myself, or for Lily, or for Dominic, or for Palinar. I suppose I cried for us all, and for the farewell that I should have had with Dominic.

I was waiting with my bags in the entrance hall before dawn broke. I had hardly slept, and Tara had been crying over me since I awoke. Even respectful Lottie had broken down and begged me to return, but I did not want to give them false hope. I had no idea what my future held.

When Tara asked me tearfully if I was leaving because I was in love with Cole, I shook my head in frustration. Obviously, Lottie hadn't passed on our conversation.

"Of course not," I snapped. "I'm leaving for my sister." I hoped they would all remember my words and understand my meaning if I should end up married to Cole.

His sneering, cruel expression when we parted flashed before my eyes, but I couldn't tell them the true source of my hatred for him. "He was a party to his father's plans to kill my sister's new family and destroy Marin. I could never love such a man."

A gasp sounded on my left, just as I heard the soft sound of a closing door to my right. I frowned at the small front door carved from the larger ones. Had it been open a moment ago?

More servants arrived and began carrying my bags out to the carriage. I shook off my distraction and followed them. This time I was able to greet the coachmen by name, not at all unnerved by the carriage that appeared to drive itself. I hadn't worked out how I would break the news of our true destination to them yet, but that was a job for after we had left the castle grounds.

Just as I was about to step into the carriage, however, I noticed a familiar head among the rose bushes. Telling the servants to wait, I hurried toward the garden, almost running through the spirals.

"Dominic," I said softly as I reached him in the center of the roses.

He started and spun around, seeming to drink me in with his eyes. *I had hoped I would see you again, but I did not like to intrude.*

"I couldn't leave without a proper farewell. I am...I am grateful for what you've done for me."

He shook his head. *Too little, too late. I see that now. I did not believe you would be able to see past my appearance, so I let my anger and my hurt pride control me. But you have taught me better, and for that I am grateful, even if I am never to see you again.*

I opened my mouth, but he held up a hand to silence me. *I am not looking for reassurances. I know we will not meet again. And I do not deserve anything else. But I have something for you. A proper birthday gift for you to remember me by.*

"I do not need a gift to remember you, Dominic."

He smiled slightly at my words, but reached for something behind him anyway. When he turned around, he held a single rose. I took it with a trembling hand, breathing in its sweet perfume. It was pure white at its center, the white softly blending into a cream with the faintest blush of pale pink, becoming deep pink only at the tips of the petals.

I stared at it in wonder. "I have never seen such a rose."

*I have worked with the gardeners to develop it as a gift for you. I feared it wouldn't be ready in time, but when I came out this morning, the first rose had bloomed. It is called Belle Sophia.*

I couldn't speak, my breath trapped in my throat and tears springing to my eyes. How long had he been growing it? I looked around the garden, trying to regain my composure, and sucked in a breath.

"You said it bloomed overnight?"

He nodded. *Ironic, isn't it?*

I looked around in shock. How had I not noticed as I rushed through the spirals? Overnight, the roses—the one remaining piece of the enchanted garden—had withered and died. Not a single bloom remained on the bare bushes.

*I will have the gardeners prepare the bush itself for travel, and when my carriage returns I will send it to you in Marin. But at least you can take this rose with you now.*

"Thank you, Dominic." I reached to touch his arm, but he pulled away from me, and I let my hand drop, hurt by his rejection. "Well, then…I suppose I had better be going."

*Yes. Goodbye, Sophie.*

"Goodbye, Dominic." The words felt at once too little and too much. I gripped the rose to my chest and hurried into the carriage, not looking back.

# CHAPTER 26

*J* watched the castle disappear in the back window of the carriage. Surely, they would discover Cole had escaped at any moment. What would Dominic do when that happened?

I still hadn't worked out *how* Cole had escaped. I had actually crept down to the dungeon in the middle of the night, afraid there might be guards down there in need of medical attention. I knew I should tell someone else what had happened, since I had no way to see the guards myself, but I didn't know who I could trust to keep my secret.

To my astonishment, I had been greeted at the entrance by the voice of the guard who had agreed to give Cole my letter. He had joked that he was becoming a postal service, although he had sounded slightly disapproving behind the levity. When I assured him that I had not brought another letter but had merely come to check if the prisoner wished to make any reply, he had informed me that all had been quiet since my previous visit and that no such request had been made by Cole.

I had left in shock but also grateful since it meant I could keep my secret a little longer. Cole must have gotten his hands on a godmother object, despite how rare they were supposed to be here. It was the only explanation for the ease of his escape. Twice now.

As soon as we passed through the now open gates, I thrust out a projection, searching for Lily with all of my mental strength. This time I burst through the lingering blockage on the first try, connecting with Lily instantly. Either I had become stronger or it had become weaker.

*Lily! Lily! Are you all right? Has he hurt you?*

*Sophie!* She groaned. *Cole made it to you, didn't he? I was hoping he would be eaten by a bear.*

*Don't say that! If he had been, his men would have killed you.*

*They could have tried,* she projected in a mutter.

I sighed. For all her defiance, she sounded tired.

A glance through the front window showed we had nearly reached the main road through the forest. *Just a minute,* I projected to Lily. *I need to talk to the coachmen.*

I banged on the roof of the carriage until I heard one of the coachmen call out, *Whoa!* and the horses slowly came to a stop. I clambered out, and stared up at where I knew they must be sitting. "We need to go to the Palinaran capital."

*I don't understand.*

"We're not going to Marin, we're going to your capital."

The second coachman spoke, sounding as uneasy as the first one. *I don't think His Highness would like that.*

I put my hands on my hips and glared at them. "He told you to take me to my sister, did he not? Well, my sister is in the capital."

*I suppose...I suppose he did say that.*

I sensed their capitulation and smiled at them. "Excellent. How long will it take us to get there? We need to hurry, you know."

*About two days, Princess Sophie.*

I frowned. Two days. Even if I could defeat Cole, I had no hope of returning to Dominic before his opportunity to claim the throne had disappeared. I bit my lip; there was nothing I could do.

"Let's be on our way, then." I climbed back into the vehicle, and we were soon back in motion.

*What was that all about?*

*I lied to Dominic. He thinks he's sending me back to Marin, so I had to give the coachmen new orders.*

*Dominic? Oh! You mean the Beast.*

I frowned again. *Please don't call him that.*

She sent me an image of her shrugging shoulders. *If you wish it.* She didn't ask for an explanation, although I could feel the curiosity in her mind, and I was grateful for her restraint.

*You know you can't possibly marry Cole, Soph,* she projected instead.

*I will if it's the only way to save your and Jon's lives. You know you would do the same for me.*

*I refuse to let that slimy, stinking, lying low life win.* I had known Lily would be mad, and I couldn't help but smile at the outrage in her voice. It was just such a relief to speak with her again.

*Well, we do have one advantage he doesn't know about. I assume you didn't tell him about our connection.*

*Of course not!*

I snorted. *He tried to convince me to agree to come with him at first, saying that you had hatched the plan together. He would have received a shock when we got outside the castle grounds, and you started screaming in my mind that it was all a lie.*

Lily sent me an affectionate smile. *I knew you wouldn't be taken in by him, no matter what he said.* I shifted uncomfortably on my seat, aware of how close I had come.

*What happened?* I asked her. *How did he capture you?*

She groaned. *I had taken to riding up into the hills around Marin every day and gazing out into Palinar. Eventually I noticed changes in the wilderness. They were subtle at first, but I became increasingly sure of them. Like trees in the distance that hadn't been there before.*

*I decided to ride out a short way and see what I could find. Jon insisted on accompanying me as long as I promised to turn back at the first hint of something dangerous. He only let me go at all because he knew I was going crazy wanting to try, and he thought we would have to turn back within minutes of the border.*

She sighed. *Only we didn't. Not within minutes, not even within hours. We kept waiting for howls, or paw prints, or something. But instead we found streams and trees, even deer and rabbits once we got far enough in.*

*By the time either of us realized I was actually right, we had gone so far in that we couldn't get back that night. We made camp as best we could and debated what to do next. I wanted to keep going to find you, but Jon insisted we turn back for reinforcements. He promised we would come straight back out again.*

*Except that night Cole and his men found us. They had been watching Palinar from across the border in Talinos and had noticed the same thing I did. They had already been exploring the reclaimed wilderness area for some days before we arrived, apparently. It hadn't occurred to us we might need to keep guard while we slept—we hadn't seen a single other person, after all. They easily overpowered us before we were even properly awake.*

She gave a silent scream. *I feel like such an idiot.*

*You're not an idiot,* I reassured her. *How could you possibly have known something like that would happen?*

*I knew Cole was still loose. I should have been more wary.*

*It never occurred to me he might try to get into Palinar, either, if that's any consolation.*

She laughed. *A little, perhaps.*

*I'm surprised he didn't try to force* you *into marrying him, with Jon as his threat.*

She sent me a disgusted expression. *He thought of that as soon as he had us safely restrained. But betrothals are as serious a legal bond here as they are back home. They can only be dissolved by agreement between the two parties, and even Cole doesn't want to risk violating the ancient laws.*

*He was furious when Jon said that he would die before he would dissolve our betrothal. And if he actually killed him, he would have had no leverage against me, as well as risking war with all the kingdoms for killing an heir. Obviously, they couldn't threaten to kill me, so then Cole had to come up with a new plan. He's completely convinced that your betrothal to...Dominic will be severed when he ceases to be the heir. I'm not sure if he's right or just deluding himself.*

*It doesn't matter,* I projected glumly. *Dominic dissolved our betrothal before I left.* I knew I should be glad because it meant I didn't have to choose between Lily and Arcadia, but I couldn't muster the emotion.

*Wait, really? Then you're free! Well, as soon as we work out a way to escape Cole...*

Yes. Free. I felt strangely depressed at the prospect, although it was possible that was just my anxiety over Cole. *It's a long story,* I warned her.

*Well, you have a long journey, I assume...*

And so, I settled in to tell her the whole story of everything that had happened to me since leaving Marin. Not surprisingly, she bombarded me with questions throughout, but when I finally finished, she fell silent.

*It's been over three months, and I still have no idea how to save Palinar,* I projected, failing to keep the dejection out of my voice.

*So, what do we actually know?* she asked. *Other than that old King Nicolas broke his covenant with both his people and his family and was, what...killed for it?*

I shrugged. *I don't actually know how he died. Only that he's dead. And I'm only guessing that he killed Queen Ruby.*

*He was clearly a man who would stop at nothing.* I could feel her studied concentration. *And Princess Adelaide is missing—fate and whereabouts unknown. We know she outlived her father, though, so he can't be responsible for her disappearance.* She hesitated. *Do you think Dominic could have killed her?*

I frowned. Once I had wondered the same thing, but my doubt had long since slid away. *No, I'm sure he would not have. He never talked about her current situation, but when he reminisced, he always sounded protective. And the servants said they were always affectionate toward each other.*

Lily accepted my judgment call without comment. *So, our best theory is that the curse was only against the royal family. It could even have been the curse itself that killed the old king.* I received an image of her shaking her head. *We were all so sure the entire kingdom had been cursed. It never occurred to anyone it might not be a curse, at all.*

*How could it have?* I projected. *Who would possibly guess that the people had merely been shifted sideways into another realm, and the wasteland put in place to protect them from outsiders who might try to come in and take their land?*

*But it has still affected them negatively,* projected Lily. *Surely there is some means to rescue them and bring them back.*

*There must be,* I agreed. *The godmothers have been involved, and they always leave a way out from such things. But no one would talk to me about it.*

*Wait!* Lily gasped. *You're telling me that the capital isn't empty like it appears, but full of invisible people? And that I can learn to hear them?*

*Maybe.* I spoke slowly, trying to think it through. *I'm not completely sure. The godmother who intervened for Dominic changed something to allow him to interact with his servants. It's possible I was only able to hear them because of whatever she did.*

*You mean, like she made some sort of extra bridge between the two realms, or something?*

I shrugged. *Maybe?*

*And you think when she did that, she also cursed him to look like a beast and took away his voice. Oh, and trapped him in the castle* grounds. *So, there are possibly two different curses—or, at least, pseudo-curses—to find a solution for.*

I shrugged again. *Yet another guess. There are just too many guesses. Not least of which is why the snow melted at the castle and the wilderness disappeared. In fact, for that one I don't even have a guess.*

Lily was silent for a moment. *I do.*

*Really? What?*

She hesitated again. *I don't want to say, I might be wrong.*

I snorted. *When have you ever worried about being embarrassed in front of me?*

She sent another image of her shaking head. *It's not that. I just don't want to give you a false idea. It might lead you down the wrong track.*

I rolled my eyes but couldn't be bothered arguing with her. Not when we had more important things to discuss. *But none of that matters until we can get you and Jon free from Cole. We need to come up with a plan.*

We talked about it for two days straight. Lily wanted to incite the invisible people of the capital to fight against Cole and his men. Only, there were several problems with her plan, as I kept reminding her.

One was that despite trying over and over again, Lily couldn't hear anything. If there were invisible people anywhere around her, they were either silent, or too separated from us to be heard. And she and Jon couldn't try speaking aloud to them, because there was a guard in the room where they were being imprisoned at all times.

Another problem was that the invisible people of Palinar were completely separated from us physically. I explained my experiments with my maids to Lily. *If I'm right, the whole point of the reverse curse was to ensure no one in the normal world could hurt them.*

*But the same seems to apply in reverse as well. The servants couldn't actually touch me. I suppose it's possible that they could still wield a weapon of some sort, but it's also possible that any attempt would simply slide away, like happened in our experiments. And that's all assuming you could actually communicate with them. Let's just say it's not a solution I want to be relying on.*

Eventually I succeeded in moving her attention to other strategies, and we came up with several tentative plans. It was difficult to decide anything for certain, however, when we didn't know what Cole would do when I arrived in the capital.

The one thing we did know was that he could not act immediately. Dominic's window to claim the throne would remain open for at least a day after I arrived in the capital, and Cole would not act before that. He didn't know that Dominic had dissolved our betrothal, and he still feared the ancient laws enough not to risk breaking it himself. Which meant I couldn't marry anyone else while Dominic remained the heir to Palinar.

However, he would surely be poised ready for the ceremony as soon as the window closed. He wouldn't want to waste any time making me Palinaran, as well as royal. Which meant I needed to find a way to rescue us all before Dominic ceased to be the heir.

I asked if a squad of guards from Marin might show up at some point, but her reply wasn't very hopeful.

*If the duke does decide to send out a search party, they would surely head to Dominic's castle. Everyone knew I was trying to go after you, and they have no reason to think we would have diverted to the capital.*

*Perhaps they would bring trackers with them,* I suggested hopefully.

*Cole went to fairly extreme lengths to hide our tracks on the way here, unfortunately. I don't think we should be holding out hope for rescue from Marin.*

Eventually we had come up with every variation of plan we could think of, and there was nothing left to do but wait.

# CHAPTER 27

*I*t took the full two days the coachmen had predicted to reach the capital. Eventually the city appeared on the horizon, and not long afterwards we acquired two silent outriders. I could only assume they were Cole's men, sent to ensure I entered alone and proceeded straight to him. Their presence destroyed several of the tentative plans we had made.

The capital was the largest I had ever seen, dwarfed only by the city-state of Marin. Even the buildings were built on a grander scale, with elegant arches and fountains every few streets. I could see why people in Marin talked about the magnificence of Palinar before the curse.

But now it felt eerie, the streets unnaturally deserted. To make the sensation worse, I kept thinking I saw flashes of movement down alleys and behind windows. But whenever I focused on it, I could see nothing. It reminded me of my first few days in the castle and the terrifying whispers that had followed me around. But for all I strained, making myself as receptive as possible, the only conversation I could hear came from the two coachmen.

Still, I couldn't deny the prickling at the back of my neck. And the memory of the terror, loneliness, and insecurity that had accompanied my first encounters with the whispers came flooding back. But I realized I had grown stronger in the last few months. The threat I faced now was even greater, but I successfully resisted the helplessness and the fear. I was here with a purpose, and I didn't have time for doubt to slow me down.

It helped that if ever it became too much, Lily was there, her comforting presence a mere thought away. Surprisingly I found myself glad of the time apart—it had allowed me to find my individual strength. But I also rejoiced at being reunited now; we had always been stronger together. And we would need all our combined strength to defeat this threat, just as it had taken our combined strength to defeat the Tourney.

When we entered the city, our outriders pulled in front of us, and I leaned my head out the window to instruct the coachmen to follow them. I didn't want to cause trouble yet. Thankfully, it soon became apparent they were heading for the palace. I breathed a sigh of relief. Lily had told me they were being held in one of the rooms there.

When we pulled through the great castle gates and into the courtyard, I alighted from the carriage and spoke quickly to the coachmen, keeping my voice low, unsure how much time I had. "Tell me, can you see people here, in the capital?"

*Certainly, Your Highness. Although none here in the palace grounds. I suspect no one lives here now. We will have to find a stable for the horses elsewhere.*

If they could see and hear the locals, and I could hear them, could they act as a go-between for us? I briefly considered the plan, but I could hear someone beginning to unbolt the palace doors, and too many obstacles stood in the way of the plan. Perhaps if I could speak to them as I did to Lily…but I had only ever been able to speak aloud to the servants because they were not truly communicating in their minds. From their perspective, they both spoke and heard like normal. I had long ago concluded it was the reason I couldn't feel their emotions or connect privately with any one individual, like I did with Lily.

Another thought occurred to me, and my words tumbled out in a rush. "Never mind a stable. You must return immediately to the castle. Let everyone know that if they hear word of a new king, or if your curse lifts, you all need to get out of there. At least for a while. It might not be safe."

*A new king? But, Princess Sophie, His Highness is still back at the castle.*

The palace doors opened, revealing Cole, flanked by several armed men.

"Just go!" I snapped in such a sharp voice that they obeyed. As the carriage started to move, I thought for a moment that I could see a vague outline of the two men, but then I blinked and it had disappeared.

I fixed my eyes on Cole, listening to the carriage turning in the courtyard without breaking my gaze. I didn't want to draw his attention to it, hopeful that his men would let the magical driverless carriage leave unobstructed. From what he had said in the castle, he seemed unnerved by all the objects that moved on their own, so I didn't think he'd want to interfere with one that was attempting to remove itself from his vicinity.

I allowed myself a tiny sigh of relief as I heard the wheels clatter away over the cobblestones.

*Is he there?* asked Lily, and for an unthinking moment I thought she meant Dominic. A sharp pang shot through me at his absence.

*Ugh. I could run him through myself.* Her anger made it clear she meant Cole.

*Be quiet for a minute. I need to focus.*

"Ah, my bride." Cole spread his arms wide. "How lovely to see you. And all alone as instructed. I think we're getting off to an excellent start."

I glared at him, but he merely laughed back. "Please," he

stepped back and gestured toward the entrance hall, "come inside."

I stuck my chin in the air and mounted the stairs, sweeping disdainfully past him. Halfway inside, I realized my bags were in the disappearing coach, and I had to work to maintain a neutral expression. I supposed it didn't really matter. In a few days, I would either be queen, or free to leave here and fetch them. And the most important item I still had, tucked into my dress—the rose, which had somehow survived the journey in full bloom.

Cole led me to the throne room. Sprawling himself across the largest throne, he smiled at me. "I admit I had my doubts. I thought I might have to send out a squad to skewer that prince of yours. But it seems you have successfully shaken him free."

I stood as straight as my short height allowed. "I don't know what you mean."

He laughed. "I am not an idiot. I would have thought that much was apparent." He gestured at the throne behind him. "I have studied all the emotions, or I could not simulate them so well." He laughed again. "Not that it took much expertise to see that monster's jealousy." He regarded me dispassionately. "You are beautiful enough, I suppose. Although Dominic was always a proud one—the only heir to the great kingdom of Palinar." He sneered. "But he has been brought low now. Perhaps after his years of exile as a beast, it was inevitable that he would fall in love with the first girl to cross his path."

I stared at him. Jealous? In love? Dominic had been protective of me, certainly, but he had been the one to pull away from our kiss. Cole must be wrong. Why would Dominic dissolve our betrothal if he loved me?

Because if he truly loved you, he would free you, whispered a small voice in the back of my mind that for once didn't come from my sister. And if he truly loved you, he wouldn't take advantage of the situation to kiss you.

Terror washed over me, making it hard to breathe. If Dominic loved me, then he was in terrible danger. Because when he realized Cole had escaped, and when his coachmen returned with my message, he would easily put the two together. Nothing would stop him coming after me. And then he would die.

"I'm glad to see you looking sufficiently horrified," said Cole. "I was a little afraid at that castle that you might actually have feelings for him back."

But I wasn't listening. I was grappling with a second terrible realization, made far too late. I loved Dominic back. He was more than an intelligent companion, whose company I enjoyed. He stimulated my mind and awakened my emotions in a way I had never experienced before.

When I had first arrived at his castle, I had seen only his inconsiderate pride. But in the months since then, the care he showed to Spitfire had extended first to me, and then to his servants. I had seen his passion, previously warped by his anger, transform into something else—a protective instinct that complemented the good governance he had previously dispensed with so little feeling. No one was better equipped to rule Palinar.

And I could imagine no one else so consuming my heart. I loved him and would do so even if he remained bound by the curse, trapped in his beastly shape forever. The thought of his inevitable death cut through me with a pain so deep I could barely breathe. My fear of finding myself married to Cole paled beside it.

"Now," Cole continued. "Did you manage to find out when the old king died?" He eyed me sharply and added a warning. "If you lie to me, I'll know, and your sister will be the one to feel my wrath."

"It's been three years, three months, three weeks and two days," I blurted out, my mind still distracted by my amazing and despair-filled revelation. I immediately wanted to shake myself.

Since Cole and I couldn't be safely married until Dominic was no longer the heir, I could have lied and given Lily and me a couple more days at least.

A smile spread over his face. "Excellent news, indeed! And that lines up exactly with when the curse fell over Palinar, so I'm even inclined to believe you. I can't imagine you want to be bringing down curses on your head any more than I do. Which means we don't have long to wait."

I eyed him coldly. "I would like to be shown to my room."

"Your room?" He raised both eyebrows.

"I assume you do not intend for us to stand around here for hours and hours. And I am to be queen, am I not? I assume the queen has a suite of chambers somewhere in this palace."

I waited to see if he would explode with anger, but he laughed at me instead. "Regal and demanding. I like it." He jumped to his feet and stepped down to stand beside me. Leaning forward he whispered in my ear. "It looks good on you."

I suppressed a shiver with difficulty, forcing my voice to remain steady. "My chambers?"

He waved over two of the men and directed them to take me to the queen's chambers. He eyed me. "They will remain outside your door...an honor guard as any queen should have."

I glared at him but said nothing. It would have been too much to hope that he would leave me unguarded. And even with their presence, the first step in one of our more outrageous plans had just succeeded.

The two men led me silently through the palace, and I couldn't help looking around curiously. It was magnificent, yes, but also a little cold. I found myself adding some warmer touches in my mind, as I had once found myself doing for the prince's castle.

I shook my head at my foolishness. If I ended up queen of this castle, I would have other things to think about than redecorating. I would have to expend all my energy to keep the people safe from Cole's selfish whims. But still, I examined the rooms as closely as I could, walking as slowly as the guards would allow.

Eventually they stopped, and one of them opened a door, gesturing for me to go inside with a grunt. I hurried through and pulled it shut behind me. For a moment I leaned against it, catching my breath, and then I looked around.

I had entered a sitting room, although I could see a bed through an open door on the left wall. These rooms had none of the cold feel of the rest of the palace. In fact, the hints of gold leaf and the elegant white marble were largely obscured by the soft fall of warm rose material. The chairs all had cushions scattered across them, and a basket overflowed with embroidery.

I walked over to a well-worn table of soft wood, and ran my hand along the book that lay there, lying askew, as if dropped in haste. Everything here appeared exactly as it must have when Queen Ruby left the room for the last time, just with a thick added layer of dust. Had she known her coming fate? Nothing I could see suggested it.

I sat in a chair and tried to breathe in some of the calm of this room. No large portrait dominated the wall here, but the queen's presence seemed to linger all the same. She had so clearly made the space her own.

*Sophie? Where are you? Are you still with Cole?*

*I told him I wanted to be shown to the queen's chambers. I wasn't sure he would let me out of his sight, but he seemed to find the request amusing.*

*Ugh. He would.* She seemed to be enjoying having some small outlet for her disgust of Cole.

*I memorized the route here, though.* I relayed it to her. *Do you know specifically where you are?*

*We do, thankfully. Cole never made any attempt to blindfold us. He went on and on about how complacent we all were, but he seemed pretty sure of himself, too.*

*Do you know how he got out of the prison in Marin? Does he have a godmother object?*

Lily sighed. *He wouldn't tell us. But it's the only thing I can think of. There was no sign of how he did it—the cell was just empty.*

I stood. *It's time we were getting out of here.*

*Past time!* She chuckled. *You should see the look Jon is giving me. He's going crazy wanting to know what we're saying. I've whispered as much to him as I dare, but I don't want the guard to realize something is going on.*

*It's just the one guard, right?* I asked, nerves hitting me. *Is Jon sure he can deal with him?* The plan we had decided on if we ended up in this situation required Jon to be able to take the guard out on his own.

*Yes, there's only ever one. We would have overpowered him before now, except that there wasn't any point. He's only here to make sure we can't plot anything. There are three more outside the door at all times. And the locked door itself, of course. Naturally he doesn't have a key on him.*

*Remind me what you're wearing again?* I walked through into the queen's dressing room.

Lily described her clothes, and I looked through the largest wardrobe I had ever seen for a match. I found one that seemed close enough and pulled it out. Slipping it on, I discovered that the late queen had been taller than me, but thankfully not smaller. If anything, it was a little baggy, but not so much as to look ridiculous.

*Is your hair up or down?*

*It was up originally, but it's mostly come down now.*

I looked around the room while we went over the plan one last time. Crossing over to one of the curtains, I ripped off a braided pull cord. It was gold, but I hoped that it would pass for rope at a hurried glance. I looped it awkwardly over my wrists, twisting it around several times to ensure it wouldn't fall off while keeping it loose enough that I could pull my hands out quickly if I needed them. It didn't look convincing close up, but I didn't need it to.

I slipped my hands out, and stashed the makeshift rope inside my dress. Pulling my cloak over the new dress, I straightened my shoulders and opened the door. The two guards were standing on the far side of the corridor, and they both stepped forward at my appearance.

I ignored them and turned down the corridor. In my peripheral vision, I saw an arm reach out to grab me, and I froze. Wheeling around, I stared at the stretched-out hand with as much regal disdain as I could muster. The guard let it drop and exchanged an uneasy glance with his companion. I arched an eyebrow at them both.

"Well? Aren't you coming? I wish to go for a walk, and Cole said you are to be my honor guard." I looked them up and down disdainfully. "As disappointingly inferior as you are, I suppose you're better than nothing."

The two men exchanged another look, and then the one who had tried to stop me gestured awkwardly for me to continue. They fell into step behind me, and I suppressed a grin. It had been a significant gamble, but my haughty disdain had thrown them off too much to protest. Especially after Cole had been so supportive of my demanding the rights of a queen. They were off-balance, unsure to what extent they were supposed to be treating me as a prisoner.

I strode quickly down the corridor, heading back the way we had come, looking for a particular room. When I saw the open door to the small, intimate dining room, I paused briefly in the doorway. I scanned the walls, holding my breath until I saw what I had been hoping to find.

Without hesitation, I sprinted for the far side of the room. One of the guards gave a shout, but they were as slow to respond as I had hoped they would be. Partially due to surprise, I was sure, and probably also due to the mistaken belief that I had dashed into a room with no other exit.

I flung myself into the small wooden box nestled into the wall, only just fitting inside. I gripped the brake with both hands, pulling it loose. As I began to sink down, faster than I had expected, I saw the astonished faces of the two guards disappear from view.

# CHAPTER 28

*I* plunged toward the ground two floors below so fast that I felt my stomach whoosh up into my mouth. Clearly, I was significantly heavier than the food the counter weight usually balanced. The opening into the kitchen appeared, but the top half of the box still opened only onto a wall when it jerked beneath me and came to a shuddering halt. The wood creaked ominously as I bounced hard against the wooden bottom.

I hadn't made it all the way down, but I thought there might be enough of an opening for me to squeeze through. As I moved to slide out, however, the box jerked again and began to move back upwards. I gulped and scrambled in the small space until I crouched on my feet, head bent and shoulders, along with both my hands, pressed against the top of the box. I grunted and strained with my legs, pushing upwards with all my strength.

The wood creaked and groaned, and then splintered apart. I plummeted down, fast, landing hard on my rear, and the top of the box shot upwards, now carrying almost no weight. I heard the guards curse, but I didn't wait to see their next move. My plan had worked better than I could have hoped, the wood obviously starting to rot with the years of disuse. But it was only the first of the obstacles that had to be overcome.

Clambering to my feet, I shoved my cloak into one of the large empty fireplaces and ran from the room. I pulled my hair down around my face and slid my hands into the bundle of cord. As I neared the part of the palace where Lily and Jon were being held, I slowed, checking around each corner first. It wouldn't do to be discovered too early.

Finally, I reached the corridor where Lily had said I would find them. Sure enough, three guards loitered around a door half way down.

*Are you ready?* I asked Lily. *I'm here.*

*Ready!*

I took a deep breath and knocked a candle sconce on the wall with my elbow. It rattled loudly enough for my purposes, and I ran along the passageway past the opening to the corridor with the guards. I stopped just out of sight, pressing myself against the wall.

"Hey!" shouted one. "The prisoner!"

"Impossible," said another.

But the third one spoke over the top of him, "I saw her, too."

"Here, I'll show you." I heard the rattle of a key as the disbelieving one spoke. I held my breath. This was the moment when everything needed to work perfectly.

Inside the room, I knew Lily had thrown herself against the wall on the inside of the door. I could picture it all happening in my mind. The confused guard would be flinging the door open and scanning the room. Inside he would see Jon and the other guard, but no Lily since she was blocked from view by the now open door.

I heard the guard inside call out a muffled question, at the same time as the guard with the key called out, "It *was* her! She's escaped somehow. Quick! After her!"

I heard the pounding of two sets of boots and took off

running as fast as I could down the corridor. I ran heedlessly, my knowledge of the castle's layout exhausted. All that mattered, though, was that the two guards continued to pursue me, and that Jon and Lily now had only two guards and an open door between them and freedom.

The second the two guards had taken off, Jon would have leaped up and incapacitated the guard in the room. Hopefully by the time the guard in the doorway realized what was happening, and that he was needed in the room rather than in pursuit of me, Jon and Lily would have been able to attack him together.

I ducked through a small indoor courtyard and burst into another corridor.

*We're free!* Lily's jubilation rang through my mind. *You did it! Now all we need is to get into the city, find each other and find somewhere to hide while we come up with the next plan.*

*That's all, hey?*

I slammed a door behind me, but it was being pulled open before I was more than four steps away. I was losing my lead.

*I don't know if I'm going to make it out, Lil.*

*What! Where are you? We'll come for you.*

*No!* I snapped the word as I tried to push some extra speed from my now exhausted legs. *Cole can't force me to marry him unless he has you and Jon. You're the ones who need to get away.*

*He could still kill you!*

*But he won't. Not right away, anyway. He'll be hoping to recapture you. Make sure he can't!*

As I projected the final word, a hand landed in the center of my back, and I sprawled forward across the floor, a heavy weight falling against me. I tried to push up and crawl away, but strong hands gripped me.

"Oh no, you don't. I don't know how you managed to get out before, but we've got you now." The two men still assumed I was Lily then.

"I demand to see Cole," I gasped between shuddering breaths, my lungs burning. Anything to prevent them returning to the room they had been using as a prison and seeing that both prisoners were now gone.

"He's not going to like it that you tried to run," said one of them, dragging me to my feet and pushing me roughly down the corridor.

I stayed silent, keeping my hands tucked against my dress in the hope they wouldn't notice the strangeness of my apparent bindings. When they shoved me through a small side door into the throne room, I tripped and nearly fell, but one of them caught me by the arm. He pushed me forward to where Cole still sat on the throne, talking quietly with a man beside him.

"The door never opened, we swear it," said one of the guards. "But somehow this one escaped. We ran her down half way through the east wing, though."

Cole stood up and strode over toward us. "Lily, Lily, Lily. Don't tell me you still have some surprises left in you after all. But where is the oh-so-tiresome Jonathan? I cannot believe you have escaped without your ever-faithful swain."

I spat at the ground at his feet, since it seemed like the sort of defiant thing Lily would do. He raised an eyebrow at me.

"Really, was that necessary?" Then his eyes narrowed, and I saw his gaze fasten on the gold cord looped loosely around my wrists. It moved up to my dress. "What is this?" His eyes flew to my face.

He yanked me away from the guards and turned on them. "Fools! This is Sophie! Where are Lily and Jonathan?"

They looked at him in bewilderment.

"Go!" he screamed at them. "Check on the prisoners!"

Both men lumbered around, still clearly confused, and raced out of the room.

Cole turned on me, his face white with fury. "How have you managed this? By what magic have you switched places with your sister?"

I shrugged. "My sister is long gone and her betrothed with her. You may have caught me, but you no longer have any leverage over me. I won't be telling you a thing, and I certainly won't be marrying you."

Before he could reply, the two guards who I had left behind in the dining room came rushing in, their faces red.

"We've lost her..." one of them started to say before trailing off as he looked with confusion between me and Cole. "Wait. Is that...?"

"Yes, idiots!" Cole's volume had dropped, but the menace still lingered in his tone. "This is the girl you were meant to be guarding. And now I find that somehow she has helped the other two to escape."

"Escape? But how is such a thing possible? She didn't even know where they were being held. I swear we did not take her near that wing."

"And why does she look like the other one?" The second guard seemed to be struggling to catch up.

"Obviously it was part of the ruse that allowed the others to escape," Cole snapped. "Believe me, one way or another, I will discover how it was done. But in the meantime, I want every guard out searching the palace for the prisoners. If they are not found, you will pay the punishment."

Both men paled and hurried from the room. The guard who had been talking to Cole earlier made as if to follow them, but Cole signaled for him to stay. I felt a small stirring of pride that I had unsettled him enough that he wanted backup.

He must have seen something of the emotion on my face, because he shook my arm, hard. "Don't think this is over, Princess Sophie. I am not so easily defeated."

I remained mute, so he towed me over to the throne and threw me to the ground at its foot. Sitting down, he gestured for his remaining guard to come and stand over me, sword drawn and pointed down in my direction.

I pulled myself slowly into a sitting position, rubbing at several new bruises I could already feel forming. That was twice I had ended up on the stone ground in the last few minutes.

I reached out for my sister in my mind. *Sorry, Lily.*

*No, I'm sorry.*

*Don't worry.* I tried to keep my tone positive. *You'll find a way to rescue me, I'm sure of it.*

*No, they...*

Before she could finish the sentence, two guards strode through the double doors on the far side of the throne room. Between them they dragged my sister, her feet barely touching the ground.

She looked up and met my eyes...*they caught me, I'm afraid. I'm so sorry, Sophie.*

# CHAPTER 29

*I* leaped to my feet. "Lily!"

"Ah!" Cole also came upright. "Well done."

*What happened?*

She looked dejected and guilty as they half carried her forward. *We had nearly made it out of the palace grounds and were taking turns scouting a short way ahead. I was distracted, worrying about you, and stumbled straight into a group of guards. I bolted, to lead them away from Jon, but I couldn't outrun them.* She paused. *He's going to be so furious that I left him behind! And you, Sophie. You should be furious with me, too. I've ruined everything!*

I sent her an internal glare as she arrived in front of the throne. *Don't be ridiculous. This situation is not your fault. All of the guilt belongs with Cole.* I glanced at the guards who tightly gripped her arms. *And maybe some on these henchmen of his, too. Who in the kingdoms are they?*

She glanced at one of them and frowned. *Honestly, I have no idea. I don't think they're Marinese, though.*

"Where's the prince?" asked Cole.

One of the men shrugged uncomfortably. "We haven't seen any sign of him. The others are still out looking."

Cole's eyes narrowed, but then he shrugged. "It doesn't matter. There is nothing he can do, and Lily is the important one." He turned to me. "I told you I would not be so easily defeated Princess Sophie. And you have now worn out every shred of my patience." He gestured at the guards, and one of them grabbed both her arms, holding her firmly in front of him, while the other drew his sword and placed it at her throat.

"No!" I leaped to my feet and lunged forward, but the man who had remained behind with Cole held me back.

"Carefully now, Princess," said Cole. "You wouldn't want to go startling my guard here."

I froze.

"We will be married immediately," he continued.

I swung around to stare at him. "Immediately? But Dominic is still the heir."

"We will be married now, to ensure you don't get any more foolish ideas. You will be able to claim the throne soon enough."

I gaped at him, my mind racing. This couldn't be happening. Everything had gone wrong, and now it was all moving too fast. I couldn't marry him. But when I looked at the sharp blade pressed against Lily's throat, I knew I couldn't refuse him either.

*Don't do it, Sophie!* But I could feel Lily's fear, as sharp as my own.

Cole seemed to have lost all caution in the face of our nearly successful defiance. It was a dangerous move since he didn't know that Dominic had dissolved our betrothal. I suspected Lily and I weren't the only ones afraid—I could sense the fear lurking beneath the surface of his actions. He didn't understand what had happened, and he no longer trusted his ability to keep us secured.

"But how?" I asked, searching for any way to delay him. "How are we to be married?"

He eyed me coldly. "Surely you didn't think I had come unprepared? In Marin, I befriended an official from Palinar, one stationed in the duchy with a small liaison role before the curse hit. He has accompanied us and stands ready to perform the ceremony. He is eager to assist in freeing the kingdom from the curse of the Beast and his family."

The thought of Dominic brought tears to my eyes. If only I could have found a way to save him. Would I ever get to see him again, or have the chance to tell him how I felt? What would happen when Dominic's coronation window closed? Would he remain a beast forever as I feared?

My stomach churned. If he came after me, it wouldn't matter. He would be dead.

And yet, still I wished he was here with me.

Cole was shouting orders for the official to be brought to the throne room, but I was only listening with half my mind. A strange flash outside the window kept distracting me. I remembered the flashes I had seen earlier while driving through the city, but this one was different. This one actually looked like a human form.

There! I saw it again. This time I felt sure it had been a person. How many guards did Cole have with him? My heart sank. He would not allow us the opportunity to escape again. And Jon would be hard-pressed to assist us, even if he remained free. Not when he was alone and had no way to communicate with us.

The official eventually arrived, and I noticed that he looked nervous at all the drawn swords and angry-looking guards. Perhaps he would refuse to conduct a ceremony so clearly done under coercion? But Cole clapped him on the back and murmured something in his ear. His face cleared, and my hope withered.

Cole had the official stand in front of the throne and arranged the two of us at the bottom of the three steps that led up to it. Lily he positioned to one side, within my eye line, still held by one guard, another holding the sword to her throat. He pulled a ring from his pocket, and I shivered, feeling it already like a prison chain around me.

*Dominic!* I cried in my heart, my eyes filling with tears. *It should have been you.*

As if called into existence by my desperate wishes, a deafening roar shook the throne room. Everyone started and looked toward the double doors. They had been flung wide and, standing between them, stood Dominic. Fury radiated from every line of his body, and death was in his eyes.

"Guards! Stop him!" shouted Cole, a tremor in his voice. And then chaos broke out.

The guard who had been holding the sword to Lily lowered his blade and moved to stand between Dominic and Cole. A group of guards poured in from the small side door and rushed to join him. My stomach churned to see Dominic facing them all alone, growling and striding forward, a sword gripped in each hand. But a moment later, a small crowd poured in behind him, most of them dressed in the official uniform of the Palinaran guard.

Before I could even begin to wonder who they were, or where they had come from, Lily seized the opportunity afforded by the absence of the second guard and bit down hard on the arm that encircled her shoulders. The guard yelled and pulled his arm back while Lily kicked him hard in one shin. He stumbled backwards, and she launched herself forward.

I thought she was coming for me, but Jon appeared instead, sweeping her into his arms. He must have come in with the wave of Palinaran guards although I hadn't seen him.

Meanwhile, the Palinaran guards clashed violently with Cole's men, attempting to pull them away as they tried to swarm the prince. Dominic's swords flashed, clearing a path ahead of him, his focus never leaving Cole.

My stomach churned at the sight of him, overwhelmed with both love and fear. How could he be here? How was it possible?

"Dominic!" His name fell from my lips involuntarily, just as he broke through the last of the guards. He faltered, his burning eyes turning to me, and for a moment no one else existed in the room but us.

*Sophie! Behind you!* Lily's scream ripped through my mind just as rough arms jerked me backwards, and something sharp pricked my throat.

"Stay back!" yelled Cole, dragging me off my feet and immobilizing me with a dagger at my throat.

Dominic paused, but I could see his whole body shaking with contained fury, and his growls rolled over one another, deep and threatening. His menacing gaze remained fixed on Cole, but his words could only be addressed to me.

*If he harms you, I will kill him.*

His face was the last thing I saw as Cole dragged me backwards out of the room.

# CHAPTER 30

*C*ole seemed to recognize that he couldn't drag me all the way out of the palace alone. Instead, he took one quick look around the antechamber we had entered and then tugged me over to a slim door. Moving without hesitation, he yanked it open, thrusting me into the darkness inside. His shove had unbalanced me, and before I could recover, he had joined me, pulling the door closed and pinning me back against him.

The bite of metal on my neck stopped my struggles, and he leaned forward, breath heavy, to whisper in my ear. "If you make a sound, any sound, I will slit your throat. Don't doubt me." He sounded angry enough to mean it, too. "In fact," he added, "if that door handle so much as rattles, you'll be dead." He clearly had not forgotten our earlier seemingly magical escape.

*Sophie! Sophie! Has he hurt you? Where are you?*

I swallowed and tried to form enough coherent thoughts to respond. *He hasn't hurt me—yet. But he's threatening to kill me if anyone even approaches us. I don't even know where we are. It's very dark. And it feels small.*

I could sense her confusion. *You mean like a cupboard?*

*Yes!* I must have been shaken indeed not to recognize our

location myself. *I think we might be in a cupboard. In the antechamber of the throne room. I suppose he's hoping you'll all assume he's run for it.*

*Too bad for him we can talk.*

*Yes, except that now we're at an impasse. If any of you try to come in here, he'll kill me. I don't much fancy having to wait and see which of the two of us faints of dehydration and exhaustion first.*

*We'll call through the door,* she suggested. *Demand he hands you over.*

*No! If he realizes you know where we are, I really think he'll kill me. You saw Dominic. I'm sure Cole thinks that the minute he loses hold of me as a hostage, he's dead. I can easily imagine he'd want to take me down with him in that scenario.*

*What can we do then?*

*I don't know. What's happening out there? Oh wait! It sounds like some of the hubbub has died down, and I can actually hear you all. This cupboard must share a wall with the throne room, and you must be standing very close to us...*

"Dominic." I recognized Jon's voice. "That was a well-timed arrival."

Dominic growled, but only I could hear the question behind the sound.

"I heard...I heard that you can't speak." That was Lily. "But I'm guessing you want to go after Sophie, and you're wondering where he might have taken her."

*Don't forget, if I can hear you, Cole can too!* I reminded her.

She ignored me, responding instead to Dominic who must have nodded, or something. "I don't think it's a good idea to go racing after them. I think Cole meant his threat." A pause, and then she added, "Don't look at me like that! I'm as worried for her as anyone."

*Can you hear me, Sophie?* Dominic's voice had never sounded so welcome in my mind. *Don't give up. I won't rest until I find you and make him pay.*

"We should go and consult those guards of yours," said Lily. "I assume they can speak, at least."

Cole's armed tightened around us, the tip of his dagger nicking my skin as the sounds of the others moved away. His message was clear—for my sake, I had better hope they didn't try searching this cupboard.

*Can you hear us still, or are we far enough away?* Lily asked me.

*I can't hear anything but general muffled noise.*

*Then I'm going to tell them where you are and what's happening. It's a good thing that Dominic of yours can't speak, or I imagine he would be asking me some difficult questions about how I know so much.*

I felt my face flush, a surprising reaction given my current circumstances. *He's not* my *Dominic. He dissolved our betrothal, remember?*

She just laughed at me and then fell silent, presumably because she had started talking to Jon and Dominic. I pictured them all out there. Where was this going to end?

I bit my lip, trying not to swallow against the blade which had already broken my skin. Dominic didn't seem sick, but then he hadn't succumbed immediately the last time he had left the castle grounds either. It had taken more than a day despite his significant wounds. How long would it take the sickness to overwhelm him this time, when he had started off healthy and strong?

I tore my mind away from the thought, needing to focus on my immediate situation if I was going to escape alive. I breathed slowly, in and out, while I thought. After everything I had been through, both Dominic and Lily were a mere wall away. I refused to lose them both now.

"We can't stay here forever," I whispered as quietly as I could. "You know that."

Cole tightened his grip, but kept the knife still. I breathed a little easier. He must recognize the truth of my words.

"If you let me go, you might have a chance of escaping on your own."

I could feel his head shaking behind me. "Do you take me for a fool?" he breathed into my ear. "I saw how many guards that cursed prince brought with him. I just don't understand where they came from!"

I stayed silent, equally mystified.

"I will not walk away with nothing now, after all this work, all this planning."

"You would be walking away with your life."

"Silence!"

He shook me slightly, and I felt a small biting pain and then a drop of blood running down my neck. I shut my mouth. I had pushed hard enough. Now that I had planted the seed, I needed to provide a spur.

*Cole knows we can't stay here forever,* I projected to Lily. *If you all come back over here and have a conversation that suggests there might be a free path for him to get us both out of here, I think he might take it. Only you'll have to be extremely careful to keep everyone out of sight when we emerge. He's going to be jumpy, and I'd rather not die just because he was startled.*

Lily moaned. *I do NOT like this situation.*

*Just get all the guards out and hide yourselves somewhere. I'll have a better chance of getting away if we're on the move than if we stay stuck in this cupboard.*

Reluctantly she agreed, and I soon heard the group return.

"Look, we're wasting time," said Jon, sounding frustrated. "He could be anywhere by now. I'm dividing the guards into search parties and sending one to each floor. We'll flush them out."

"Don't send all of them!" said Lily. "We can't leave the throne room undefended."

"Why not?" Jon sounded impatient and dismissive. "What's he going to do, sneak back in and steal the throne? They're clearly long gone from here, it's about the one place in the palace we know they're not."

Dominic growled, a dark, threatening sound.

"See," said Jon. "Dominic agrees with me."

"Don't be ridiculous, he could be saying anything!"

I could feel Cole's tenseness behind me and knew he was listening to every word. I wanted to applaud their little charade.

"Dominic, leave off all that growling for half a minute and nod your head if you agree with me," said Jon. There was a brief pause, and then, "See! I told you."

"Men! Ugh! Fine, send out your search parties. I just want to find my sister."

Their voices faded away again, and then we heard barked orders and the sound of many moving feet. A number of boots tramped through the antechamber, and both Cole and I held our breaths until the door closed and silence fell.

It stretched on and on, and I began to wonder if he would need another prompt. But finally, he stirred, prodding me forward. "We're leaving," he whispered. "Just don't forget. One sound, and I slit your throat."

I groped in the darkness for the door handle and managed to open it silently. We walked out slowly, Cole holding my back pressed hard against his chest, his knife unwavering. As expected, the antechamber was empty, both doors shut. He paused, which I hadn't expected, and spun me around.

"Don't try to run," he warned. "You won't get far."

The gold cord was still tangled around one of my wrists, everything having happened too fast for me to bother removing it. He pulled it loose and commanded me to hold both hands in front of me. Placing his knife in his teeth, he quickly bound my wrists, before spinning me away from him again.

He placed a hand on my shoulder, and I felt the tip of the knife press into my back, between two ribs. "Don't worry, Princess," he whispered. "I know what I'm doing with this thing. Your death will be no less inevitable, it will just be considerably slower."

I swallowed, but relayed the news to Lily in my mind. Hopefully this would make my rescue easier.

*We're in here, out of sight,* she told me. *We're ready.*

Except when Cole pushed me roughly forward, he didn't turn toward the door into the apparently empty throne room. Instead he propelled me to the door out into the corridor, and checked it quickly before thrusting me through into the passageway.

*Lily! We're not going into the throne room. He's gone the other way.*

My breathing hitched as I started to panic. This hadn't been the plan. What would happen if we stumbled on some of the guards? I kept imagining I felt the pressure of the knife increasing.

Cole pushed me down the corridor and into another. I didn't recognize the route and had no idea where we were heading. We saw one group of guards, far in the distance, and Cole pulled me back, pressing me against the wall until they disappeared in the opposite direction. He became a little more confident after that, pushing me forward at a faster pace.

I had been keeping Lily informed of our progress, but she seemed almost as panicked as me, scrambling now to get into place for another plan. Finally, we reached a small door that looked like it might lead outside. Cole directed me to open it, and I did so awkwardly, due to my bound hands.

I pushed the door, and it flung open faster than I had expected. A flash of brown and red filled my vision and then something jerked me forward and flung me to the ground.

I fell, only just managing to twist my bound hands into a position to take the brunt of my landing. A familiar roar sounded as I rolled onto my back in time to see Dominic lift Cole completely off his feet. He shook him, roaring again.

But Cole still held the knife, and rays from the dying sun reflected off the blade as he lifted it over his head.

"Dominic!" I screamed, struggling to push myself up.

His eyes flashed up and saw the danger, and he flung Cole

away from him with all his strength. He landed against a wall, hard, and fell to the ground. He lay there, still, his body bent at an unnatural angle.

I slumped back against the ground and closed my eyes. I expected to feel hands helping me to my feet, but instead I heard a loud thump. My eyes flew open, and I saw Dominic crumpled in the dirt a short distance away from me.

# CHAPTER 31

"*D*ominic!" I screamed again, twisting over and crawling slowly toward him. I added a mental scream immediately afterwards. *Lily! Where are you?*

*What? What's happened? We're still trying to follow you, but I think I must have gotten one of the turns wrong. Dominic took off a while ago.*

*He's here. I think Cole's dead. But something's wrong with Dominic.*

*I thought he was starting to look weak.* She sounded grim. *Where are you?*

I looked around. *I don't know. In the palace grounds somewhere. Just outside a door in the...east wing, maybe?*

*All right. We're coming.*

I had reached Dominic and now knelt beside him. I had been sure he had acted before Cole's knife struck, and I could see no sign of an injury. His collapse must be the result of his curse. Leaning over him, tears streamed down my cheeks as I searched for a heartbeat, or breathing, or something. He stirred.

"Oh!" I gasped. "Dominic!"

He gave me the smallest of smiles. *Are you hurt?* he asked, his voice weak.

I shook my head. "How did you know where to find me?"

*I grew up in this palace, I know it well. Once I realized the direction you were going, his destination was obvious.*

"You saved me."

He smiled again. *I told you I would.*

I gave a shaky laugh that cut off abruptly as his eyes fluttered closed. "No. Dominic, no!" I gripped his jacket as best I could and shook him. He didn't respond although I could still hear his labored breaths.

I dropped my forehead down onto his chest. "I will not lose you now. Your kingdom needs you. *I* need you."

He seemed too weak to speak, but I refused to let him go. If he could not speak, allowing me to hear him as I did the servants, then I needed to connect directly with his mind. I needed to communicate with him as I did with Lily. I had no idea if such a thing were even possible, but I was determined to succeed.

I closed my eyes, and concentrated my mind. I could feel how much my powers of mental communication had grown in the last months, honed and strengthened by my time at the castle. I shaped my thoughts as I would do to send them to Lily, but instead of sending them out to her, I focused all my attention on Dominic. I breathed in the smell of him and felt his warmth beneath my hands and head. I thought of how he made me feel—infuriated and exhilarated, cherished and so alive. I reached into my dress and pulled out the rose he had given me. Somehow it had survived being stored in two different dresses now. It hadn't even wilted—the last piece of our enchanted life at the castle, the deep color and the pure white of the spirals in the rose garden combined into a single blossom. I pressed it against his chest and sent my thoughts flying in his direction.

I felt my mind connect with the essence of him, so like to what I had always done with Lily, and yet so unlike at the same time. Her mind felt safe and familiar, at times like an extension of my own. His felt wild and barely tamed, full of pain and grief.

*Dominic,* I projected. *I will not let you die.*

Dimly I heard the arrival of Lily and Jon, and part of my mind knew they had pulled up my hands and were cutting the cord from my wrists. But I ignored them, too focused on my new connection with Dominic.

One of his hands twitched, and for a moment I thought his eyes would open, but he did not seem to have the strength.

*How...how are you here, in my mind?* he asked.

*This is the connection I have with Lily, have always had with her. This is how I learned to hear you and the servants at the castle. I'm sorry I didn't tell you sooner. I was cut off from her at the castle, and it made me angry and afraid.*

*No, Sophie. You have no need to apologize to me. We have both of us had our secrets.* He paused. *I know that you could never forgive me for mine. Could never...love me. But I want you to know that you have taught me so much. You have shown me what it is to love. And even if there was never hope for me to be freed from my curse, you have freed my kingdom, and that is enough.*

The tears continued to pour down my cheeks as I stared at his still face. *Saved your kingdom? What do you mean?*

Somehow our connection seemed to give him a small burst of strength. He opened his eyes, the bright blue that had always captivated me, capturing me once again. He smiled. *Didn't you notice the snow melting? Or the wolves disappearing? Or all those guards I had with me?*

I gasped. *The people have returned?*

*They have returned—thanks to you.*

*But...I don't understand. I was never able to figure out how to save them.*

*I already told you. You taught me to love. The people of Palinar were moved to a place of protection until their ruler could learn the true meaning of love.* He paused as he drew a particularly labored breath. *I did not understand self-sacrifice, or how to value myself last.*

259

*And then you came. I should never have forced you to come as I did, and yet how could I regret it?*

I felt his emotions wash over me, a wave of love so strong I could barely breathe. For a moment, I choked on my tears.

*So, I was right. It was a protection not a curse on the people.*

He grimaced. *It was only the royal family who were cursed. Twice cursed in my case. But now you have freed my people from my curse. No one could have freed me, however. I see that now.*

*No!* I projected, my hands clasping at his jacket. *I cannot accept that. There must be a way to free you.*

*You must find my sister. She has been missing for more than three years now, but I cannot believe she is dead. Find her, and help her claim the throne. She has a good heart, like yours. She will make an excellent queen.*

I shook him. *And what of your heart?*

*It is yours. And you shall have to keep it safe for me when I am gone.*

*I don't want you to leave,* I sobbed.

He went so still that I feared he had died, but then he breathed again, and me along with him. *You would not feel that way if you could see what I have done. And you should see it, it is only right.*

I felt his mind wrap itself around mine in a way I had never experienced before. And then in my mind's eye I could see a series of memories, as vividly as if they were my own. I saw King Nicolas, exactly as his portrait had shown him, strike down villager after villager.

I whimpered at the sight. So, Dominic had been there. I wanted to cover my eyes, but the images were in my mind, and I could not turn them off. Thankfully Dominic had looked away after a few moments, but his feelings from the time continued to assail me.

Shock at his father's actions, anger that he would attack unarmed people in such a way, and underneath it, fear at where his father's rage might be directed next. And over all of it, confusion. It didn't seem just, what his father was doing. But wasn't it a ruler's right to do with his people what he willed? They all of them lived to serve him, did they not?

I could feel his revulsion, his urge to intervene, and his shame that he did not. And then Dominic spoke over the top of the memory. *I was there, Sophie. I stood by and let him kill all those people, even the babies. I said nothing. I did nothing.*

I remained silent, too overwhelmed to speak.

*It gets worse,* he projected. *I wish I did not have to show you, but it is the only way for you to understand.*

The memories shifted, and I saw the palace as it had been more than three years ago, shining and full of people. The servants scattered before the king as he strode through the corridors, and I knew—as seventeen-year-old Dominic had known—that news of the king's massacre had preceded them to the palace. By the time they approached the royal wing, not a single servant was anywhere to be seen or heard.

King Nicolas made no comment, his face cold and detached. Until Queen Ruby appeared at the top of the stairs. Dominic's shame returned at the sight of his mother's ashen face, and the way she met his eyes only to quickly look away. His mother would have at least tried to intervene. He knew it. She did not believe the people lived to serve them.

A spasm passed over the king's expression. I could not have guessed at its meaning, but the young Dominic interpreted it as a sign of the king's emotions for his wife. Of his love. Except that over the top of that sensation, I could feel Dominic's current opinion. It had not been love. His father had not known how to love. He had valued his wife because she was beautiful, and because at times the people's love for her had been useful. But he did not love her.

*What have you done?* asked the queen in Dominic's memory. *Tell me it isn't true. It cannot be true!*

*They defied me. All of them. They got only what they deserved.* The king attempted to brush past his wife, but she clutched at his sleeve.

*Even the babies?* she whispered, horror in her eyes.

King Nicolas turned on her, anger transforming his features. *How dare you question me?* He raised his hand and hit her, hard, across the face. She fell backwards, losing her footing and tumbling down the long flight of marble stairs.

A young girl whose presence Dominic had not even noticed, ran forward and grabbed blindly at her father's jacket, attempting to shake him, despite his solid bulk and her slender frame. *How could you?* she screamed.

Her father, for it was Princess Adelaide, raised his hand as if to strike her, too. But, quick as a flash, Dominic interposed himself between them, catching his father's wrist. For a moment, the two men stood facing one another, both of their chests heaving. And then all three of them looked down to the bottom of the stairs. The queen lay completely still, and Dominic's certainty of her death washed over me.

I gave a gasping sob, overwhelmed with the horror of his memories. But they did not stop.

I felt the young Dominic's determination to push his father down after his mother. But before he could do so, a flash of light blinded him. When his sight slowly returned, a figure he had never seen before stood at the top of the stairs. All three royals stared at the woman I recognized as a godmother. And yet, despite similar features, including the gray hair, the woman looked nothing like the godmothers I had seen. Instead of a humorous affection, almost grandmotherly in nature, this being radiated wrath and power.

Dominic and Adelaide drew back, the princess clinging to her brother, but their father stood his ground. A thunderous rage built in his face as he listened to her words.

The godmother rebuked him for his actions and for the evil he had brought to his kingdom. Young Dominic's confusion made me wonder what royals were taught about the godmothers in these lands. Didn't he know that the rulers were responsible for the prosperity of their kingdoms? Why else would the godmothers go to such lengths to ensure true love ruled?

King Nicolas had just demonstrated that no love remained in his heart. Dominic should not have been surprised to find a godmother intervening before he brought about the complete destruction of his kingdom.

She explained the protection that had been placed on the people of Palinar, and the conditions for it to be lifted.

*How dare you seek to work against me?* the king raged at her in the memory. And then he actually lunged forward to strike the godmother as he had just done to his wife.

The godmother, sadness on her face, stepped back to avoid him. And it seemed, in his anger, the king had forgotten who he dealt with. The winged woman's steps took her from the top of the steps into the air, and the king's momentum caused him to lunge head first down the stairs. Within seconds, his broken body lay motionless next to the queen's.

Dominic and Adelaide retreated another step, their eyes now on the hovering godmother. She looked at them both and sighed. *There was always hope,* she said, *although I did not entertain much. And now the burden of freeing your people will fall on you, young prince. I hope you will prove a more worthy student of love than your father.* And she was gone.

But the younger Dominic knew only the pride his position had taught him and the anger toward his father which had been whipped now into a rage so burning hot that there was room for nothing else.

*I did not know what love meant, though my mother had tried to model it to me,* Dominic whispered in my mind. *My exile at the castle calmed me somewhat, but it was only in watching you, that I began to remember the lessons of my mother, so different from those of my father.*

My heart ached for him. I could not imagine growing up without my father's love. It had been an anchor for Lily and me during the years that our mother had been distant from us.

A succession of short memories flashed through my mind. An angry Dominic, eaten up by guilt and shame and grief, roamed the castle, rejecting his sister's attempts to speak with him. It wasn't until a week after their parents' death that he realized he hadn't even seen her in days. He searched the castle for her, but could find no sign of the thirteen-year-old. Fear gripped him, and he called on the godmother he had so recently seen for the first time.

To his surprise, and mine, she actually came. This time she looked more like the godmothers I had met, her no-nonsense air obscuring an underlying vein of sympathy. *Princess Adelaide is gone from here. She is no longer your concern.*

He pressed her for more information, and she placed her hands on her hips, narrowing her eyes. *You have a whole kingdom of people who are your responsibility, young prince. What thought have you given to them? I had hoped that you might take my words to heart, and yet so far you have shown too much selfishness even to consider your own sister.*

*What consideration—or love—can I show to my people when they have all of them disappeared to a place where I can neither see nor hear them?* he asked, angered by her rebuke.

She sighed. *You are not your father, and you have not yet committed his crimes, though you bear the responsibility for correcting them. I can give you some assistance, but it will come at a price.*

*A price?* I could feel the injured pride in his memory, that this unknown woman should dictate such terms to a prince of Palinar. *Why should I pay a price?*

For a moment, the wrath she had shown toward King Nicolas reflected from her eyes. *Inside you are in danger of becoming more beast than man, young prince. As your father was before you. Perhaps if you see this reality always before your eyes, you will be spurred to consider your responsibilities toward those in your care.*

*As for my offered assistance, you will now find yourself able to see your subjects. But the only ones you will be able to hear are your own personal servants.*

*But my servants all reside at my castle.*

*And that is where you also will be confined. So often you have retreated there—now you must remain there until you are ready to step out and take up the mantle of kingship. If you step outside the grounds while your curse remains, you will be struck with a deadly illness.*

A terrible, grinding pain ripped through the memory, as Dominic's body transformed into the Beast. He opened his mouth to protest, but only a growl emerged.

*You must transform your insides back into a man again,* she had cautioned him. *Because only when you have so completely transformed yourself that a woman will value you enough to marry you, despite your beastly state, will you be free.*

The memory died away, and I could once again only feel Dominic's current emotions. The strength of his mind seemed to be weakening, and I desperately tried to cling to our connection.

*I heard you, back at the castle,* he told me, and I frowned in confusion at the change of topic. *I had come to find you, to give you the rose and wish you farewell. But I heard what you said to the servants. How you could never love a man who stood by and became a part of his father's evil. I know you could never love me.*

My eyes widened. *Oh, but...* How to explain to him that I had been ready to forgive Cole until he proved himself just as evil as his father. I had only said that because I could not tell them the whole truth.

*When I discovered Cole had escaped, I knew instantly that some-thing was wrong, and that I must pursue you. Must protect you from him. It did not even enter my consideration that such a course of action would mean my death. I only hoped I could retain my strength long enough to save you.* His voice filled with wonder. *And then, as I traveled, I began to hear flashes of my people around me. By the time I reached the garrison of guards inside the gates, I could hear them clearly. A good thing since I needed them to follow me straight into action.*

*As I grew closer to you, as you helped me change, the protection had begun to weaken. But only when I was truly ready to sacrifice myself did it entirely lift.* He shook his head weakly. *I did not realize that self-sacrifice would be so easy. When I thought of you in Cole's hands, it was no decision at all.*

*You're right,* I projected, staring into his eyes. *It is too easy.*

His brow wrinkled, his eyes narrowing in surprise.

*Dying is far too easy. If you wish to prove your ability to love, you must go on living and show that you can sacrifice every day, in the small things as well as the big.*

*I would live if I could,* he projected. *Even though I would never see you again. Merely to be in the same world with you would be enough.*

The tears flowed unheeded down my face, as I knelt over him. *It is evening, Dominic, and you have not yet asked me your nightly question.*

He reached up a hand to stroke the side of my face. *I do not deserve you.*

*I don't care what you deserve.* I gripped his jacket with both hands and leaned closer. *Ask me.*

The fading light in his eyes rekindled for the briefest moment. *Will you...*His chest stilled, and I stopped breathing until his own labored breaths began again. *Will you marry me in the morning, my love?*

"Yes! Yes!" I spoke the words aloud as well as in my mind, in case it made a difference. "I will engage myself to you in truth this time, Dominic, and I will marry you in the morning, or any day you like. Just don't die!"

Amazement transformed his face, as he covered one of my hands with his own much larger one. *But, why, Sophie? Why would you marry a beast like me?*

I stared at him. There were so many ways I could answer that. So many reasons I had been wrong, and he wasn't a monster. But every moment he grew weaker. I decided to give the simplest answer possible.

*Because I love you, Dominic.*

An exhalation, half cry, half groan broke from him, and his whole body began to shake. I fell back from him. Light roiled across his hands and his features, making it impossible to see through to his face underneath. His loud roar sounded all around me, only to be suddenly cut off.

The light faded, and his shaking stilled. Dominic looked up at me out of the face from the portrait, aged slightly, but easily recognizable. He pulled himself into a sitting position, gathered me into his lap, and lowered his face to mine, our lips so close that I couldn't be sure whether they actually touched or not. He paused there, and heat rushed through me as I remembered our previous almost-kiss.

His hand reached out to stroke my hair as we hung in that moment, consumed by memories and shaken by love. I had known then that I wanted his kiss, but not why. I knew now that I wanted not only his kiss but his forever, too. We both moved at the same time, pressing our lips together as we clung to each other in joy.

# CHAPTER 32

could hear Lily laughing and applauding in the background, and when we finally broke apart, I looked up at her sheepishly.

"Don't give me that look, Sophie. You enjoyed every second of that."

I looked back at Dominic, and he could clearly read the truth of her words in my face, because he leaned in to do it again.

"Whoa, whoa, whoa," said Lily with another laugh. "Just hold on there."

Dominic glowered up at her, but she was unmoved. "I don't think we've been properly introduced. I'm Lily. And that's my twin you're holding so possessively."

He gave a reluctant laugh, the sound almost as rough as it had been when he was the Beast. He lifted me gently from his lap, and stood, pulling me up with him. "I am Dominic. And I can assure you that I have no wish to start my new betrothal at odds with my bride's twin."

"Oh, excellent. You can speak now." Lily gave me a significant look. "Wasn't there something rather important—and time sensitive—that needed to happen once you could speak?"

I gasped. "The coronation vow! Quick, Dominic." I ran back through the still open doorway, tugging him along behind me. Lily and Jon trailed after us.

"What's all this?" Jon kept pace with us despite his confusion. "Is there really such a rush?" Obviously, the coronation hadn't been one of the things Lily had been able to explain to him while they were under guard.

I shrugged and didn't slow down. "I don't know if anyone has been keeping track of the number of hours it's been since Dominic's father died. And I for one don't want to discover we've arrived too late because we dawdled on our way there."

"Very well, then," said Dominic and, without warning, swept me into his arms and took off at a jog.

I giggled and swatted at him. "Put me down!"

"I thought you said we were in a rush?"

I rolled my eyes, but secretly I liked the way he carried me, as easily as if I were made of cushions. He might have become human again, but some things hadn't changed. His shoulders were still broad, although correctly proportioned now, and his arms were still strong.

After a whispered conversation between Lily and Jon that I didn't attempt to catch, Jon broke away from us. However, he had joined us in the throne room within minutes of our own arrival, with someone else in tow. Lily had already explained that they had stashed the terrified official in a dusty sitting room, and that Jon had gone to fetch him.

"If he was official enough for a wedding ceremony," she said, "we're hoping he's official enough for a coronation oath, too."

The man seemed extremely nervous to be confronted with Prince Dominic, but he made no protest to our request. I expected that performing the ceremony in such a fashion would feel rushed and irreverent, just the four of us gathered around the official. But Dominic stood tall, and his strong voice spoke the words of the ancient vow with such meaning, that the moment achieved a solemnity I had not expected.

And when he finished, cheers broke out all around us. I had been so transfixed, I hadn't even noticed the hall behind us filling with the guards and other inhabitants of the city who had made their way up to the palace to find out who had broken the curse.

For a long time after that, Dominic was busy talking with important citizens and the occasional noble who had remained in the capital. The guards, members of the single company he had ordered to remain in the capital when the others had been dispersed, were ordered to round up any of Cole's men who still remained free and return to their barracks.

Several of the people who had arrived identified themselves as palace servants who had been living in the city while the palace stood unoccupied. I received the strong impression that no one in the city had stepped foot in the palace since the curse. That they had, in fact, feared the place. Since they had initially fled at the return of King Nicolas from his massacre, none of them could have known the curse's true nature.

But if they had been afraid before, they now seemed happy to have returned. They quickly put themselves to work cleaning out the kitchen and several of the bedchambers.

"You'll have to hold a proper coronation ceremony, with the actual crown, at some point," I said to Dominic. "But I suppose you'll have to wait for the nobles to gather first. How in the kingdoms have you been ruling them all this time if you couldn't hear anything they said?"

His eyes looked sad as he answered me. "My father's was a harsh rule. He had trained his subjects to immediate and unquestioning obedience. With the mirror at his disposal, the nobles dared not break his commands even on the privacy of their own estates. The godmother allowed me a week to make my way to my castle, and I used the time to issue my orders. I knew the kingdom needed to go into sustainment mode."

He frowned. "Since I couldn't hear them, I had no choice but to find each noble and issue my orders without conversation or discussion. I must have looked terrifying to them, too. I can only suppose they thought I meant to rule as my father had done. They did not know of the protection they had been given, or that I would be confined to my castle. I have watched them through the mirror, understanding as much as I could from observation alone, and sent further orders as seemed necessary."

"Did you bring the mirror with you?" I wondered if it could be helpful now as we tried to bring the kingdom back together.

"No," he said. "I'm afraid I didn't squeeze it into a saddlebag when I leaped on Spitfire's back and charged off to rescue you."

Lily rolled her eyes. "Men. They never think of the practical things."

Dominic stiffened, offended, until we both burst into peals of laughter, and he relaxed.

"I think having the two of you together is going to take some getting used to."

"Well, get used to it," said Lily, slipping her arm around my waist. "Because I intend to be around for a while."

Jon slapped Dominic on the back. "Don't worry. You'll get used to it. Mostly. Just don't be surprised if she starts breaking off mid-sentence or staring into space for protracted periods in the middle of a conversation because she's been distracted by a voice in her head."

Lily shook her head at him, but fixed her eyes on Dominic and me. "Speaking of the practical things." She put her hands on her hips. "I hope you weren't serious about that getting married in the morning thing. Because I cannot possibly put together a royal wedding overnight. And just think of our family. Mother and Alyssa would be heartbroken if they missed your wedding. I've already sent them word to come—so they could save you and attend my wedding—but it will take them weeks to arrive."

"Ha!" I grinned at my twin. "You don't fool me, Lil. There's the real reason—you don't want me getting married before you."

"Well, I am the older twin," she said with dignity, although her eyes laughed back at me.

"And I've already been waiting patiently for several months," said Jon, slipping his arms around her waist from behind and pressing his face briefly into her hair.

I glanced back at Dominic. "The curse doesn't require we be married in the morning, does it?"

He pulled me close and leaned down to whisper in my ear. The sound of his familiar voice speaking aloud, the growl still lurking behind his words, thrilled me. "Would you believe me if I said it does? I don't like this talk of months."

I chuckled and shook my head. "You've waited for years, you can wait a little longer." I looked over at Lily. "I don't think Dominic could possibly leave Palinar right now. Do you think the people of Marin would stand for their heir being married here?"

Lily's eyes lit up. "A double wedding! As soon as Mother and the rest arrive." She turned to Jon. "Oh, Jon. Can we?"

He laughed. "If it means finally setting a date, I will use all of my persuasive powers. We can have some sort of ceremonial event when we return to Marin to commemorate it." He tried to suppress a smile. "I know you're a little sick of balls after the Tourney, but…"

Lily groaned. "I said my birthday ball was the only one I would attend this year." She bit her lip, but I could see excitement in her eyes. "But if it will convince your parents, I suppose I might be persuaded to dance…"

"Dance?" asked a familiar voice behind us. "But you dance so beautifully, Princess Sophie."

"Oh, no…" said Lily, as I swung around to confront the girl.

"Oh!" she exclaimed, looking wide eyed between the two of

us. "I'm sorry. I didn't realize...You must be Princess Lily. My apologies."

"Tara!" The short girl looked close enough to my imaginings that I suspected I might have recognized her even without her voice. I rushed forward to embrace her, and she squeaked in surprise. "Sorry!" I stepped back. "But I had no idea you were here in the capital, and I'm just so excited to be able to see you."

I glanced reproachfully at Dominic. Why hadn't he told me he had brought my friends with him? But he was regarding Tara with a raised eyebrow and an expression of resignation. "Tell me," he said. "How many of my servants have gone rogue and defected to the capital in my absence?"

Tara flushed, looking a little scared. "Oh, no, Your Highness! Only, I couldn't sit around at the castle, not knowing what had happened to the princess."

"Ignore him." I told her. "That was extremely sweet of you, although probably foolhardy. It could have been dangerous."

She shrugged. "That Cole made it through, didn't he? And I didn't ride here alone, or anything. Lottie's Samuel has turned out to be far more resourceful than I would have imagined. He was on duty in the entrance hall and overheard His Highness talking about riding to the capital because he had seen Cole there in the mirror and also your carriage heading in that direction. So, Samuel convinced one of the coachmen to bring us here in one of the unused carriages." She looked a little guilty. "We may have given poor Thomas the impression that you were expecting your maids to follow you."

"You mean Lottie's here, too? Where?" I looked around, eager to see if my mental image of her had been equally accurate. My eyes fell on Lily who appeared to be suppressing a laugh.

I gave her a glare. *These are my friends!*

She grinned back at me. *I'm only laughing because she's so exactly like you described her. You have to let me come and meet Lottie, too.*

Tara had already started leading me away, and Lily ran to catch up without waiting for my response. Tara apologized profusely for mistaking her for me, but Lily waved away her apology and had soon entirely ingratiated herself with my maid.

We found Lottie with a tall man, dressed as a footman, who hovered over her protectively. I immediately recognized the truth of the assessment Tara had made of him months ago. Samuel looked trust-worthy and easily approachable. And I also realized that Tara had been right about Lottie.

My image of her had been quite wrong, although her basic features and coloring were as I expected. I had allowed her general attitude and her lack of confidence in herself to override Tara's description, but it turned out she was indeed willowy and graceful. I couldn't be surprised at the way Samuel looked at her.

All of the introductions were quickly made, and Lily was soon winning over Lottie as well. I watched her with amusement, somehow suspecting that I would now be expected to share their services. But in truth, I was merely glad to be so quickly reunited with my friends from the castle. With so many new people to meet, I appreciated the familiar voices.

All three were full of thanks to me for breaking the curse, although I tried to deflect their praise onto Dominic, since he had really been the one to free them.

"But he couldn't have done it without you," said Tara. "He hadn't broken it in all the years before you came."

I considered telling her the details of the double curse but hesitated. I didn't know if Dominic would want it widely known, and I wasn't sure I had the energy for such a complicated explanation, anyway.

"Of course, we don't really know what the curse involved," said Lottie, "and we weren't supposed to talk about it. Except you can't stop rumors, not completely. We were all sure you must have come to break it, and at least half the servants were convinced that if you couldn't break it before the coronation window closed, we would all be stuck forever."

I shuddered to think of the truth to that guess. Now that I knew the truth of the curse, I knew that it would never have been broken with Cole as king. Would the wilderness have returned once Dominic had no longer been heir and regent?

I shook myself from such gloomy thoughts to ask after the rest of the castle servants.

Tara told me that Gordon had begged to come, claiming that his work helping Matthew with Chestnut qualified him to assist our coachman. When Gilda roundly refused his demand, he had even attempted to stowaway in the carriage. Lily exclaimed that she wished he had succeeded since she was dying to meet him, but I couldn't help feeling relieved he had failed.

There would be enough going on over the next few days without my feeling responsible for whatever unintended mischief he would have been sure to land himself in. I told Lottie she should write to them all, though, and let them know that I would visit the castle as soon as possible to meet them properly at last.

# CHAPTER 33

There turned out to be a great deal to be done to return Palinar to order and prosperity again. I forced Dominic to go to his bed before he had even finished making a list of the tasks which needed to be completed immediately. The servants had somehow managed to dust four chambers for us, but Lily and I insisted on sharing a room. We weren't ready to be parted after our long separation.

We both slept deeply, far beyond normal levels of exhaustion. But we awoke early, excited to finally be able to talk in person again.

"You know, I've been thinking," said Lily. "About the Tourney."

I nodded. "Me too. We knew that each Tourney was shaped by the prince who called it, so we assumed Dominic must be evil and twisted. Only then we learned that the darkness of the curse had corrupted the Tourney through him. Looking back, I can't understand why it never occurred to me that it was the darkness that made the Tourney so awful, and not Dominic himself. I suppose it was because I thought he was responsible for bringing the darkness in the first place. It never occurred to me that he might be trapped, as well."

Lily shook her head. "How could you have foreseen any of this? We knew nothing about Palinar or Dominic." She looked across at me. "And don't bite my nose off, but I think he must have been responsible for at least some of the difficulty of the Tourney events. Because think how perfectly it's worked out. You were exactly the right person to come here. In fact, you might be the only person who could have broken both curses." She bit her lip. "We knew that some of the original magic of the Tourney remained, enough to keep us all alive at least. But I think there must have been enough to ensure the right winner, too. The whole time we thought we were cheating using our projections to give us an advantage. And yet, it's only because of that ability that you were able to communicate with Dominic. In the end, all those horrible events ensured the right bride won."

I couldn't deny the truth of her words, or that there had been at least a little darkness lurking in Dominic when we first met. "I guess I wasn't ready to believe that Dominic and I could be a perfect match until now."

Lily spoke in my mind. *And you're completely sure he is? You didn't agree to marry him out of pity or...or a sense of responsibility or something?*

I grimaced at the concerned look she gave me. *I understand why you're concerned. You haven't had the chance to get to know him like I have. But you saw the way he saved me, the way he sacrificed himself for me. I just wish you could see some of the other things he's done...*I broke off, my eyes going wide as an idea occurred to me.

*What is it?*

*When Dominic was too weak to speak, I managed to connect with him in my mind, like we do.*

*Wait—what? You can talk to him in your mind now, too?*

My face fell. *Not any more, sadly. The ability must have been somehow connected to the curse. But while we were connected, he did something we've never done. Something it never even occurred to me to try.* I explained the way he had shown me his memories.

Lily's eyes lit up with excitement. *I guess we never even thought of it because before now we never needed to do something like that—all our memories were shared. But let's try it right now. I want to see that magical castle of yours!*

We ran late for breakfast because it took more experimentation than we hoped. But the important thing was that, in the end, it worked. Hurrying through the palace, we both tripped more than once, distracted by the inundation of shared memories. Neither of us spoke it, either aloud or through projections, but I knew we were thinking the same thing—this new connection would make our inevitable separation easier. Because by falling in love with Jon and Dominic, we had ensured that our lives would be lived apart.

We only stopped practicing when Jon demanded our attention. "You have to be firm with them," he told Dominic, as if imparting a great pearl of wisdom, and Lily threw a piece of half-buttered toast at him.

"I have a question for you, Dominic," she said, after choosing another slice. "When you arrived you never seemed in the least confused between Sophie and me, even though we were dressed nearly identically."

Dominic looked disdainful at the suggestion that he might not have recognized me. "You may look something alike, but I could never mistake anyone for my Sophie."

I blushed and looked down at my toast. I still hadn't quite adjusted to my wonderful new reality.

Jonathan raised an eyebrow and glanced between the three of us before leaning down to half-whisper in Lily's ear. "I could tell you apart from the beginning, too, remember."

She glared at him, also keeping her voice low. "Jon! This is hardly the time."

"What?" He shrugged innocently. "I'm just making sure I get full credit. You know, since I'm not dark and brooding, and I don't have a whole castle of my own. Several castles, in fact, now that I come to think of it." He looked despondently around the room, his face so comical, I almost laughed despite everything.

Lily rolled her eyes. "Because you're so insecure."

He reached over and dragged her from her chair, dumping her in his lap. "I can be very insecure. That's why I need you to constantly tell me how important I am. And how much you love me."

She wrinkled her nose, and he dropped a kiss on it. "No? Too much?"

She laughed and nestled against his chest.

I shook my head and glanced at Dominic. His horrified expression made me chuckle. "Don't worry, you'll get used to them," I assured him. When his expression didn't change, I laughed again.

Several hours later, when we finally managed to steal an hour alone in the palace rose garden, I refrained from pointing out that we were sitting in a similar manner to Jon and Lily at breakfast. I didn't want to say anything that might make him rethink having me snuggled on his lap.

Not when we were having such an enjoyable time finding out exactly what the other had been thinking at crucial moments throughout our relationship.

"I was a fool," said Dominic, when I asked why he had called the Tourney and then proceeded to treat me so rudely. "More than a fool. I hoped that an engagement through the Tourney would be enough. But clearly it was not. So, I ordered for you to come to my castle, thinking perhaps we just needed to be in the same vicinity. But clearly that didn't work either."

He sighed. "So, then I decided I needed to get you to actually marry me. Each night I asked you, desperate to get you to agree but not really believing it possible that you could see past my appearance. I had been intrigued by you from the start, but you were terrified of me. In my despair, I made no effort to make myself lovable. I let my anger rule me at each instance of hurt pride."

I shook my head at him. "What if I had said yes? If I had married you out of obligation, because of the Tourney, you would never have had the opportunity to be free."

"Thank goodness I was so repulsive, then," he said wryly.

"You weren't all bad. You came to save me from the wolves, remember?"

"I've told you already that you reminded me of the goodness I had seen before in my mother and sister. I never stood up to my father for them, and I failed Adelaide in the end, but I had a chance to save you. It was an act of atonement, I suppose. Only then you came to my sickroom and ordered around my servants and read to me—even though you turned up your pretty little nose at my mathematics." He chuckled, the sound close to a growl, and placed a kiss on the offending article. "I saw the way you controlled your fear and your anger toward me. And I began to learn that I could do the same. You made me choose to be different."

"That's funny," I said. "I don't remember being so controlled. I remember getting rather angry at you, in fact."

He smiled ruefully. "Only when I deserved and needed it."

"Oh, no disputing that."

He shook his head at me before resting his forehead against mine. "I love you, Sophie. You have saved me from myself."

I smiled, feeling as if my heart would burst. "When I rode into Palinar, all those months ago, I told Lily that I wouldn't be coming back until I could free the kingdom and bring the light back with me. It never occurred to me that I might want to stay."

His arms around me tightened. "We would lose half our light without you as queen."

I flushed, but then my thoughts turned dark. "Lily and I are both convinced Cole must have gotten his hands on an ancient godmother object. I only wish we had found it on him. And that we had found that man he was speaking with."

Somehow, in all the confusion, the man Cole had been speaking to when the guards dragged me into the throne room dressed like Lily, had disappeared. I was convinced he must have taken the object with him.

Dominic cupped my face in his hands. "I thought Lily was supposed to be the worrier. Let it go, my love. You have freed an entire kingdom, as well as my heart. Let that be enough for one day."

A chill ran up me at his endearment, and I pressed my lips against his. Within moments I had forgotten every other thought except wonder that I was sitting here surrounded by roses, kissing my Beast.

# NOTE FROM THE AUTHOR

You can read about Celine's adventures in the icy kingdom of Eldon in A Crown of Snow and Ice: A Retelling of The Snow Queen. Turn the page for a sneak peek!

And if you missed the story of the twin's childhood, read it in the first book in The Four Kingdoms series, The Princess Companion: A Retelling of The Princess and the Pea.

To be kept informed of my new releases, please sign up to my mailing list at www.melaniecellier.com. At my website, you'll also find an array of free extra content.

Thank you for taking the time to read my book. If you enjoyed it, please spread the word! You could start by leaving a review on Amazon or Goodreads or Facebook or any other social media site. Your review would be very much appreciated and would make a big difference!

# CHAPTER 1

*I* grumbled under my breath as the carriage bumped over a particularly large hole in the road. Prince Oliver's chestnut stallion flashed past the window, and I directed my ire toward him, although I lowered my voice even further so as not to be overheard by the other passengers.

I would have been riding too, if I was anywhere but Eldon. I hated being cooped up in the carriage, especially with no one but Emmeline and Giselle for company. They weren't exactly scintillating conversationalists.

"We will reach the capital by sundown, Celine," said Giselle, as if in answer to my inaudible grumbles. Her tone suggested she had no complaints to make about several more hours trapped on the uncomfortable seats. I waited for her to go on, but she directed her gaze out the other window, returning to silence.

I sighed and looked out my own window. Perhaps I should have ridden, after all. But a moment's glance at the landscape reinforced my original decision.

Despite asking everyone I could find, I hadn't been able to garner much information on Eldon before my departure. The one thing everyone had agreed on, though, was that it was cold.

Really cold. And if there was one thing I hated, it was being cold. Not a problem I usually had in my tropical kingdom of Lanover.

So far in these new lands I had visited Marin, Palinar, and now Eldon, and none possessed the clinging warmth of my home. But Eldon still stood out from the others. Here we were only an hour's drive from the port, and already patches of snow covered the ground. We'd hardly even begun to ascend yet. I hated to think what it would be like once we hit the capital.

Eldon was so mountainous that it had apparently always been on the colder side. Or so the inhabitants of Palinar informed me. Like their own barely inhabited eastern region. But the Eldonian capital, located in the foothills rather than the true mountain ranges, had once been pleasant for a good portion of the year.

And then things had started to change across the kingdoms. I shivered and rubbed my hands together, although the fur rug across my lap was actually keeping them rather toasty so far. On reflection, I thought I would have preferred dealing with wolves and bears and invisible people—as Sophie had done in Palinar—over this icy cold. Why couldn't I have been sensible and gone to visit Gabe in Talinos—or even better, Millie on the warm southern isle of Trione?

"We seem to be making good time," said Emmeline, out of nowhere. Like her sister, the princess's tone suggested she didn't much care one way or the other.

I resisted the urge to glare at her. After all, this was exactly why I had come to this awful place. Something was decidedly not right about Princesses Emmeline and Giselle. The same something that wasn't right about their older brother, Prince Oliver. And something wasn't right about their kingdom either. That was the one thing everyone I asked could agree on. Ever since the darkness had spread its way across these lands, Eldon had grown more and more icy. And from what I could see, it wasn't just the weather.

The young Eldonian royals were as cold as their kingdom. I

had never seen either girl display anything I would consider an emotion. With my own eyes, I had witnessed Giselle fall, apparently to her death, in the Princess Tourney the year before. And yet neither her inseparable older sister, nor even Giselle herself, seemed in the least perturbed by the terrifying accident. Decidedly not normal. And I intended to find out why.

When I was drafted into the Princess Tourney, along with my friends Lily and Sophie and all of the local princesses, I had been newly arrived from the Four Kingdoms. I had known no one from these lands, but I had made plenty of friends during the months of the Tourney. Emmeline and Giselle had not been among them.

So it had shocked me when the sisters invited me to visit them after the Tourney ended. What could possibly have motivated them to do so? The whole thing smelled of adventure—and if there was one thing I couldn't resist, it was the prospect of an adventure.

*Idiotic. That's what I was*, I reflected sadly as I watched the snow build up beside the road. Why couldn't I have found an adventure somewhere with a warm climate?

I had already put off the invitation until after Lily and Sophie's joint wedding, remaining behind in Marin when Emmeline and Giselle returned home after the Tourney. And then my mother, along with one of my brothers and his wife, had sailed over from the Four Kingdoms for the twins' wedding. They couldn't sail home in winter, and my mother insisted I remain in Palinar with them for the duration of their visit.

I think my mother was surprised at my acquiescence. My brother less so. At least once he heard the stories about the climate in Eldon.

But, come spring, I had grown altogether tired of being back under my family's wing and decided it was time to follow through on my promise to visit Eldon. It was spring, after all. How cold could it be?

I shivered again, this time directing the grumbles at myself. I glanced at the girls across from me. How would they react if I made my complaints aloud? So far common courtesy had been holding me back, but my curiosity to see their reaction was growing by the minute. It was horribly tempting to see how far I would have to push to get a response from the detached princesses.

I had actually been a little touched when all three of the younger Eldonian royals had traveled down from the capital to meet my ship at the port. Touched enough that I had even insisted on taking the front seat so that I faced backward, and they were both able to travel forward. But we had now been stuck in the carriage together for some time, and I could no more see a reason for their coming to meet me than for their making the invitation in the first place. They certainly weren't expending any further effort to make me feel welcome. And Prince Oliver had managed no more greeting than a murmured "Princess Celine" and a head nod.

My mother had wondered if the icy kingdom was hoping for a marriage alliance with my distant kingdom of Lanover. But after meeting the Eldonians at the wedding in Palinar, she had been forced to admit that neither the Eldonian delegation, nor Prince Oliver himself, seemed in the least interested in either the Lanoverians or me, their youngest princess.

A pang in my right ankle made me scowl. The broken bone had healed months ago, but it still sometimes ached in the cold. An unpleasant reminder of the ordeal of the Tourney. My mother seemed to think the Tourney should have been adventure enough for her seventh child and couldn't understand what pulled me to visit Eldon. But the Tourney hadn't been my adventure. Not really. At least not after I had broken my ankle in the first trial. The Tourney had been the twins' adventure, and I had been nothing but a burden on the eleven other princesses.

At least my mother knew me well enough not to argue. With

six older siblings, I had long ago determined to find my own path. I had always longed to get out of the shadow of a family full of far too many outstanding royals. My one fear had been that my mother would insist the Duchess of Sessily accompany me to Eldon. The older noble was far too canny for my taste, one of the few who could see through whatever scheme I currently had underway.

But it seemed the duchess was needed back in the Four Kingdoms, so I had received a reprieve. I had been saddled with the usual collection of guards and maids and such, of course, but I didn't mind them—none of them would attempt to manage me.

For the first time ever, I was truly on my own. And I relished every moment of it. At least until a fresh blast of freezing air somehow swept its way through the carriage. Hopeless dreams of Lanover's bright, sandy beaches filled my mind until a sudden lurch sent me tumbling off the seat and on to the two other princesses.

The tangle of girls and rugs took some moments to straighten out, our efforts impeded by the strange new tilt of the now-stationary carriage. Emmeline was the first to free herself, moving over toward the door. But instead of opening it, she shifted back toward us.

"Perhaps it would be best if we stayed in the carriage for now." Her calm voice didn't fool me.

"What's going on?" I finally kicked free of my rug and half crawled over to have a look myself.

"It also might be wiser to keep away from the windows."

I ignored Emmeline, and she made no further move to stop me. The scene that greeted my gaze would have been accompanied by a great deal of noise in any other kingdom. But the coachmen, grooms, and guards all filed along in near silence, dropping their weapons in a pile in front of a masked figure. I pressed myself against the window to get a better view.

We appeared to be surrounded by mounted, armed men. Only

my own two Lanoverian guards looked appropriately horrified, but I could hardly blame them for falling into line. Our party was vastly outnumbered. For a moment I wished I hadn't left the rest of my guards to follow with the baggage, but even their number wouldn't have been enough to tip the balance.

I scooted to the other side of the carriage, hoping to spot an opening in the circle of assailants. But, if anything, there were even more of them on this side, stretching out into some sort of field on the side of the road. Prince Oliver's stallion danced uneasily, and the prince seemed wholly occupied in keeping the animal calm.

I sighed. Clearly I could not expect any heroics from him. For the first time, real fear gripped me. Who would dare attack a royal carriage traveling the well-used road between the port and the capital? And what did they intend to do with us?

I glanced back at Emmeline and Giselle sitting calmly on the carriage seat, despite the awkward new angle. A warmth ignited inside my chest, the pity that surged through me taking me by surprise. What could possibly have made them this way? They seemed more like empty shells than people.

I looked back outside and met Prince Oliver's eyes. He watched me without any sign of fear or perturbation. My pity transformed into something more closely resembling anger, and the spark grew into a burning sensation. If they had no care for themselves, they should at least have some concern for their guest, surely?

If it was up to me to save myself, I didn't know what hope I had against a large company of armed guards. Especially when they were mounted, and I was not. I had a small dagger hidden in each boot, but I couldn't see what good they would do me. Reluctantly, I decided my best hope was to wait and watch for a better opportunity of escape.

But, as I thought it, one of the attackers moved forward to attach a lead rope to Oliver's mount. The prince's calm acquiescence caused the fire inside me to leap into an inferno and, without thought, I thrust out my hands as if I could push the attackers aside from inside the carriage.

A rush of hot air shook the vehicle, nearly toppling us all again. Outside, it looked more like a gale. Those on the ground stumbled, some falling, and the horses screamed and snorted as their riders desperately tried to control them. Some failed, and their mounts took off, scattering in all directions.

A half-second before the unexpected gust, Oliver had looked up, his gaze meeting mine. And I could have sworn that as I thrust out my hands, something sparked between my eyes and his. For the first time, a glimmer of warmth filled his blue eyes, lending animation to his pale face. But a moment later his horse reared, and I lost sight of his expression.

The man holding the chestnut's lead rope lost it as he attempted to control his own mount. When the prince's stallion found his feet again, he charged forward. Again I couldn't be sure in all the commotion, but it looked as if more than random chance directed the horse toward the newly opened gap in the circle surrounding us. The prince appeared to be actively guiding him as he leaped through and disappeared from sight. So there was some life in the prince, after all.

For a wild moment I considered flinging myself out of the carriage and scrambling after him. But on foot I wouldn't make it far, and already the gaps were closing as riders returned with their now calm mounts. One of the returning men focused his gaze on my face as I peered out of the window, and I drew back hurriedly.

Retaking my seat as best I could since it still sat at an angle, I hid my trembling hands in my lap. The idea of escape had momentarily distracted me, but now my thoughts whirled back to the source of the sudden and violent wind. It had not been natural, that much was obvious. The temperature, even in the carriage, still lingered several degrees warmer than it had before.

But that wasn't what scared me. The timing on its own would have been uncanny. But it had been more than that. The moment I had thrust out my hands, I had felt the fire raging inside me rush down my arms and out of my hands to heat the air around me. And now, although the air felt warmed, my insides had returned to their usual cool state.

My stomach roiled, to be sure, but it carried no unusual heat. It made no sense, and I couldn't explain it, but I couldn't help thinking that somehow that hot wind had come from me. When I thrust out my arms to push away our attackers, the air itself had moved to obey me.

Read on in A Crown of Snow and Ice

# ACKNOWLEDGMENTS

I didn't expect it, but this book turned out to be one of the hardest I've ever written. Beauty and the Beast is a beloved fairy tale—possibly the most beloved—so retelling it comes with a lot of pressure. It's also unlike many other fairy tales, with the adventure overshadowed by an intense and complex romance. I've done my best to make the story my own, bringing it into my Four Kingdoms world, while keeping all the elements that have been beloved by so many generations.

There is so much that is enchanting in the story of Beauty and the Beast—that the worst of circumstances can somehow lead to the best; that we are all worthy of being loved, no matter what we look like or what hurts we have either caused or endured; that self-sacrifice will be rewarded; that love can conquer all. And despite the stress of the writing, I've enjoyed seeing Sophie and Dominic living out this tale.

But I couldn't have done it without the support of those around me and, in particular, my husband, Marc, and my amazing friend Katie, who kept me and my family alive, fed and sane while I wrote, agonized, edited and agonized some more. Thanks for listening to me and taking me seriously, however crazy I became.

A special thanks, too, to Rachel and Greg who read the book chapter by chapter as I wrote it and gave both encouragement and excellent feedback. This book is for you, as much as it is for Elodie.

Also helping me through this book has been my new community of writers, each of whom encouraged me at some point during the process (even if it was just with a funny gif and far more confidence in me than I deserved). Thank you Kitty, Kenley, Shari, Aya, Brittany, Diana and Simone for understanding this crazy journey that is the life of a writer and for welcoming me into your own journeys.

Once again, my editor Mary brought insightful improvements to the story, and I am so grateful to have the opportunity to work my books through with her. I am thankful, also, for my other editors—my Dad and Deborah—who are dedicated in their work and incredibly patient with my changing timelines.

The same is true of my cover designer Karri, who designed and brought to life the stunning cover. It seems to embody the brilliant sun dress worn so effectively by Beauty in the Grimm Brothers' strange version of this tale.

Our life takes so many unexpected twists and turns, and I am so grateful to God for helping me to keep writing through the most recent ones in my own life. I only hope that I will have the opportunity to write through many more.

# ABOUT THE AUTHOR

 Melanie Cellier grew up on a staple diet of books, books and more books. And although she got older, she never stopped loving children's and young adult novels.

She always wanted to write one herself, but it took three careers and three different continents before she actually managed it.

She now feels incredibly fortunate to spend her time writing from her home in Adelaide, Australia where she keeps an eye out for koalas in her backyard. Her staple diet hasn't changed much, although she's added choc mint Rooibos tea and Chicken Crimpies to the list.

She writes young adult fantasy including books in her *Spoken Mage* world, her *Mage's Influence* world, and her various *Four Kingdoms* and *Kingdoms of Legacy* series that are made up of linked stand-alone stories that retell classic fairy tales.

www.ingramcontent.com/pod-product-compliance
Lightning Source LLC
Chambersburg PA
CBHW030627110726
47901CB00002B/345